Summer '24

Copper Snow

Brett Walpole

Lovely to meet you, on the Aldrich Beach. Scaravelli!

Cheers, Brett x

Copper Snow
Brett Walpole

ISBN

A CIP catalogue record for this book
is available from the British Library

Published 2023
Tricorn Books
Treadgolds
1 Bishop Street
Portsmouth PO1 3DA

Printed in UK

Copper Snow

Contents

1

For Each Colour, A Note

Daybreak, 27th December 1945

Kodaikanal Solar Observatory in the Palani Hills of Southern India

I am waking. I don't think I was really sleeping though, not really and I'm not sure I was really dreaming either. I was just playing with remembering everything.

I was matching up all the notes from the piano with all the colours in my glass prism and I suppose it must have taken me all of the night. Every note now has its own colour but now I think I really am asleep and that maybe I should wake up.

Somewhere in the future there is a place where I will be awake and that's where I want to go today. Yesterday it was Boxing Day and Boxing Day is always my birthday.

I probably am dreaming now but I have a very good memory of the place where I want to go, a place where I can wake up, where all my senses will wake up too. It is this memory which makes me want to get up, so that is what I do.

I get out of bed and slip on my shoes which have no laces, so it is very easy to put them on. I pick up my little copper cymbals, which are joined together by a bright purple ribbon, and I leave my bedroom.

Going downstairs I pass the gramophone at the bottom by the door. There is no record on it and the arm is up but pieces of the melodies I heard flowing from it last night come back to me in fuzzy faded parcels of sounds and words.

Chiming my cymbals together, they let out a high pitch note which echoes around the hall, bouncing off the walls before coming back to me.

I go outside, leaving the door open. The note lives for a while in the room as I walk away from the Observatory. It is not quite sunrise yet, but it is warm. But then it is warm here most of the time.

The moon lights my way, he seems shiny and friendly. He owns the night and everything under it, our house, our garden, and our telescope. Of course, the whole mountain top also belongs to him, surrounded by the forest as it is.

I am going to the forest to claim my gift. It is just me and my cymbals and as I'm walking along they make a chiming sound whenever I bring them together. The little note is high and pure and rings without echo as it dissolves into the still, clear, enormous air which must reach all the way up to the stars, and the moon too I should think. Can he hear me I wonder?

The stars are incredibly pretty, really they are, but they are so very tiny too. They must be a long way away, or maybe they are actually very close, but just so very, very small indeed. Whatever the case, I don't think the stars will be able to hear my cymbals chime. The moon can hear my music, of course he can. Obviously he watches but he is also able to listen, he just chooses not to say anything.

Maybe one day he will whisper in my ear the stories he has made from all the way up there. It's a very good place from which to make up stories, I imagine.

I'm at the edge of the forest now and the garden changes to trees suddenly. I didn't notice the colours of the rhododendron flowers which I passed on my way here. Moonlight is funny like that. He only lets you see what he wants you to see. Sometimes this is all you need to see but he won't show everything to you, whatever the case. He hides everything he believes to be unimportant so that you can concentrate on where you are going, so you won't get lost.

He has brought me safely to these trees with his light and I must say I think he has worked very hard to do so because his light is fairly weak, if I'm being truthful.

The sun will be up soon, and she will blast away the moon and there will be colour everywhere suddenly. She will creep up on him, overpower him and send him to sleep. He will still be up there of course, with his big shiny face all wispy and white, but the blue sky will surround him and hide him, and everyone will forget he is up there unless they really look for him. Even if they do, they will surely find him asleep in broad daylight, all lazy and peaceful and quiet.

Everyone forgets how he guides them through dark nights but whenever he decides not to be there at all, then people get scared and a bit blind and become fearful of falling. I don't forget him though because I know he is always there, always.

He is beaming as I enter the forest. Even as the treetop roof closes over my head his light still manages to find a way through, and he shows me where I can walk. I pass through patches of shadow, but his puddles of light are quite enough for me to see my way.

My feet crunch the leaves on the ground and the sound echoes a little bit, around and back and between the trees as their trunks become closely packed together.

I chime my cymbals and make the most of their sound. It is only a light note but it has some strength and I feel the spaces around me as it bounces off wood, as it both travels up high and disappears below me into the ground. There is moss on the ground here, I can feel it all spongey beneath the soles of my shoes.

The man with the sore throat is singing his songs now, the ones he was singing yesterday at my party. The words and the sounds of the instruments and the whirly rhythms and rhymes are all blending together as one. I like his voice because it is so deep and strong and powerful and beautiful and funny and old. I love him and I don't even know what his name is or what he looks like.

I am singing it to myself now as I'm walking through the forest but I'm singing quietly so as not to wake up any friends of mine who might still be asleep.

No one to talk with
All by myself
No one to walk with
But I'm happy on the shelf.
Ain't misbehavin'
I'm savin' all my love for you.
I don't stay out late,
Don't care to go.
I'm home about eight,
Just me and my radio
Ain't misbehavin'
I'm savin' all my love for you.

He is only one man, but he is singing with his heart and this is why he keeps on singing I think. But some of his words aren't even real words! They're nonsense words like, "Do dee bop da do be do," and he sings them very quickly so that you can hardly catch them. However, they are actually very good as words because they are quite easy to sing along to and remember, being so funny as they are.

I can see the song as clearly as I can see all the colours of the music in the forest. They are all as one.

Even though the sun's rays from the horizon are not much stronger than the moon's, in this moment I can see her colours mixed together with all the sounds and the music. They are inside me and outside me, too. That is to say, the outside is inside. I don't think there really is an inside and an outside, not really, or if there is they are the same thing.

I am quite dizzy when I arrive at a small patch of very tall grasses. The sun is getting stronger, every second now she is more powerful still. I can feel her warmth and the forest is waking up. It is a shower of light and sound raining on me, all around me. I step into the patch of tall grasses and then stop walking because I am thinking of lying down to rest.

The grasses are tall, as tall as me, and they surround me as I stand in them. If anyone were looking for me here, I would be completely hidden, especially if I were to lie down, which is what I do.

On my back I look up to the sky and make a note with my cymbals. The sound goes straight upwards and disappears into the sky through a big hole in the roof of trees. The thick strong blades of grass are stripy. As they reach up, they sway about a little, quite a lot in fact as it is rather breezy now.

The grasses are the walls of a house which has not yet had its roof put on. I am lying on the floor looking up through a roof which isn't even there!

This blue sky is turning a much lighter blue now. It was completely black and full of the stars only a moment ago, then it became the darkest of blues and the stars started to vanish, and then they disappeared altogether, very suddenly. Now the sky is soft and light, like thin blue paper onto which I can throw all my colours, because of all the music.

Way up through the roof I can see an aeroplane and the sunlight is bouncing from its windows one by one as if they are mirrors. Each window takes it in turn to shine as the sun beams reach my eyes. The plane moves slowly and draws a straight, chalky white line across the space above. It looks like a big blue circle with a white line going from one side to the other.

I chime and wait.

The aeroplane has gone but the line stays for a while longer.

Then it begins to dissolve slowly, from one end to the other. When it has completely gone, I chime again. I don't know where the aeroplane is going or why the line has disappeared.

The bright colours I was making are getting quieter and softer and more pale until they are all gone. I make another note with my cymbals which are very good for making notes at any time.

The cymbals are small and round. They are like tiny, shiny, copper dinner plates and the ribbon which ties them to each other is purple silk.

I decided to taste the copper, so that I know what is tastes of. The taste stops everything moving for the very longest of seconds. It is both good and bad at the same time and it buzzes on my tongue and in my head, along with all the other sounds and colours and smells and feelings.

The giant blades of grass feel very alive. It's as though I can hear them growing. It is a bit damp and wet down here though, so I stand up. The tops of the grasses are dry and soft and brushy. I spin around in them for a while, stretching out my arms with my hands facing down and I can feel the light gentle swoosh of the grasses on the skin of my arms and my wrists and my palms and my fingertips.

I'm dizzy again. My ears are all blurry inside and so I stop spinning and stand still for a long while. When it is peaceful and quiet again, I look at my cymbals and, bringing them together again, the note leads me home.

I walk back the way I came. It is perfectly light enough now to see all the colours of all the flowers as I reach the garden and I remember another song. My mother was playing it last night as I was falling asleep. I'm humming it to myself and thinking of the words as they move along and I move along with them. They take me all the way home.

Gee, how I miss
Your tender kiss,
And the wonderful things we would do.
Now I run my hands
Through silvery strands
You left me blue turning grey over you.
You used to be
So good to me
That's when I was a novelty.
Now, you've new friends in view,
You've found someone new,
And left me blue turning grey over you.

When I get home, I go up to my bedroom, I put the cymbals next to my glass prism on the bedside table, I take my shoes off and I get into bed.

I sleep and later I wake.

2

The Gift Of The Forest

The previous day (Boxing Day)
Ananya's Sixth Birthday

The Solar Observatory at Kodaikanal had been built on a high plateau in 1899 and by now it was recognised worldwide for its work. Sophie Rondel currently occupied the position of the leading astronomer at this foremost of Indian facilities. She was the first woman to have been appointed to this prestigious role having proved her value at the Greenwich Observatory in London in the years immediately prior to World War II. Her application was strongly supported by references from several renowned colleagues.

'Kodaikanal' can be translated as meaning 'The Gift of the Forest'. Within the idyll of this mountain-top paradise, Sophie's daughter Ananya was born. It was here that her senses came to life, and she learned of them as being as one.

Sophie's husband, Callum Rondel, was a geologist. They had met, fallen in love and married while studying for their PhDs in Manchester several years before moving their lives to a land so far away. When his wife had suggested this future for them both it was with huge drive and enthusiasm that he took on the adventure.

After some extensive research, he believed with a deep and intellectual passion that there was the possibility of finding great quantities of copper ore in this region. When Ananya had come into the world to join them, being born in Kodaikanal, the combined strength of the love they felt for each other was an incredible force, one felt also by all who worked and lived here.

Callum's search to find copper ore in viable quantities had become increasingly successful towards the end of the War and, now the destruction had ceased, reaching its terrifying conclusion with the atomic explosions over Japan, he had at last been able to open his first commercial mine. It was scheduled to commence operations in the coming weeks.

The mine had been surveyed recently and their meeting with a government official there tomorrow was a formality as much as anything. However, it was a significant milestone and marked the culmination of years of hard work. The mine would give his family a solidity and a permanence now the war was over, and he felt sure their future here had only just begun.

The Rondels lived together as their family of three in a small house adjoining the main Observatory building. The local people here liked them very much because they shared many values with them. In this small scientific community, people were highly intelligent and perhaps a little introverted with it, but they were all kind and generous.

There were staff including a cook, cleaners, and groundsmen. The telescope itself was currently staffed and maintained by a small, efficient and well-trained team of academics and technicians numbering less than ten, some of whom also lived on the site. The combination of specialist telescopes at Kodaikanal looked outwards and upwards, away from the problems of men on Earth. These instruments and their caretakers were asking only to learn, and so be able to understand.

Callum was already up busying himself with preparing the car. The mine was a three-hour drive away on good roads and he and his wife had decided to leave later that night as they wanted to spend as much of the day as they could celebrating Ananya's sixth birthday with her, along with everyone else at the site.

Six years ago on this day, in the very building where the telescope was housed, Sophie had gone into labour and given birth to Ananya.

As part of her work here at Kodaikanal, Sophie Rondel was required to take a photograph of the sun at the precise moment when it had fully cleared the horizon. She did this every morning at sunrise and yesterday had been no exception. Christmas Day means little to the celestial bodies, as the sun and moon and the stars are indifferent to the holidays and festivities of mankind.

Ananya was born prematurely, most likely because she had wanted to see and hear the world outside as soon as she possible could. It happened to be at sunrise, when Sophie was carefully going about her work taking her daily photograph.

The main telescope was mounted on a frame some twenty feet high and made of heavy cast iron beams, painted white. It stood bold and proud, with its gaze trained on the sun through a long gap in the dome above. For Sophie it had the character of a benign giant, a sentinel, and from the day of Ananya's birth a guardian for her baby daughter.

This morning Sophie was up a little earlier than usual because she wanted to play some music for Ananya as the sun rose. However, moving the gramophone outside had taken longer than anticipated as it was heavy and an awkward shape. It was still dark, which had not helped but Louis Armstrong had now begun to sing. It was a song called 'Blue Turning Grey Over You'.

The Victor gramophone had originally belonged to Sophie's mother who had first heard recorded music at the Paris Exposition of 1889 where, as a child of a similar age to Ananya, her parents had taken her to show her the marvels of a new age.

On that day, Thomas Edison had a display of his latest electrical devices on show and was aided by his wife, Mina, in demonstrating these inventions to the public. News of the phonograph was the talk of the city as was Mina's gown which was reputed to have cost some three thousand dollars.

When seen together, the music and the gown, were a heady mixture for the young girl on this warm summer morning. She was surrounded by an excited crowd of well-heeled Parisiennes and it was a giddy moment where sight and sound were fused together as one. The experience had clearly moved her greatly. The memory she made of it had never left her, and when she grew up, as soon as she was able to afford it in fact, she had bought the model 'V' Victor V in 1907 from a specialist shop in London. It had been very expensive and soon she had begun buying records in significant numbers, mostly imported from America and of a substantial price.

Sophie lost her mother to the Spanish flu in 1919 and inherited the gramophone, bringing it with her here to India in 1938. She and her husband Callum had made the decision to leave England with great deliberation, followed by a passionate flurry of activity and then the epic journey itself.

The entire family record collection had been transported here with them and now these beautiful objects sat in the hall at the bottom of the stairs, containing within their design a vibrant hidden universe.

Several hundred brown-paper sleeves formed a neat row, stacked on their edges along a custom-made shelf which ran the entire length of the wall. Advertising material covered most of the paper sleeves, but some were bare. These bland envelopes made the records seem anonymous and each the same as the other, but the hidden truth was very different.

Brittle and prone to cracking or breaking if dropped, many records in the collection had been damaged in transit on their journey here by ship. The large brass horn had also been badly damaged, but Callum had repaired it himself. Yesterday it had been polished and buffed. The deep orange and pink of the copper within its alloy, all shiny and bright, caught the first few rays of the sun as it appeared over the distant skyline to the east.

Sophie had wanted to wake Ananya with her favourite song, but the idea to move the music outside only came to her as she woke to the harsh sound of own alarm clock. She got out of bed quickly, dressed, and then gently woke Ananya, carried her down the stairs, half asleep as she was, and made her comfortable with some blankets and pillows on the swing chair out on the veranda. There was a chill in the morning at this time of the year.

It had been a race against time as the sun does to wait, and Sophie had her duties to attend to. She had to run to the telescope in order to prepare the photographic plate for its timely exposure and make her recording with her usual scientific professionalism. On this occasion it was to the sound of jazz.

Louis Armstrong was now in motion at seventy-eight revolutions per minute. The spiral span quickly around, the soft metal needle sitting in its groove tracing its arc from the outer edge towards the inner label. His distinctive gravelly voice carried far in the still air. Across the wide-open gardens of the Solar Observatory and then out and beyond into the Palani Hills, music played and the day began in earnest.

The employees at the Observatory began to stir, at first with confusion and then with smiles. They were familiar with Sophie's music as she played it every day, but never before quite so early. Some began remembering that today was special and that there was more than usual to be getting along with.

There were no other children living in this remote hill station and she was somewhat of a star here, the soul of place one might say. Perched on its elevated mountain-top plateau, it was a perfect high-altitude island. Under a thin atmosphere it was a clear window through which Sophie could study her chosen subject.

Sophie Rondel's life's work, to observe and understand patterns of sunspot activity, was highly ambitious. The cause of the little black spots, which appeared on the surface of the star in apparently regular cycles, was yet unknown to the scientific community. She hoped the photographs she made would help to answer the questions scientists had asked but somewhere along her journey the project had begun to represent an attempt to understand her own soul as well as that of the sun.

The eyes of the astronomer rested for a moment, closed and relaxed, as she faced the first light. The rays falling on her face were gentle, but already they warmed her skin.

Ananya knew how to turn the record over, and indeed to wind the handle which coiled the spring which powered the motion of the turntable. She had been shown how to do this, she had learned, she did it very carefully and this morning she had by now already performed this operation no less than five times.

The sun rose quickly. Ananya was fully awake now and barefoot, twirling around on the sloping lawn in front of the main telescope building. The low, yellow rays caught in each tiny bead of dew on the blades of soft grass was glinting like a sea of stars. The water and light tickled the soles of Ananya's feet as she lost herself dancing to the music. She was happy and in love with a man whose image she had never seen but whose voice somehow reached her soul through a mechanical miracle which had transported it to her through great spans of time and across huge distances of space.

3

Mining For Life

The Morning of the 27th December
The Rondel Copper Mine

I remember I like this Callum Rondel man very much. He is quite happy as far as an Englishman can be said to be properly happy. I helped to survey his copper mine only a few months ago and we hit it off very well I thought.

For myself, I am a fairly humble man I suppose, quite a lowly person to many I would think. My name is Anish. I am not even a surveyor, only a surveyor's assistant, but I am not lowly to myself. I have my qualification and I am young and I like this job. I like the people I meet, most of them, and the people I work with, most of them.

When I was here last, Mr Rondel said to me, "You know Anish, the life of a surveyor must be a very good one I think!"

Of course, I asked him straight off the bat why he should say such a thing, bearing in mind that I was only the assistant to a surveyor.

He said in reply, "Well, you walk from place to place in your country, and you put down your theodolite, in the spot you think it right, and you have a good opportunity to really look at the land, really look at it and let it make you feel what it will."

I understood his sentiment perfectly.

"Mr Rondel, forgive me for asking, how do you think I should look upon this land of mine, in order that I might profit the most?"

He looked at me knowingly. I had heard that he and his wife had come to India from Manchester just before the war. I wondered if his accent was a Manchester accent.

"Yours is a beautiful land indeed. These mountains, the forests, the plateaus and the plains. It is not like this where I was brought up. It is hard for me to explain the differences they are so great, hard too for me to explain why I am here, in your country. Perhaps all I am saying is that to be able to stop and see, to look at the shape and lie of the land, to look deep into it and to have this as part of your job is a wonderful perk, is it not?"

"Ah yes, the perks of the job indeed! But I imagine your country is also a very beautiful place, in certain places."

"It is, Anish, it is ... Tomorrow Sophie and I are travelling back to England for the first time since we came to India, since before the war started. We have a daughter here, Ananya, she was born in Kodaikanal, she is six now and she has never stepped foot in England. I hope to show her some of the beautiful places I remember from the time when I was a child."

"But you will be returning surely?"

"Oh, yes. We will only be away for a month. Sophie has a sister in London who is going to be looking after us all, then it's back here to get this mine into working order, my friend."

"Will you be able to visit your family in England as well, Mr Rondel?"

"No, Anish. I have no brothers or sisters and my parents died many years ago. This is home."

He looked at me with eyes that were tired I thought. The war had taken its toll on all of us but there was something else. He sighed a little.

"There will be a huge change here, very soon I think, for your people, for your country. I think it might be very painful for everyone. I am not sure what the world will look like a few years from now, but my life is here. I hope I will always be welcome here and that my life will benefit your country and its future. I cannot imagine what it has been like for you, with us here for so long. Sometimes I am very sorry, but I wish to be a force for good."

After saying that I remember he turned and slowly walked away. He was ashamed in some way I think. He seemed like one of the good ones to me although many people I knew felt them all to be bad and wanted them all to leave our country. I was looking forward to seeing him again nevertheless as I felt we had much that we could talk about.

I like his wife too. This is partly because she is so beautiful but also because she is an astronomer. She looks at the sun all day through her telescope and oversees the Solar Observatory at Kodaikanal.

The whole idea of her life seems very romantic to me. She is tall and graceful, elegant and charming. She has light brown hair, woven into a single loose plait. She is fun but intense too.

On my last visit I was also able to talk with her for a while. One moment she was laughing and joking with me about the puny lens on my theodolite but the next she was interrogating me about the manufacturer of the lens, where it was ground and other such matters. Then she asked me about how one would go about measuring the circumference of the equator and I was a little bit stumped as I am only an assistant surveyor. I'm not sure whether she was trying to teach me or test me.

Even if I did not have the answers to her questions, she kept asking them in different ways. I have done some research into these particulars since our last meeting, such was the strength of her curiosity, so I shall feel well prepared. It will give me the chance to speak to her for a lengthier duration, which will benefit me as she really is quite beautiful.

Callum Rondel is not as beautiful. He has a strange face, even for a white Englishman. It is mostly full of nose and moustache, but the ears are quite generous also. There are some quite spectacular eyebrows as a bonus I must say.

Sometimes, when he talks, I find it hard to contain my mirth as these hairy protrusions rise and fall to highlight certain words and parts of his speech.

He had been told there was no copper in these mountains but still he searched. It is said among the local people here that he walked in the Palani Hills for years before he discovered this small, exposed seam where he has located his mine.

A local farmer sold him these few acres, he applied for permission to excavate and set up his business and I was here only a month ago to survey the land with my boss Mr Chandra who is a very experienced surveyor. I met Mr Rondel and his lovely wife that day. The results of the survey proved to be extremely promising. His permission to mine has now been granted and I am here again but this time with a man called Mr Jai.

Mr Jai is a government official for the district. I don't like him very much. I am only here just to drive him to the site, having been before and knowing the way. He has been treating me like his personal chauffeur all day.

He is here to make sure all 'I's have been dotted, every 'T' has been crossed and to make sure all the paperwork is just so. Only then will Mr Rondel be able to commence his operations. Mr Jai likes paperwork very much indeed.

It is the very earliest part of the morning. It rained heavily here all night, and although we started out before sunset and have come from only ten miles away, it has taken us several hours. The road was treacherous and Mr Jai is clearly an accomplished backseat driver. I don't like him at all if truth be told. He makes me nervous, and this affects my driving abilities.

We are arriving now. Mr and Mrs Rondel's copper mine is nothing much at the moment. They stand by their hastily erected wooden temporary residence. I will not say it is a shed for it is larger than a shed and I believe also contains the embryonic arrangements of an office. Their car is parked nearby, and I see he must have recently bought a brand new mechanical digger, a generator and some other machinery. I wonder how he might have had those transported all the way out here. I shall ask him during casual conversation when I find the opportunity.

I can see Mrs Rondel over there. She looks very pretty. How does she stay so clean, surrounded by all this jungle, in such a flowing white dress? She is like a lotus flower growing in muddy water.

"Stop here, Anish! We have arrived. Help me out of this ridiculous motor vehicle of yours. Really it is like an old elephant!"

I applied the parking brake, stopped the engine, and stepped out of the car. It was slimy mud underfoot and I slipped slightly on exit. Opening the rear door, I removed my annoying passenger. He was overweight – considerably so – and encumbered by a large leather briefcase and an ebony cane.

I took a good look at this walking stick. He was always with it. The length of it was patterned with inlaid ivory and its handle was made of silver. It seemed pretty to me at first glance but on a closer view I saw it was fashioned into the shape of a snake's head and suddenly I was at once repulsed by it and looked away.

He was out and very nearly slipped over himself. I smiled to myself as he did so, just wishing it would happen.

Mr Jai has a very pronounced limp, for which the cane was an assistance. Apparently this limp had been gained some five years ago when a large granite boulder had fallen on him on a construction site in the south.

Supposedly he had been an agreeable man of some considerable humour until this event but having been pinned under the rock, isolated with his leg broken for a full twenty-four hours before assistance appeared, he had never been the same since. By all accounts, his character had changed completely and even his close friends could recognise no trace of the jovial chap they knew.

He had become a miserable, mean-spirited, and vindictive sort, quick to a vicious temper and never short of abusive words for all, women or children included, overnight it seemed.

His former friends had left his company after only a short few months feeling sorry for him, his sudden metamorphosis so complete as to exhaust all possible sympathy.

I did not know him prior to his unfortunate accident but I could only dislike him with an intensity and this was annoying because it would only leave me when I knew he was not nearby.

The Rondels were waving at us and I could hear music coming from their shelter. It was American jazz music! Yes, for certain, and it was quite loud! What a lovely counterpoint to this dismal, gloomy, muddy day.

Mr Jai waddled towards them. I followed, but he quickly turned on me.

"You stay here Anish, you are not needed."

"But I …"

"Look at the suspension on the rear offside of the motor car, it is making horrific clunking noises!"

I stopped and watched him walk away. The suspension was truly in a very sorry state and I had meant to have a look at it yesterday. He was technically my superior, so I complied. I watched him totter gingerly on his cheap white shoes and suspect cane, hoping he would slip base over apex in a comic way, with arms and legs flailing around all over the place, and be horribly and embarrassingly covered in mud head to toe.

I took an old blanket from the boot of the vehicle and laid it on the floor by the wheel in question. It was on the far side of the car from the Rondels but before I lay down, I stood for thirty seconds or so watching the interaction of the three people. Out of earshot of their conversation, I could nevertheless hear the music clearly.

Rising immediately behind them was the substantial cliff face where Callum Rondel had discovered azurite. This near-vertical outcrop jutted straight up some eighty feet or so I guessed, clearing the trees. It was a spectacle of beauty I thought. Perhaps to a geologist it would be even more so. As I scanned my eyes, I fancied I could see the rich dark blue seam running horizontally along it some fifteen feet above ground level. I did not know what this meant as regards the size of his find, as Mr Rondel supposed it, but I would be sure to ask him if I had that chance after seeing to the blasted suspension. Hopefully I would also be able to converse with his beautiful wife again and relay the new knowledge I had acquired concerning lenses and measurements of the equator.

Before lying down under the rear axle, I saw Mr Jai reaching up at the cliff face, poking away at it with his cane.

It was with a sudden instant revulsion to his body language which caused me to get on with my work. I squatted to the ground and then, turning onto my back on the blanket, crawled under the back of the car, shuffling along until I was in a good spot to look at the condition of the suspension.

Water dripped on my face. The leaf springs were muddy of course, but I could see the problem immediately. The connecting bush, a large piece of rubber acting as a stop for the spring, had completely perished and hardly any of it was left intact.

It would be an awkward and time-consuming job which I would have to do myself when I returned. It would be hard to get the part and I received no extra pay from my employer for being an amateur mechanic.

I lay there peacefully for a moment, relaxing. I breathed deeply several times thinking I had been neglecting my yoga recently. Life was good for me I thought, I have a job and I have friends.

All I was aware of in that moment was the music. It seemed to be sad and melancholic, sentimental even, certainly it was not as joyful as I thought jazz was supposed to be. It was beautiful though and of this I was in no doubt. The Rondels must have a good radio to get reception out here. What a good idea.

I did not see the accident, but I heard it and felt its vibrations through my body.

It was a fearful primeval sound of Nature, of the Earth, and its impact was by virtue of its size and its duration. It was a huge dull sound, one I had never heard before, but its duration seemed impossibly short. A crack and growl were followed by an incredibly powerful bass rumble. A slump, a gigantic groan caused by a movement of incredible mass.

I lay motionless as I experienced the force of it, my eyes open wide and still staring at the underside of the car. I could not twist my head toward the source of this sound, this vibration, and when it was over, so soon after it had begun, all I could hear was the music, the same song drifting through the air. I could not find the wherewithal to move. The crystal-clear sound of the birds in the canopy up high came into my consciousness. I had previously been completely oblivious to this music but there they were, insistent high-pitched notes, shrill and demanding both attention, and then action.

I moved quickly.

Clambering from beneath the car, I stood. Before me was a site which was at once so clear yet made no sense. A huge section of the cliff face had come away, a landslide. A triangular fan of mud interspersed with fine rocks and a few larger boulders strewn between reached all the way up to where I was standing.

The place where Mr Jai and the Rondels had only moments before been chatting was no longer there. It had been replaced by a vast slope of dark wet earth, full of rocks and at least thirty feet high. The new machinery was nowhere to be seen.

The wooden building stood perfectly intact to one side, the music still emanating from its windows and doors. In this mad scene it stood as an insane musical island, surrounded by a brand-new topography of motionless mud, which had a lethal, natural beauty all its own.

I was in an horrific shock, from which it was hard to break free. Once again, the crying of the birds in the trees broke my trance, forcing my muscles to act.

I ran to the wooden shack and climbed up to the spot where I imagined the three last to have been. I climbed higher. I was where they had been, I thought, but many feet above. I kept looking down. For a while, I don't know how long, I found myself gazing at an enormous piece of azurite, which was now freshly exposed. Its blueness was so deep I felt myself falling into it. Did I break free of its spell to begin digging or did its pull compel me to dig?

With furious energy, my bare hands were my only tools, and I was soon covered in the mud of the Earth. Not knowing if I was in the right place, I was relentless in this digging for many hours. I did not rest.

They may be alive, but it is not possible. How could it be possible? They are covered and crushed and buried. But could there be large rocks forming a space? A space which contains a volume of air?

I threw stones and rocks, as I scooped mud and earth away to go down deeper and closer to them, to find them. It became a lust for life, their life and mine. I would not and could not stop. If I hesitated it was not through a lack of faith or belief. If

I had to find them only dead I must find them nevertheless and I could not let myself think until I had done so.

If any of them were alive they would be in pain, and their pain would overwhelm their thoughts. It would be black, they could be still alive, but unconscious.

The music played and this replaced my thoughts with a sound which seemed to be the sound of a friend. This friend didn't care about anything except love and life and joy. The tone of this singer had changed now. He was happy, vibrant, wonderful, and alive. He kept me in a state of alertness because his words were so far away from my own plight as to be an extreme and a balance to my own extreme. I didn't know who he was but in that isolated hell of a place, he was my only friend.

Without him I might have lost my mind because I knew as he sang that he sang of a world which was not connected to my own except through a random coincidence of fate. It was important for my sanity in those hours to know such a world existed.

I was not singing of course, at least I don't think I was. I did not know why this American man kept singing all the time, it seemed odd that song after song on the radio should be dedicated to just him. I began listening more closely to the words he was singing and this helped me to separate my mind from my body.

There was one song which made me imagine that they could hear it too. It was called 'A Monday Date'. Little piano notes danced in the background of the song, and they played in my ears as the sun grew higher and stronger.

Don't forget our Monday date
Oh little baby, don't be late
I said don't forget our Monday date
At the same little place, about half past eight

Now I'm gonna press my suit
I'm gonna shine my shoes
I'm gonna spread the news
And I'm gonna chase away the blues
So don't forget our Monday date
Please, baby, don't be late.

Mr and Mrs Rondel had died here today. I found them and when I did the music came to an end. On the radio a male voice, a British Eastern Service voice, began to speak. He announced the end of the selection of songs by Mr Louis Armstrong and the beginning of the World News. It was 9am exactly as I listened to the news.

They had died in this dark and muddy landslide and the only way I found them was by luck and persistence. They were together. As I uncovered them it was less with the pain of sadness but more with exhaustion and then suddenly some incredulity.

They lay next to each, pushed together with no space between them. They were not on their backs looking up, but on their sides, and face to face. It made no sense but there was a beauty in their death. What's more, it seemed they were at peace, and there was deep blue azurite all around.

I had no energy to cry. I was exhausted to the point of collapse and had nothing left with which to express how I was feeling. I did not know as to the whereabouts of Mr Jai. I did not think of him really, I must say. It was as though he were an incidental character, an extra in a movie scene who was killed in the background and quickly disappeared off screen.

When I came to my senses, I knew what I had to do. Before long, I entered the wooden building to turn off the radio, which had begun covering a report from a correspondence in Japan. I turned the switch, and all was instantly quiet, except for the sound of the songs of the birds in the canopy. This seemed to have acquired a greater strength and as I left the hut the sound was all around.

I climbed into the car and drove in a numbness which defied the difficult terrain to Dindigul where I parked outside the central police station. I entered and gave them my account of that morning.

I had the telephone number of the Rondel's residence in Kodaikanal on some of my surveying paperwork which I gave to the police chief. He called the number upon completion of my report of the incident. Then I stopped talking.

Caked in dried mud and without strength for any emotion, I sat and listened as the call went through. Someone must have answered because the police chief spoke with them for quite a time, relaying the tragedy and explaining to them that he would be sending men to the site immediately.

4

A Memory Sleeps

The world I had searched for so tirelessly, the place which had taken so long to find, fell in on Sophie and me and buried us alive. On this beautiful morning we died together at the copper mine, leaving Ananya to live out the rest of her life without us. Her sixth birthday was just yesterday.

After a night of continuous rain, a massive landslide of ore-laden mud slipped from the side of the quarry. In this dark moment, the exotic adventure of our wonderful lives came to an end as did any future with our beautiful daughter. The story we might have shared together was left forever unwritten because of a seemingly meaningless act of fate.

A local man by the name of Anish was the sole witness. He was a surveyor, a surveyor's assistant actually, who had the fearful task of desperately trying to find us, to dig for us, so that he could be sure for himself of what he already knew to be true.

There was no warning, only a sudden inexplicable sound, a giant slump of enormous scale and then an immense pressure on our bodies which pushed all air from us, extinguishing the anima and light of our souls.

Sophie and I were standing there, side by side, and we fell as one. In the final instant there was a sharp inhalation of breath, a gasp of physical, panicked reflex. Our breathing failed us both quickly in the following seconds, but within this dense abyss we had been thrown together tightly in a final embrace.

The wind in the sails of our lives moved us forward only a short distance but in the blackness, I went into myself. A memory showed itself to me with such incredible clarity that

I was lost in its replay. It was the night Sophie and I had first met, the night when we had first kissed.

I arrived late at the concert, alone, and the music had already begun. I squeezed through a group of people in the packed audience to find an empty seat just as Louis Armstrong was about to finish his first song.

There was huge applause and cheering as I sat down but I had to stand up again almost immediately as everyone took to their feet to clap and shout out loud. It so happened by chance that I found myself standing next to Sophie, who was also at the concert on her own. She looked at me as we sat down again for the next song. She had only happiness in her eyes and neither of us were ever alone again.

The Nottingham Palais was sold out for this one-off performance during Louis Armstrong's visit to England in 1932. He took the adulation with grace and humour and then came a pause as his mere presence on stage subdued the ebullient noise of the assembled crowd.

He addressed his audience with an American style and panache, and we were transfixed and silent as he spoke. His charismatic bass growl put each and every one of us into an hypnosis, a state of focus on the sounds and meanings of his every word. He was an entertainer of great experience, but when there was laughter, I found my attention drawn to Sophie, who occasionally looked back to me with a beautifully flushed face full of incredulity and love.

For some three hours Louis Armstrong and his band played. Sophie and I flirted with glances to one another and stole a few moments of unexpected touch. Then she held my hand. In between the maestro's performances of unforgettable songs, we shared only a few spoken words with each other and even these were lost in the cacophony of appreciation made by all around.

By the end of the night we were enraptured, by the music and by each other.

The presence of Louis Armstrong that night was something of a dream in itself. The way he played his trumpet, alive, powerful, expressive, and so much richer in tone and timbre than any recording might try to do justice. His singing voice alone was a miracle but the lyrics to his songs were full of a simple meaning, a universal genius of soul and depth. And he was just so funny too!

He talked to us directly in between each number, just as if we were his friends or his family. We were reached by him, and touched by him and he fused us into one.

It didn't seem as though this could really be happening or that it could really exist, or that we should have found ourselves being here. The venue itself was a world which contained us all, but this world seemed to be outside of all other worlds with no longitude or latitude.

The film of it runs through the auditorium of my mind now in a technicolour vision. It is a flawless reproduction, stored somewhere hidden within and now it is being projected from this place. I recall it not so much as a memory but as a fresh and highly enriched experience. It destroys the blackness which would have otherwise consumed the end of my life.

As a record it is a metamorphic rock, laid down in rich layers in the first place and then compacted and changed by temperature and by time. A flint finally cracked in this rock, perhaps opened by the incredible force of pressure on my mind, and the interior revealed its content, this fossilised memory.

Its compressed detail is in front of me now. Wth each word Louis Armstrong said, each note he played, each phrase he sang, all of these sounds arrive to me now as they did then, the distance in time and space between us apparently of as little relevance now as it was then.

The recording in my soul plays only once. When it finishes playing it will never play again for I will no longer be here to be the medium through which it plays.

The cheers of the audience subside, there is a hushed murmur and then a pause of pure silence which Louis Armstrong exploits before speaking … It is the end of this night of jazz …

"Thank you ladies and gentlemen, thank you so much. Thank for your kindness and your warmth and all the love and energy you've been givin' me up here. It's hard work I can tell you! You see me sweatin'! This little 'kerchief has had its day, it's soaked right through, take a look! Phew!

"You folks here in England are amazin'. But I gotta go now, we all gotta go home now … Yep! It's time for bed … we's all gotta go.

"I been thinkin' though. You see I got secret … I've been wanting to share it with you all of the night, but I didn't know if I was gonna … You want to hear a secret? I don't usually talk about this sort of thing, but this is kind of special.

"All of tonight I've been trying out a new trumpet on you. See this here horn, well it's a brand-new one, I thought I'd try out and wear it in a little at the same time, see what kind of sound it makes, see how I feel about it you know. I like it, I do, sounds kind of sweet don't you think?! … You like it?

"I mean I go through these things fairly regular. I give 'em about five years usually. I look after them, of course, I run hot water through them every night after I been playing 'em, so you know it going's to percolate right.

"Now, you see, I formed a nice friendship with these nice people from a cool French company called Henri Selmer who work out of Paris. They's all cool over there, not that you ain't cool over here of course! Anyway, recently I've been using a 'Challenger' – that's the name of one of the models they make. But this one here it's a special one, you know, a one-off, like tonight here in Nottingham. Makes it kind of 'unique' I feel … Like all of you good folks … each of you, all different, and there's never been any one quite the same as each one of you and there ain't never gonna be! Ain't that special, and don't you forget it!

"And you know I didn't even have to buy this here horn, it was just given to me, just earlier this year in fact, in May … by your very own King … Yep, I know … George the 5th no less! Yep, Yep, that's the truth!

"I played for him and his lovely wife Queen Mary at the Buckingham Palace and I called him 'Rex' in that concert and a few of your journalists didn't like it too much when I did. Maybe you read about that in your newspapers?

"Anyways, I don't think the King himself minded too much because he gave me this here trumpet, which was very good of him I thought … Cos you know, I'm just starting out in this music business and I ain't got so much to be spending on fancy new horns … And it's nice when good folk help you out, and this one here is gold plated! That's the truth!

"Cos you see, when I started out in life as a boy, I grew up poor as a church mouse, with a Lithuanian family, the Karnofskys. They were very good to me and treated me as their own. They would pay me money for the odd jobs I did for them, it was not much, hardly anything, but it was money and then they leant me some more to buy my very first instrument and it was a tin cornet which cost me all of five dollars!

"I don't know exactly how much your good King had to pay the cool Mr Henri Selmer of Paris, France, to have this beautiful thing made but I do know it must have cost him more than five bucks!

"I just want to say to you. I love this thing, I love your country, I love your King and I love every one of all you folks too! I want to thank you.

"This is my living, and this is my life. I love the notes. That's why I try to make them right. Because I love playing them to you people. And it ain't what you got, it's what you do with it, right!

"But this is just a thing. Sure it's made of gold, but underneath it's just brass like any old trumpet, and brass is mainly just copper, with a bit of zinc. I gotta say though it sure does shine up nice … Look, I got my fingerprints all over it now. I've got some polishing to do.

"But this trumpet ain't a person, and that's what's it's all about, people, you people and you got to make the most of each other, you know, appreciate each other. If you've got someone that is … If you've got someone, think about how you were before you found each other, look after each other, imagine how you'd be without them. You've got to love each other, that's the whole deal right.

"But if you ain't got nobody, don't worry too much, don't get too blue, someone will come along, and in the meantime, while you're looking for them and living your lives, I've written this song just for you, and it's going to be our very last song. It's called 'Ain't Got Nobody'. Good night, and God bless you."

The song has a beautifully slow melody. It is perfect, clear, and precise yet full of emotions of all colours, extremes, hues, pitches, tones and textures.

He bows and the final applause is staggering. There is cheering and a riotous atmosphere fills the space all the way to the ceiling and back as though sound is falling on us from above. Mr Louis Armstrong says no more. He walks from the stage, and despite shouts for an encore he does not come back. He was clearly exhausted from his performance and as we realised the night is over many throw their arms around each other in joy and farewell. People finally begin leaving the auditorium, but Sophie and I sit and talk, and get to know each other, and kiss for the first time.

As our breathing grows faint I have another memory of us

which also appears as an inner vision of a kind. It is from a much later time and in a much different place. On a warm and hazy afternoon, shortly after arriving in India, we are next to each other amidst the long, lush grass of a hidden glade in a far corner of a vast botanical garden and we are making love under a copper-coloured eclipse of the moon.

I can no longer feel the pressure upon me as there is only one feeling left in my body. My heart is still strong, I can feel it pounding and fighting for a last chance to continue with life, but then its rhythm becomes erratic and then it is slow and growing slower.

Ananya is here now, and she becomes my final memory.

It is yesterday, her birthday at the end of the day. We are all tired as the festivities came to an end long ago and Sophie and I have been preparing for our drive to the mine. We must leave very soon, so that we can reach our destination before the sun has set. There is no electricity at the mine yet, there are no lights there and I do not wish to navigate the treacherous little roads in the dark.

All day I haven't been able to give Ananya the present I made for her because I could not find the piece of ribbon which I needed in order to complete it.

However, in my office I have found the purple ribbon in my desk drawer, pushed to the back and I am now tying it to the little copper cymbals I have made. These I cast and hammered last week from the very first copper I managed to extract from the first test batch of ore we found. It is of such high purity and I still cannot believe how it happened that I came across such large quantities of it.

When I become aware of Ananya, her soul seems to announce itself slightly before she does so in person.

I notice moving lights on the far wall of my study and have no idea where they are coming from. My curiosity is captured by quick, multicoloured moving flashes which appear and disappear.

They are reflected from a large mirror on the far side the room and are coming through the half open door.

I stop for a few seconds, I hear a 'pitter-patter' noise from the hall outside.

"Ananya?"

There is no reply. I swivel in my chair. I stand and walk over to the door and open it fully.

She is there in the hallway, spinning around barefoot on the wooden parquet flooring. The steps she makes as I watch her dance are small and quick and a blur and make a sticky noise. Her tiny feet are on a patch where I saw lemonade spilled during the party. Indira must have forgotten to clean it up. Ananya whirls in circles.

Held above her head is the glass prism Sophie gave her for her birthday.

The setting sun is warm and orange and finds its way to the prism through a gap in the trees opposite the Observatory. Its beam travels through the window above the front door into the glass and throws its stars and rainbows everywhere. She is lost in its play and delirious with rotations.

She is a tiny lighthouse, a rotating beacon of happiness lighting every corner of her world. Inside a ball of her own energy, within herself and surrounded by a larger space also. I too am in her world hypnotised by it, by her.

Was she aware I was there? She slows and brings the prism down in front of her, slightly lower still, until she is gazing deeply into its heart.

She has found something in there, slowly shifting her look this way and then the other, bringing the prism close and then holding it at arm's length. Finally, she puts it right up to her eye.

Is she looking straight through it? No, her gaze is fixed on a point inside. An imperfection, an inclusion, a crack, or perhaps a bubble has seized her focus. She is standing perfectly still.

The two of us are only ten feet apart. Ananya is a whole world as a person, a person as a world. A vision of the world where we live, its light, its sky, the painterly strokes of clouds, so thin and delicate running through the life-giving air itself, the aura around her soul. She is the Earth.

She spins again with a carefree style. The Earth's surface, the deep hues of undulating lands and ocean blues, the natural beauty of her face.

Ananya is the core of the Earth, a swirling, chaotic molten flux, spinning an invisible magnetism in a field around us all. She is life and she protects life.

Who protects her? I am this protection. She will always need me.

I call to her softly, hoping not to startle her or break her dreams …

"Ananya …"

She looks up from the prism with a serious expression and, seeing me standing in the doorway, her face lightens. In a blink she becomes all smiles and bubbling laughter and walks towards me. She is tired after such a long day, and I hold her tight before giving her the cymbals.

Sophie walks in as it's time to put Ananya to bed. A promise is made that she can hear Armstrong sing one last time to end her birthday as it began. She wants to fall asleep just as she was woken.

I say goodnight and Sophie takes Ananya from me, carrying her up the stairs to bed.

5

True Reflection

The phone rang. I was in Mr Rondel's study as it did so, but it stopped just as I was walking towards it. I quickly realised Indira must have picked up the call on the other phone as I heard her answering it in the hall. She likes to answer the telephone and it was with her characteristically buoyant and bright voice with which she greeted the caller.

I listened with some indifference as I was in the middle of some rather pressing paperwork, but she said nothing further for a while to the caller. At a certain point I suddenly had the thought that her silence was unusually long, and it was in this moment that I heard her say, "I am simply the lady who looks after their daughter."

There was great anxiety in her voice and it sounded broken and unsure of itself. I left the study and stopped at the doorway as I saw her. She turned to me with terrified confusion across her face. I could hear a voice still talking from the telephone as she held the handset towards me.

"It is a policeman, I think you should talk with him Mr Kumar, I think a horrible thing has happened, I don't know, he ..."

I walked to her quickly and took the receiver from her.

"Hello. To whom am I speaking please?"

He was the police chief of Dindigul, he said his call was regarding the residents at this address. He wished to know my name and my relationship to them.

"I am Niral Kumar. I am Mr Rondel's partner in business. Could you please tell me what this is regarding?"

My eyes had come to rest upon several items which lay on the polished hall table, their energy calmed my mind as I was told of the nature of the tragedy which had taken the lives of Mr and Mrs Rondel. I was somehow able to start thinking about new opportunities which began revealing themselves to me as possible consequences of this terrible event. From all things bad can come goodness, even from death there is life.

There was a glass prism which threw its rainbow across the shiny mahogany surface of the table. This colourful light caught two tiny copper discs, tied together with a dark velvet ribbon. I had seen Ananya put this object there just a little while ago before going to her piano lesson with Indira but I had not seen them before this and did not know their function. I thought them perhaps to be new playthings, toys or presents from her birthday yesterday.

Next to them, face down, lay Mrs Rondel's hand mirror which I knew very well indeed as she had it often on her person, using it to adjust her hair pins which often slipped. It was as much a part of her as a watch was to a man. I had always had a keen interest in it, but I had never before held it myself.

As it transfixed me, I began thinking that perhaps it was I who had a spell over it, the owner of the mirror being unclear to me in this moment. The prism and the copper discs clearly belonged to Ananya and of course she would have them. I would give them to her when Indira came back with her from her piano lesson but not the mirror. I picked it up, it was mine, it would bring us luck.

The policeman finished saying what it was he needed to say, and I made appropriate noises to show that I understood him. By the end of the call, as I replaced the handset, I was staring at the objects on the table with greater intensity. I was saturated with sadness for the loss of Callum and Sophie naturally, but my focus now was for the future of their daughter. My own life would now be changing considerably, and I heard myself thinking that perhaps this might eventually all end up to be to my significant benefit.

Ananya was at her lesson, playing the piano. The decision I arrived at was clear and came to me quickly, almost as though I had run through some similar possible scenario at an early point in time.

I looked at Indira who had been staring at me since I had taken the phone. She was overcome with shock as I confirmed what she feared and then she began to collapse. I caught her. She began to cry out. I shook her by the shoulders and explained to her what was going to happen, that I had a plan.

"You and I are all little Ananya has in this world right now, Indira. We are responsible for her. As you know, Callum made me her godfather and so all legal responsibilities are mine, but you are the closest to her. You must be her best friend because she will depend on you. Do you understand? Ananya must go to England. She will live with her Aunt in London. Do you understand Indira? Indira!"

Indira stood there, eyes wide open but her face now began to change as she nodded and began to prepare herself for the task I put to her.

"It must come from you Indira, you must tell her what has happened and what is going to happen to her. She will be lost but she trusts you."

Only a few moments after my words were finished, she began touching her headscarf to her face in a nervous way, to dry the tears on the skin around her eyes. Then she looked at me as if to say something. But clearly she could not.

"Go! Make her understand that she will be taken of. Indira, go now!"

Indira seemed to be staring at me in an odd way, but she would not say what she was going to say and remained frozen and quiet. I told her firmly to go again and she left in a panic.

6

Tears On Lilac Silk

I walked at erratic speed to the piano teacher's house, so much so that my gait became a terribly broken run. It was not far, perhaps only thirty minutes to walk at a good pace, but my steps were in a desperately troubled rhythm which my body did not recognise. Time itself ran in an unfamiliar way, taking me to places in my mind I did not wish to go. Hips, ankles, knees, feet, waist, torso, arms and neck were estranged from each other, and this awkwardness was as unknown to me as my state of mind.

The thoughts of the deaths of Mr and Mrs Rondel darkened all available light, and Mr Kumar's specific behaviour added to the shadows around me. His change in energy was of a sinister type, it seemed to me, and kept returning to my mind to disturb my soul. His aura was of a dark and silent quality and its insidious presence had no volume within me. The way he had spoken and the way he had held Mrs Rondel's hand mirror in the way he did, it was as though he was no longer corporeal but only pure image. It was upsetting to my senses, and I couldn't shake the nauseous feeling which it created.

Previously I had not formed any emotions regarding Mr Kumar as I was quite new here but on reflection it was odd that I had felt nothing, neither good nor bad of him. I had instead only the neutral acceptance of the position he held over me. Now I would be greatly wary of him as there was no trust in my heart for him. I hated that this dark spirit he had could so influence my thoughts for Ananya and the way I wished to be when I found her.

I hurried and my haste made the short distance feel even greater still. With an irregular beat in my heart, anyone who saw me would have seen a woman out of step with life itself.

I could not think in a rational way at all. The thoughts I managed to make were as irregular as my steps, but they were somehow able to push me forward towards the task Mr Kumar had instructed me to perform.

Ananya at her piano, Sophie and Callum no more… The girl without protection, a future nowhere, her life with no shape or path.

It was too much pain. Her heart must be kept safe, and I must try to take her pain from her. Ananya will return to England as Mr Kumar has suggested, he knows best surely. She will be away from the death and she will be where she needs to be and where she belongs. That will be best.

Mrs Rondel's sister is a good woman, Mrs Rondel has always said so. To have a sister is an important thing and it is a good thing. To have an aunt is a very good thing.

England is the proper place for an English girl and Ananya is an English girl really, of course she is. She will have friends who are just like her, a girl needs friends like that. This place is not right for her now, not now. For her to live here is … she cannot live her life here, not without her parents, it is unthinkable.

Mr Kumar understands this. He will take her to London, and she will be safe there and will have her new life ahead of her. No, Mr Kumar is right, and I am so very near to Ananya now.

She will be on holiday in England with her Aunt Marie looking after her, just as she is expecting to be and Mr Kumar will explain everything to and she will make sure Ananya grows up to be a fine young English lady. That is how it will be.

This is it. I can hear the piano. It is a lovely sound, a slow melody and now slighter faster and faster still. Is this Ananya playing? How can her hands play so fast? I can see her through the window. There she is and her teacher and the piano. I shall wait for her by this tree until her lesson has finished and look at these flowers while I am waiting.

This music is the same as the music from yesterday from her birthday party, I recognise it. Mrs Rondel was playing her records, but it sounds more simple and clear when played on the piano.

Now the music has stopped, she is no longer playing. I think maybe she has finished. Yes, she is getting up from the piano, her teacher is walking with her to the door. She will be outside in a moment or two and I will be here waiting to collect her and to take her home.

Here she is.

"Indira! I can play jazz music!"

"I could hear you, Ananya! But I can hardly believe it was you!"

"It was me! I was playing jazz!"

"I know but I don't understand how can you play so beautifully after only two lessons? Will you tell me all about it as we walk home?"

"I shall, but Indira, why is your scarf wet?"

7

The Problems Of Being Unique

I remember standing outside the front door of my aunt's house in Primrose Hill in London in 1946 and it is the earliest recollection I have of my life in the way I believe most people think of memories. It's most definitely the first impression I made of England upon my arrival here and I can trace all later memory back to this moment in time.

My coat was dark grey and had four orange buttons the size of drink coasters running down the front in a line. The door was pale yellow in colour, primrose yellow of course I later learned.

Standing next to me was Niral Kumar, my father's business partner. It was my first time in England. Having come all the way from India by boat and several aeroplanes we were both very tired. We had made the last leg of our journey by taxi.

It was a bright clear day with a spotless crystal-blue sky and I could see my breath in the freezing cold air. It was February. Mr Kumar knocked, and we waited for a long time before he knocked again.

Mr Kumar knocked a third time. He was clearly anxious.

The two people living behind this door knew I was coming but we had not met each other before. I was scared. They would have known I would arrive on their doorstep in such a state but how does one prepare for such a visitor as this?

Mr Kumar had done his job, but I did not know what sort of a man he was. He was for me something like a bodyguard.

The people behind the door would now become personally responsible for my welfare. Kumar would pass them this burden or gift depending on how one might look at me.

The door was opened by a huge man with wild black hair, a giant with dark skin whose body filled the door frame completely but who stood there relaxed like a small boy. He was wearing a clean white T-shirt and a pair of baggy blue jeans.

He was most certainly the biggest Indian I had ever seen, Mr Kumar being perhaps one of the very smallest. It seemed I needed to say something, and this was what I said. I remember it because it was the first thing I had said since I learned of my parents' death. It was a statement.

"You are by far the biggest Indian I have ever seen in my whole life."

He smiled the biggest smile to reveal a set of perfect white teeth and then, as he began laughing, he managed to say in a big baritone voice,

"I ain't no Indian, little lady, I am an American through and through, and I ain't no American Indian neither … I'm thinking you're a little confused on account of the beautiful colour of my skin but way back in my history all of my family are from the continent of Africa!"

I was dumbfounded but that was how Uncle John and I first met each other.

He continued, "You must be Ananya. I was told you were English but from the colour of you, I'm fairly uncertain as to whether you might be Indian yourself! You sir must be Mr Niral Kumar, pleased to meet you. I'm certainly sure that you are from India!"

"Yes, I most certainly am. It has been the most arduous of journeys."

They shook hands.

"Please forgive me my manners sir, I guess you're both wondering who the heck I am. I'm John, John Jackson. Your

Aunt Marie keeps me about the house to fix up the things that need fixing, tend to the garden, that kind of thing. But you know we do just about everything else together too … if you get my drift and you know, come to think about it, she ain't been paying me lately, so you figure that one out!"

I burst into uncontrollable laughter.

We stood there with just our three bags, myself laughing, John drinking from a mug of coffee and Mr Kumar who was quite an awkward man, I think.

"Please, I just wish to get in and sit down for moment if that's not too much trouble."

"How rude I am. Come on in, please, come on in. Mr Kumar, let's get you a nice cup of tea."

This might all have happened very differently from the way I have described it here. No one has a perfect memory, certainly of events which occur at such an age, but this is the way I choose to remember it, my introduction to Uncle John. He was just so big, and his heart and the scale of the kindness he showed me from that day to this could not have been bigger.

Aunt Marie was in the kitchen but the moment she realised I'd arrived she came running out, still holding a large wooden spoon. The house is quite small, but the hall and front room are quite large so that when she picked me up and held me close and tight and span me around we didn't knock too many things over.

We loved each other from the first second. As soon as she'd stopped hugging me and kissing me and spinning me, she put me back down on the floor. She knelt in front of me and we looked at each other eye to eye.

She looked just like my mother, a year younger and her face a little smaller but her features were unmistaken shared with her sister, perhaps only slightly softer. Her hair was the same colour, a rich dark brown, but it had a gentle wave to it.

There was no mistaking our eyes. Marie, my mother, and I have irises with hues of forest, fern greens with glints of amber honey sunshine.

We did not talk about my mother for many years, but I believe this was not a denial of Sophie's life but in fact more an affirmation of mine and my Aunt Marie's.

There was a wonderful smell of cooking throughout the house.

"I didn't think that you would arrive so perfectly on time, coming all the way that you have. I had hoped of course, but that's only because I am a silly optimist. I made a lamb stew. Are you hungry? What a ridiculous question!"

"I'm a vegetarian, Aunt Marie, which means I can't eat lamb or meat of any kind for that matter. I don't want to be a problem."

Marie looked at me for a while and smiled.

"Good heavens. You know this is good for several reasons. I've never much liked meat myself either you know, it's so gristly and chewy isn't it. I can't help thinking there would be far fewer wars if we all stopped eating it too. So as of today, I think I will become a vegetarian too! You know we have rationing so meat is so hard to come by anyway, there's another reason."

Mr Kumar had been standing quietly in one comer with John standing next to him. They were both respectful of this being an extremely special meeting for Marie and myself but after so many seconds of silence in which we all just looked at each other, suddenly highly aware of the complexity of this situation, John brought us to back to a place of everyday normality. It was needed.

"Well, I for one am hungry. That lamb is not going to waste, I'll tell you that much for nothing! I've been smelling that smell all afternoon and I need to chow down. I hope you're not exclusively a vegetable person as well are you Mr Kumar?"

"I'm not really supposed to eat meat, it's a religious thing you understand, but sometimes I do. I'm a little bit naughty in this way. It's like people who say they don't drink but then every now and then they occasionally imbibe … when no one is looking."

"Oh, I see, OK. Well, now we're talking anyway. Would you like a drink Mr Kumar? I mean, would you care to er … imbibe?"

John looked at me and winked, his eyes were the darkest nutty brown but surrounded by the whitest white which flashed at me in the dark hall. I couldn't help but start laughing again.

"I thought you'd never ask … It's been quite a journey. I'm dryer than an elephant's skin in the midday sun. You wouldn't happen to have a gin and tonic by any chance?"

John looked at him funnily. "You sure? I'll go see, I'm sure I'll be able to rustle something up for you. I don't know about no G and T though …"

We ate and John and Mr Kumar drank, John more so as I remember. He had some potato whiskey which he made in a shed in the garden. With its effects, he started telling some of his more humorous, and frankly completely uncreditworthy war stories.

Mr Kumar passed out from exhaustion and the effects of alcohol. I believe he had some business to attend to in the city and left me in my new home with my new loved ones the very next morning.

8

Cannot Be Taught

I was a beautifully crazy, bizarre, and precocious ball of energy. I did not slump into some mute depression or stare catatonically at walls. I didn't scream and rage or fight. I had no disturbing mental illness or physical ticks. Sometimes I was quiet and then at other times I could not be stopped from talking. I talked about anything and everything which grabbed my attention, or indeed which distracted me from it.

My vocabulary and accent were eclectic and mixed. As an English girl I was polite and well mannered, a little lady as John had called me was right on the money. I loved to be the centre of attention and thought myself to be not only a princess but one who was significantly different from other princesses to merit special attention and privileges.

Words came easy to me to speak, and I played with them to humorous effect, even if I did not appreciate it so much when people laughed. The phrases I used were scattered here and there with Indian ways, an unusual sentence construction or styles cultivated by exposure to the Empire and its strange history.

Then I picked up John's vernacular which was not only African American but glazed with jazz and fired in the hell of war. Half the time I didn't understand a word of his 'scat' as he told me it was called, but I learned it all the same. I began hearing something similar in the Louis Armstrong records John often played and then in turn I played with these words too.

I was not interested in my past, not outwardly. I had only a few rare clues as to it even ever having existed. There were a few scant pieces of information I could recall and some blunt facts my Aunt Marie had been able to give to me. And there were a few sad personal items I possessed, things I had carried with me from India.

These objects amounted to just a few symbolic toys, trinkets really, from a childhood lost in time and eclipsed in darkness, a glass prism and some small copper cymbals which I had allowed to tarnish long since.

The prism was on my windowsill and I enjoyed its rainbow whenever the sun shone. The little cymbals were not much more than a novelty as it didn't seem as though they had been made as serious instruments. Nevertheless, they had always been important to me.

The little discs were however covered in a beautiful patina of light green, tinged with an other-worldly turquoise blue which had something of the aqua about it too. This verdigris colour grew more intense every year and I had never wished to attempt to clean it away. It did not just represent the passing of time, but indeed all of my time. Further to this, I liked to imagine that it protected the copper underneath it. I didn't think of it as dirty or in need of a polish. This was shiny new copper, clothed in a fabulous armour.

I often became so sad looking at these objects and I told myself sometimes that the little girl whom I had been in India was a fabrication, that she had never existed and that I had made her up. Perhaps I had just created her as a friend, a hand to hold on to as I grew into the young woman I am now. With no real memory of her, or indeed of anyone else from those first years of my life, perhaps inventing her had been an easy thing to do.

I couldn't just tell myself to forget about her, but I had to tell myself to stop trying to recall any memory of her. It was a memory that apparently just wasn't there and I was making myself feel terrible by seeking a taste of it.

Not being able to remember my parents, their lives or even their faces has clearly caused deep problems but I have my Aunt Marie and my Uncle John and they are the best type of people anyone could wish for. Aunt Marie is my real aunt but her and John are not even married, which is quite scandalous for the good people of Primrose Hill.

There are people here who don't talk to us even though we are neighbours, and the status of my family was the cause of persistent bullying of a needlessly cruel nature at school.

I attended a Montessori school, just a short walk from our house. This was a wonderful place, mainly I think because everyone here was just the same as me really in that we were all very different from each other. We just played, and by so doing we just learned.

St Pauls School for Girls, where I went to next, was a terrible place for me. Everyone looked the same because of the uniform but that just meant they were all trying to actually be the same, which of course is impossible. Then of course, when they realised this, they all started trying so desperately hard to be different from each other so that somehow they all became the same! They were all forgetting how very silly it looks when one tries to be something other than you are, you indeed something that you can never be! Whatever they thought they were trying to do, they were failing at it, and in my opinion at least, they were trying far too hard in the first place.

I made no friends at all there and only progressed by applying myself fully to the subjects for which I had an aptitude. I took music here for a while, but they would not let me play jazz! It was hard to believe and after a some defiance on my part and some swear words unwisely projected towards people of power, I was suspended, twice!

They let me return from my second suspension to sit my A Levels, which I completed successfully, and my entry into my first choice of university was an easy step away from all that nonsense.

However, when I arrived at the London School of Economics, I soon discovered that it was formal education in its entirety with which I had a problem and that whichever way you looked at it, I was at the centre of this problem.

The intensity of my intellectual education fed my mind with ideas and philosophies. I was in the middle of an academic whirlwind, one of my own making mostly.

My director of studies and I did not get along. She was a very intelligent and high achieving woman, and to begin with I thought she was very cool. She had succeeded in opening my eyes to a new world, one which was rapidly evolving, and I admired her very much for it but for some reason she didn't like me, not one bit.

It was, she told me, because I seemed 'hell-bent on being reactionary' and that I was always being 'deliberately and unnecessarily antagonistic' and that this was destructive to my progress. She said that I 'preferred conflict to rational exploration' and I was regressing because I believed this approach was the only way forward.

I'd explained to her that it was integral to my outlook to challenge the methods of the teaching I received and indeed the foundations of these methods, and that it was the only way I could learn, the only way I wished to learn. Her dogma was that true knowledge could only be gained through the resolution of my ideas which she told me were 'fractured' and fundamentally in conflict with each another. My essays were full of inconsistencies and logical contractions. I told her that knowledge was not of primary interest to me but that imagination was a superior tool by virtue of it being unlimited.

She did not dig my ideas, and this was only economics! Most of my ideas are from India and come from thinking about astronomy and jazz and few seem to understand them or how important they are to me.

It was my actual language with which she had the greatest problems and when I tried to simplify this for her, to translate what I was saying into form which I thought she might find more agreeable it did not integrate with her understanding. She was unable to continue teaching me and we parted company. It was a shame because in many areas we were on the same page I felt.

There was no one else in the economics department who would even give me a run for my money. Teachers and students alike were all stiff men with even stiffer ideologies, all firmly stuck in the last decade. The man who was assigned to be my ongoing tutor did his best to 'tame my wayward thinking' but then, when his effort met with no success, he began trying to ignore me.

This experience at university was incredibly frustrating from day one as I needed to acquire so much wisdom from these people. Instead, I found myself in the libraries most of the time with my head in books trying to discover some kind of description which would help me to find what I sought.

My searching was without any goals or any defined criteria for success. A lot of my reading had nothing to do with the curriculum of my degree; economics is a broad subject, but my research was invariably way off script. At that time I was concentrating mainly on the mining of copper in Chile, solar astronomy, the psychology of perception and the proposed new thinking about ideas of space travel to the moon.

9

Wild At The Keys

Experience teaches, but the only experiences which were teaching me anything I felt to be of any real, true value were those I was having when I was playing music. This had always been with John, but I had also started to find an outlet for my passion away from home.

The jazz was all over the place and not just in Soho but every part of the West End. It was in pockets of London to the north too and it had even reached some of us students at the London School of Economics. I found it here and it found me, it was always within me but now there was a way to let it out.

If you felt the desire for it, the need for it and if you looked for it, you'd find it. I'd found it already and I was only a year into my degree.

There was a vibe, a groove, a beat and vitally there were the dudes, the cats, and the movers to make it all happen for real. I'm fairly feline myself, slipping down back alleys at dusk to rendezvous with my ever-changing crews. Mainly they are French Algerians but there are some East End wise boys too.

Mixed in are some old timers left over from the war and there are plenty of these guys. Uncle John is one of them. He'd discharged himself from duties with the US military and stayed here in England to get into the scene.

They are soldiers, warriors, men of colour, of all kinds of colours, from all corners of the United States and here they use the music to unite themselves. It is a shared language, and they speak it so well because theirs is a musical conversation, a dialogue which I have now become a part of.

They are from very poor backgrounds, without exception and few have any education at all, but they survived the war and because of this they want to tell the world how they feel. I find it hard to call them black because the emotions they possess and the way they can do this has no connection to the black that I think of when I hear this word.

The black in me is a void, an emptiness and space which I fear will never be full. The musicians I meet, whatever their memories of the war they helped to win are full of experience and life. Some were treated badly by us as hosts and by their own men too. They struggle and they express this struggle with the sounds they make with their instruments. I learn from them every time we play together because they play with the rhythm in their hearts, and I know I am like them because their lives and this music are one and the same. At night, the beats they bring to this city bring this city to life.

They are from places with names I have heard of but geographies and ways of life I can only guess at; Indiana, Missouri, Manhattan, Cleveland, Kansas – wherever! With nothing to go back to they pick up a horn, some strings or get back in touch with some drums or pretty much anything and they make ends meet by doing this, by getting into what they know best.

There were even some rascals from New Orleans, they were the best. They had the jazz running through their blood, they breathed it in and then they blew it all out for us limeys, hungry for some rhythms in an England which was beginning to change very quickly.

It was 1959. The Dave Brubeck Quartet had just recorded a little song called 'Take Five' and the masterpiece 'Kind Of Blue' by Miles Davis had just been released.

I was in the middle of all this and the cats I kept meeting in the clubs just loved me, how couldn't they! I was riding free on the vibes, there's no doubt about it. I was connecting with these fellas and the way they played. Musical evolution was a fact.

No one knew about my secret forays into the darker places of London at night, the clubs and pubs, but I was learning bad as well as good in these dirty dives. I could scratch my itch and fuel my hungry need for self-expression and secrecy and anonymity were all part of this. I was unafraid, confident, and I developed an increasingly wild alter ego. I had no way to know that just as a genius inside my soul was being given a chance to inspire itself and rise to the sky, I was always spiralling downwards and at some point in time I must have started to go under.

All those years of not talking about where I'd come from, not talking about what I could remember of my parents and then with a greater and greater awareness realising that I could remember nothing at all. That is my black void and I'd started falling into it.

Here, at a trendy university in the capital I thought it would be different, free minds, free souls, all that kind of thing. But no, everyone's locked into their rigid rules, their formulaic ways of thinking, rigidly structured Western philosophies and dare I say it the restrictions they impose on themselves with their own etiquette and manners.

And then there's the little matter of being female. Things are changing but just not fast enough for my way of thinking. I don't have any male friends here, not to speak of. I see these groups of young guys, smartly dressed and hanging around together and I've tried to get in with them, but I think there's something different about me, something that quickly causes them to find me unattractive.

Do I appear to be aloof? Do I look like a non-conformist, like a 'troublemaker'? I don't know. I feel quite special and unique in many ways and perhaps this shows and puts people off, but we're all different. I'm just not good 'friend material' perhaps, at least to the people I'm drawn to and it's just stupid, for them as much as for me, because I'd like to think I'd be a pretty good friend to most, especially once they've got past the 'oddness', 'madness', 'uniqueness,' or whatever it is that they think they see in me.

There is this one person, a Japanese girl called Miyu. We found out on our first meeting that we went to that same Montessori school together. I think we remembered each other because we played together so often.

She's very small indeed and so very quietly spoken and we understand each other on another frequency from everyone else. She's also an economist in her first year too but we don't really talk about that, it's because of music that we are able to communicate. She's a classical musician and she is not just good, she is very, very good. She is a concert pianist and in the university orchestra.

Clearly our styles of playing the piano couldn't be more different. Miyu has been highly educated and has every qualification you can imagine and I, well, I've kind of made it up all the way. However, that's where we started, our differences, and that has become the focus of our interest in each other. To me she's Amadeus Mozart, to her I'm Art Tatum.

Then we've both got our interesting life stories to tell each other too and I'm sure there's much more there for both of us. Her father came over from Japan, sometime near the end of the war and married her mother who is English. She is mixed race and so very exotic to me and probably even more so to others I'm sure. People react to her just because of the way she looks and this can be very confusing for her. Miyu speaks Japanese fluently, beautifully, and when she does it sounds incredible but her English is also perfect, spoken slowly with an accent, not a Japanese accent, she has what is called a 'Surrey slur'.

To anyone who sees us together I imagine we appear as two misshapen peas in a pod, particularly as I'm quite tall. Also, although my London accent is nicely clipped and has a classy and quite sophisticated range, if I'm honest I can get a little loud and rowdy after a couple of drinks. Miyu's voice will only rise in volume slightly when she wishes to emphasise a word or phrase. I always listen to what she has to say because of this. She is tiny and perfect, and I respect her and admire her greatly, I want to be like her sometimes, but that may be because she is currently the only friend I have made who returns my feelings.

There are bad days, days when I look at myself in the mirror and I really can't say who I am, what I am, where I'm going or indeed where I would like to go. The jazz is all over the place, it's in my heart and it's in my soul but on the bad days I sometimes think it's only in my head.

Then the sun goes down and I move deep into the night. That other world opens up and I meet some guys from my band, and we drink and we smoke a bit and then we get on the stage in front of some hip crowd and I'm getting paid to do this, to do what I love, what gets me off and turns me on.

We swing, we fill the smoky air of these clubs with our sounds. We turn the heat up, we improvise, we cook it, we slow it down, we harmonise. We play the standards, and we play our own stuff, we move around these freely and in between them spontaneously. We rotate and return.

I'm often in the background, that strange young girl sitting at the piano, most unusual they say. Then it's my solo and all my heroes are with me, all my teachers inspiring me, filling me with their energy.

And I let loose. I am myself which is whatever and whomever I am. I am here and I am alive and I am whole. I am not lost, and I do not need to question, to remember or to doubt. The jazz is all over the place but in this moment, I have summoned it all here and it flows with fluctuating feelings through my fingertips.

10

Three And The Sea

I dropped out of LSE without really telling anyone, and I was getting way too far into the jazz and even trying some of the drugs that the guys used. I was drinking and smoking and leading a double life, hiding my fall from grace in academia from Marie and John. Only Miyu had any idea of what I was going through. I think I must have been close to a breakdown.

The way it all fell apart was such a surreal nightmare but fortunately, when I woke up from it, I could see it for what it was. I had embarked on an unsustainable joyride, an escapist fantasy which was realising itself spiralling upwards as well as down.

There was an incredible peak followed by an emergency descent and a monstrous crash.

I found myself in a recording studio, recording a jazz single with a mixed group of extremely talented musicians who were becoming cult figures in our underground universe. It was a full day, which ran into the night. I was on fire on the piano, my genius showed itself to me in those twenty-four hours and it delighted me, the way it took me to dizzying heights, but it scared me too.

I remembered nothing of the next twenty-four hours. There was a lot of drinking of hard spirits. I was all crazy and strung out and as the only girl in this frantic creative maelstrom there was a certain attention on me. I revelled in it, I encouraged it, and I found myself in some horrible part of London I did not know. There was bad money involved and I had been abused in a way I did not want to understand or remember. Fortunately,

I found a way to see that I had the best friend in the world to turn to and was able to confide in John.

I was sobbing, a nonsensical mess, and he held me. That's all he did, all he had to do, all I needed anyone to do. He put his massive arms around me and held me until he knew there was nothing bad left in me. Just a couple of days later Aunt Marie told me she'd made plans for a holiday, for the three of us.

She knew there had been trouble brewing for a while, but her attempts to talk with me about her concerns met with rejection. A lot of this happened very quickly and then she got some news from the dean of my faculty about my lack of attendance. It was just two days after that when I had gone to John. He'd spoken to her straight away and she did something about it.

The idea of going on holiday to Cornwall was like the sun breaking through the clouds.

We took a train from Paddington, first thing in the morning, around 7.30am. With just a couple of small bags each, every stop we made saw the considerable tension and anxiety in my mind begin to loosen.

Soon the stops had names which I didn't recognise and then the landscape began changing so much so that I started to stop dwelling on the troubling recent past. I let go of those memories, and it wasn't so hard. I thought of them as notes I could have played differently in a piece of music, and now their sound had begun to fade, I could allow myself only to be concerned with the music in the present moment. As I moved with this journey, the present became all-consuming, so much so that the past dissolved and the idea of the future was so unknowable as to not worry me about its nature or content.

It is so easy to identify with the grey of London because one can think of it as a neutral canvass on which to paint the colourful and exciting picture of a life. However, now the changing hues of the colours before me seemed to float, landing on my retinas gently without the need to think of having to choose one over another or what kind of picture to paint. The painting was coming to me and it not only calmed and soothed but energised and refreshed.

Greys became greens. Concrete edges became rounded scrolling hills of trees and grass. And I watched this whole transformation in virtually silent inner space as we rumbled along.

The rocking rolling rhythm of the wheels on the track was at times too loud and disjointed to inspire peacefulness and I smiled to myself as the thought of it sending me to sleep drifted in and out of my thinking without ever really taking a hold. I didn't sleep at all during our eight-hour transition even though I was most dreadfully tired in my emotions. The undulating wavy feel of these ragged moods was a pleasant change from the edgy harshness they had taken of late and this smoothing and rounding accompanied all the way to our destination.

The slowing down for bends and stations ahead and the pace slowly gained as we then sped up felt more natural than one might think the clunky mechanism of a train's engineering might create. The breaking and jarring of sudden moves left and right accompanied by the acceptance of my relaxing body in response. I was a taut wire becoming soft wool. An instrument strung too tight slackened off to be a lower frequency vibration, less sharp, flatter, more bass, less treble, more moderate and sustained rather than staccato or shrill.

During long periods of regular, steady speed motion, my own body rhythms began to recover a more natural state, slowing so that they might find ways to harmonise with themselves.

I suppose I was in a contemplative trance of a sort. It was such warm day and I remembered nothing else of the journey when we eventually disembarked. The passing of time in this mood produced in my thoughts an abstract musical composition. It was a lolloping jazz melody which I kept joining into loops, trying to find a way to use them as a line on which to hook the changing colours and shapes I felt as we moved along.

It was early afternoon when we opened the door to the flat which Aunt Marie's friend had said we could stay in. The key was easy enough to find, under a large stone with a hole in it just as described, but the door itself was stuck.

Perhaps it had expanded with the salty sea air and had swollen to fill its frame. We were in danger of falling at the last hurdle until John gave it a single decisive kick with his right foot tied into his size twelve army-issue boot. The door flew open, and we were greeted by light.

It was a tiny place, barely big enough for one, let alone three but almost the whole of one side of this box room was a taken up by an oversized glass window which looked out over St Ives harbour.

We staggered in with our bags and each of us became overwhelmed in our own ways by the beauty revealed before us. The bags were hastily dropped as we walked up to the window wall, which took but a few seconds the room was so small. We stood there three abreast for at least half an hour gazing, spotting, pointing out, gaping, remarking on special features of this seascape with its rare moments and events. After this time, we located the only chair in the place and two large boxes upon which we sat down for another half an hour or so to continue our active interaction with each other and this view.

John had thought to bring some army-issue binoculars which were so large and heavy as to require their own purpose-built box, which comprised almost half of his luggage. He said they had belonged to a five-star general whom he drove around in a jeep on occasion who had given them to him personally as a parting gift when the war was over. He showed us the general's name stamped onto one of the lens barrels, then he smiled and said, "Well I say he 'gave' them to me but the truth is the miserable son of a gun did in fact misplace them, and it was only later I came across them in my locker at which time he had unfortunately already departed the country for the States. I'm sure he would have wanted me to have them though, you know as something to remember him by!"

We took it in turns; a boy and his large German shepherd played with a ball on the sand; rusty old chains ran out from the harbour wall to many of the small fishing vessels moored in the harbour; some chains were hidden by sand in places, all were covered in seaweed and barnacles.

The thick stone walls, wide and squat, sat on three sides of the harbour sheltering these brave boats from rough seas which might threaten to roll in from the Atlantic. Currently it was calm, so very calm, and the sun was so near to the water as to throw its light from the sharp, immense horizon all the way to our tiny beach.

The quality of light was so strange and ethereal for me. A turquoise sheen on a glacial blue surface was hit at the lowest of angles by orange sunlight streaks, highlighting the crests of tiny rippling waves as they found their way around the harbour opening lapped up onto our shore. Their colours formed a harmony, this harmony formed a sound, this sound formed a music and this music washed magic onto me, through me and then into me to reverberate within me forever.

Before the sun had completely found its rest, a dark cloud, dense and strong and rude blew in while we were distracted by the play of lights. Rain started as silent minuscule dots on our window world and the surface of the sea became suddenly textured with an unsettling roughness.

Sooner than seemed possible, gusty whips of sea spray hit the window much harder and the echoes of this sound in the room were incredible. They seemed to be amplified by an accident of the room's dimensions.

We laughed and felt a sudden release in the joy of this unexpected change and then by some freakish chance some rays of the sun must have struck the mist in such a way as a rainbow briefly appeared for a matter of only a few moments. But we all saw it, before it dissolved into the twilight.

It was too much for us. It was dream-like, and we stopped laughing, becoming confused for a beat. It was a fairy-tale vision accompanied by a drum of rain striking glass. None of us could comment with rational words, in fact it sent us into quietness.

The sun was gone, the ocean having claimed her for the night.

It was dark inside too now, as we came to our senses. There was no electricity we discovered but we lit candles Aunt Marie found in a drawer in the mini kitchen and then played a card game with a couple of packs John had liberated from a fancy Paris hotel a few months ago.

The game we played had its roots in New Orleans he told us, but the complex rules had been 'tuned' in San Francisco. We bet cocktail sticks from a large box Marie had seen next to the candles.

I was in love for the first time, with both a place and a feeling.

These ten days which scrolled through my consciousness as fast as the weather conditions flipped and changed were deeply rich deposits of sensory impressions laid down in the geology of my being.

All my senses were touched and continuously so. Many 'events' seemed to keep occurring, happenings which normally would have gone unnoticed became of great interest to us all. These moments of observation and internal flux tended to overlap, many happening together or combinations ebbing and flowing.

There was in fact little time for thinking, rational, abstract, or otherwise. My senses took over, with my fingertips finding new textures to run over; the algae on rocks all slippery and slimy and smooth softened the rough edges of the granite on which it grew. The dry moss and lichens on the dark slate roof tops of these densely crammed together old fishermen's cottages here have bright yellows, soft magentas, and turquoise tints – I can just reach some to touch outside our window. They also grow between the heavy mortar of the stones of their outer walls and I close my eyes as I drag my palms across them walking by.

We ate little else except bread and cheese, brie and Camembert brought over from France daily. Crusty hot pasties freshly cooked and sold in the morning nearby sometimes for our breakfast. The wine we drank was white and our tea black as we found difficulty finding milk for reasons which we weren't too worried about.

John and Marie told me their stories of growing up and some of their stories together. John refused to say anything of the war and after asking him only a couple of questions, he said quite firmly with a locked stare, "If you want to know about war, it is wise first to learn a little about peace!" He then walked away.

John, I learned, could neither read nor write. It seemed strange to me that such an obvious fact should have escaped my notice all the years I had known him. When he told me one afternoon as we walked along the beach it was a moment he had clearly rehearsed and was delivered as an embarrassed confession, bordering on shame, and I realised why he had gone to great lengths to hide this surprising truth to me all these years.

I tried to joke about it, but he did not laugh, he was serious and wanted to learn. Immediately I set about trying to teach him. The results were sometimes humorous, but they were overwhelmingly suffused with a lifetime of frustration, and he became angry with himself. I suggested we leave it for another time and told him that reading and writing meant very little anyway if one had no idea of what it was that one was trying to say in the first place. He looked at me quizzically and said, "Well that's easy enough for you to say!" He followed it up with, "Just what are you trying to say anyway?"

Marie told me everything she could remember about my parents including the things she had previously held back for my own good or simply failed to mention.

There were details of her sister, who was only a year older than her, which showed how they were clearly such opposites. Marie was involved in the fashion industry before the war, the 'rag trade' as she referred to it, and was a kind of socialite in the late 1930s. She was fascinated by the high fashions of Europe and had been to Paris on two occasions. When war broke out, she had turned her skills to the design of army clothing and had herself designed some of the standard issue army, navy and air force overcoats.

On the other hand, her sister was a scientist, dedicated to the study of the night sky and was apparently quite an introverted academic. Her interest in astronomy was purely theoretical to begin with, but her PhD in Manchester had led to very practical, extracurricular work on a project concerned with calculating the position of the moon. She had used an early mechanical, analogue computer to create very accurate and reliable predictions of the moon's position extending more than one hundred years into the future. This groundbreaking work had led to employment at the Greenwich Observatory, which is why my father and her had moved to London and bought the house together in Primrose Hill. How she had come to refocus her attentions on the study of the sun, my Aunt Marie could not relate.

My father used his geology degrees to find a well-paid job for Shell, in the pursuit of global oil exploration, and worked in their newly built headquarters on the Embankment. He was dedicated to my mother who had led them to London, and who then led them to India. When I asked if they were in love with each other, Marie had hesitated for just a split second which I registered before saying, "Of course."

She then pointed out a seagull which had swooped in from the shore to steal an old man's bag of chips from his very hand. He was cursing at the bird who flew off, bag in beak, oblivious to the man's unfulfilled hunger and rage. We laughed uncontrollably but when we were quiet again, I asked her, "Will I ever fall in love do you think?"

"Of course you will Ananya, don't be so silly! Really, what a daft question to ask! Anyway, falling in love is the easy part, the hard part is dealing with the consequences of it, that takes a lifetime, if you're lucky."

John was some fifty feet away further along the shoreline, with his trousers rolled up and wading knee deep in the surf. He had found a funny-shaped piece of flotsam. It was a piece of wood which looked like a … well it looked like the funny thing that it was, and he was waving it all around and shouting about it to us.

"Really," said my aunt, "I can't take him anywhere!"

On the train on the way home I was in tears, but tears of joy. When I'd pulled myself together and we'd laughed some, I told Marie and John that the holiday was the rescue and recovery of my very soul, a renewal, and a reassertion of its strength.

John said, "Well they don't call it R&R for nothing!"

The day after returning to London I needed to go somewhere to think, maybe to write a few things down, and so I went to the British Museum Library.

I had walked past it many times on my way to LSE every day but had never thought to go in. It was a 'special' place, but it was a place where I had thought I might feel like I didn't belong. When I went, I realised there was nothing to worry about, it felt like home. In fact, I believe I may have saved this experience subconsciously until such a time as I felt equal to it, worthy of it, ready for it and with great relevance now, in need of it.

Its huge copper dome roof, some hundred feet across, created a heaven above, a ceiling to keep the lofty ideas in all the books it contained from floating upwards and escaping into the sky and then onwards and further upwards into space. It also proved to be an enormous lens, focusing my mind onto areas I had not thought of before. There were zones of awareness which I had managed to keep hidden from myself and these I now explored with the help of various maps and atlases I found in hard-to-reach places.

There were no corners in this vast round room, only the idea of a circular return to an origin. This drew me to making a detailed plan which I swiftly put into action.

After a deep discussion with both Marie and John, I booked a ticket with Imperial Airways which would take me in a series of flights to Karachi. From there I would organise travel down the coast by boat to Bombay and then onwards to Kodaikanal. Here I hoped to explore the nature of my own origin, to discover how my roots had been severed and whether there remained clues as to how I might attempt to continue growing.

The day before leaving I was so well prepared that I had very little to do. It was a nice enough day for a walk, for a little excursion even, and a Sunday too, so London would be relatively quiet.

I made my way by the underground to Greenwich and from there walked up to the hill and to the Observatory. It had been a favourite hangout of mine from an early age. Aunt Marie had allowed me to explore the capital from as young as ten or eleven as I was more than capable of finding my way around and back home again. However, I hadn't been up here for a long time, not for over a year I thought.

My mother used to work in this place, in quite a position of influence I was led to understand. Her work with her PhD had made her uniquely qualified for some of the projects which were underway, and I had been told that the employment she had gained at this famous place was the primary reason for my parents move from Manchester.

My father had not found it difficult to find work in the oil exploration business I imagine. Geologists of any competence would be an essential element to the workings of companies like Shell at that time. I often passed that building which was built as its headquarters on the river by Embankment, quite impressive it is too. As a married couple working in these prestigious jobs, I can only think that they must have been very happy with their careers, and I always came to a dead end when searching for reasons why they would have chosen to leave and venture so far away as India.

It cannot have been straightforward to do so in the late 1930s and must have been a decision they made together for some very strong reasons. The cost financially must have been great, and to leave the house in Primrose Hill for something so unknown was hard for me to get my head around. But then that was exactly what I was about to do for my own personal reasons and I'm sure they had theirs. I just wish I knew what they had been.

I can't think their decision was motivated purely by financial considerations, although clearly my father at least believed in the possibility of finding and mining copper ore. They must have been idealists of some kind, dreamers surely. That they might have been running away from something terrible had crossed my mind many times and the threat of war looming large must have had some part in their considerations and plans, but again I was oblivious as to the nature of such speculations.

All that was clear to me in this moment was that my mother must have come here, every day from Primrose Hill, making the same journey which I had just made and stood here as I did now. She must have looked out over the London skyline, perhaps next to my father and the idea of India must have filled their souls.

There would have been a decisive moment. Were they holding hands, did they kiss, was it a cold emotionless calculation based on practical necessity and realities? There would have been a point when the decision was made and from that moment their future was determined. This choice one of free will, just as mine had been, but influenced by what magic, what passions, and what kind of love?

I stood alone, deeply sad. Feelings of excitement were bubbling to the though and these were closely associated with the prospect of finding a happiness which my imagination suggested to me.

This was not a vague hope of finding answers to superficial questions. I was involved now in an existential quest to discover my true self; my identity, my meaning and my purpose as a person. Bizarrely it was pure sensations I had decided to seek and absorb as I knew the layering of textures and scents, the visions and sounds and the tastes of the vast continent towards which I now began to move to be the key to the unity of my soul.

Even as I sensed the wind picking up and the coldness it brought to my skin, it was the softness I felt of ground under my feet which moved me rather than my feet which I now discovered were moving on it and over it. This became a series of almost automatic steps which took me from this place and the contemplations and reflections I had often made here to the place where I wished to be.

11

Walking Towards A Piano

Walking the very last part of this journey, it had started to feel like a personal pilgrimage or perhaps more accurately a quest for the memories I hoped might heal my fractured identity. On turning the last corner of the winding path which leads up the side of the mountain, the Observatory suddenly came into view against its vast mountain vista backdrop revealing its beauty to my senses.

There was no accompanying rush of adrenaline however, only that generated by the long climb. There was no sudden flood of memories either. The dominant feeling was of recognition, acceptance of the reality of this place in my mind. My consciousness shouted out that I had been here before, but I could not say that I remembered it, not in the meaningful way I had hoped for having elevated its status so greatly.

It did not need my expectations because just being here did not satisfy some underlying inner criteria I must have created. However vaguely defined these conditions were in my mind, the shapes and colours of the buildings and the luscious gardens in which they were set failed to trigger the feelings I had wished for.

I did not dwell on my disappointment as it was just a fact. But throughout the few days I spent here, the neutrality of my emotions became a numbness of spirit. I saw myself as a small figure in an anonymous black and white photograph.

This feeling became a horrible indifference which I could not shake off and the difficulty for me was that it was in direct conflict with the staggering beauty all around.

I met several tourists, some of whom had travelled great distances from places such as Japan and Brazil simply to admire the telescope placed like a lofty island in the sky. These people could not help but emote, effuse, and overflow with reams of emotional superlatives to describe the impact this environment was currently having on their lives.

It was difficult to relate to them as I felt neither the joy of a child, the familiarity of a resident or the focus and discipline of an employee. This was not a holiday for me, and neither was it a homecoming. I didn't know quite what it was.

I was not angry or upset but a small character in a scene of monochrome emotions which should have been multicoloured and full of music. On several occasions I found myself sitting down wishing I had not come. After one such period of contemplation I nearly left spontaneously, an idea to slip away without saying goodbye to anyone.

However, it was the people I met who kept my interest in my purpose alive and I have to say I became fascinated by these interactions.

Almost immediately upon arrival a few people looked at me as if they recognised me, some as though they had seen a ghost, but I found it hard to imagine anyone could have put the face of a six-year-old in their memory to my own. Nevertheless, I saw those whom I felt I knew in some way.

One was a technical assistant, an elderly man whose hunched walk I felt I knew somehow. Our eyes met for a few moments as we said hello to each other but when I tried to engage in conversation he was troubled and little rude complaining that he was far too busy and had so much to do. He bustled himself away.

Then I came across Indira who was sitting on a bench outside the main telescope building. She was drinking a cup of tea and reading a novel. She smiled and I sat down next to her.

It was a smile I recognised but to say that I remembered it or remembered her would be an exaggeration.

We spoke for less than ten minutes. After we had both established our identities, a period of highly awkward conversation followed. I felt I was getting somewhere with her at last. When I pressed her for details of the day of my parents' death she was disturbed but could see I was in need.

She tried to recall what she was able to but she could only tell me that she had woken me to dress me and take me to my second piano lesson with Mrs Singh and that she had then been asked to collect me and break the terrible news to her. I wanted more and suddenly asked too much. She stopped talking and was on the verge of crying.

I relented but asked one last question, more as a kind of casual inquiry. "What kind of day was it? The weather?"

This she felt comfortable with. It had been sunny and warm the day before for my birthday party but sometime during the night it had rained lightly. The area where the copper mine was situated had much greater rainfall and perhaps, she said, this may have been the cause of the landslide. But here it had been light and when she had woken it was already sunny and it was just the lawns which were damp.

She seemed to place herself back in that time and was experiencing some moments of it in her memories as she let them play out. She recalled that the path to Mrs Singh's house was slightly slippery and that she had slipped several times, lost her footing, and made her new pair of shoes muddy.

Indira stopped her account and confusion came across her face as she remembered a detail which didn't make sense to her. When she had dressed me and had put on my little shoes, they were already wet and muddy. She had not thought much of it at the time, thinking perhaps that I had been outside late at night with my father before going to bed, before they left for the mine and that we might have been playing outside together and been caught in the rain when it had started.

She remained confused, as I was too, and then suddenly became very alert and insisted on taking me to see Mr Kumar.

I had been told a message had been sent ahead to inform Mr Kumar of my visit, but I had not had a reply from him. The journey was arranged at such short notice, and I had committed to coming. The fact of the matter was apparently that my message had never arrived and Mr Kumar had no idea at all that I was coming or indeed that I was now here.

He had a small office in buildings only a short walk away. When I introduced myself there was silence and then a strained reliance on politeness and custom. He struggled with this -default position of his for a while which was simply not designed to handle the situation.

Indira left and Niral Kumar and I sat together. We talked about my aunt, of London and the development of India since Independence. When he began to talk at length of greater global politics I had to interrupt rather abruptly, and maybe a little rudely, to address the inevitable subject of my parents. He thought it best for us to walk to the beautiful place by a tree where they had been buried.

There had been a small ceremonial funeral as requested in their joint will and it took place just two days after the accident. The skies had been dark and overcast and the air heavy and close with humidity, but it had been a beautiful ceremony, Mr Kumar said. It was a funeral where everyone from the Observatory wore their finest white clothes and both a Hindu priest and a Christian Baptist minister said words of great comfort, wisdom, and beauty.

He said there were flowers, hundreds, perhaps thousands of them brought by the local communities. But when I asked how I had been, he was sad for me but told me the truth which is what I need to hear. He recalled that I was dressed in my birthday party dress and that I had shown no emotion and had said nothing. I didn't cry, I didn't make a sound.

My mother and father and I were due to go on a holiday together, the bags were already packed. Our passage was had all been arranged in advance and we had tickets to fly to London. It was to be my first trip to England, to anywhere in fact, as I had lived only within the immediate area of Kodaikanal my entire life.

We were supposed to be going to Paris and then on to London where we would have been a family all together for the first time. All Mr Kumar knew of my aunt at that time was that she was my mother's younger sister who lived in the house my parents had bought before leaving for India in 1939.

Shortly after he received news of the tragedy, he had taken responsibility and made the decision to take me to live with my aunt and had hastily made the necessary arrangements with her via telegram. His life in Kodaikanal had been a selfless service to Rondel Mining which he had set with my father in an amicable and perfectly equal partnership. He had been running every aspect of it with the control he was empowered in accordance with my father's wishes as expressed in the will.

The tears were in my eyes, but they were less for sadness and more with the relief that this path ended here and I would have to go no further along it, I would have to journey no more to find them. In that moment I realised this had been my fundamental motivation to come here in the first place, however much I had tricked myself into thinking otherwise.

They gave me life, but still, I could not remember them with any clarity and neither could I remember Ananya. She insisted upon staying a mystery but now at least her existence had become more tangible for me. She was no longer merely an abstract idea as I could feel her spirit within me and our souls were connected, but we were not one together.

I heard music, classical piano was being played quite poorly but the sound was a reason enough to move away from that spot by the tree. I found myself walking towards the notes which were faint but distinct, Mr Kumar following silently at a little distance, respectful of my personal space. When I found the origin of the music in one of the small outbuildings nearby, I discovered with it a deep feeling of pure joy, the only powerful affirmation I had felt since arriving.

I was sure it was my piano teacher, there was something about her, an aura, which I certainly recognised. It was almost a memory. She was in a room by an open window, and she sat teaching a young boy who was perhaps ten years of age.

Mrs Singh looked at me for a long time when she realised I was standing by the door, listening to her instruction. The boy continued to play for a while until he became confused by a tricky combination of notes. It was a chord he had not come across before but his questions about how he should play it met with no reply.

She told him politely that this was the end of the lesson for the day and he left, a little bemused. With a subtle gesture and without words, I was beckoned to sit down next to her. The piano stool was plenty big enough for us both.

We sat and we played a duet. It began with the sheet music which happened to be in front of us but we soon found ourselves improvising. After harmonising for a while, I became carried away slightly and when I broke into jazz, with some overflowing happiness, and maybe to show off I suppose, she took her hands away from the keys and sat back on the stool to watch and listen and smile.

With great use of the sustain pedal I finished my improvisation with a flamboyantly comic trill and we started laughing. Then I really did cry and with such emotion that Mr Kumar became emotional himself and very embarrassed, hurrying away saying he would go to fetch us some water.

12

Copper Business Matters

Mr Kumar and I ate together that evening and the talk was mainly concerning business, him leading this conversation with great professionalism. I believe he thought I knew most of the details of the family business and that I was familiar with everything of which he spoke. This was not so as I had previously had absolutely no interest in its administration and had asked for no knowledge of its workings from my aunt Marie.

I believe Marie had long ago given up on trying to inform me of any developments in the growth of the family business because of my negative reaction to any and every effort she made.

All I knew was that our solicitor, Mr David Short, handled all the functions required of him in London and he had eventually given up on troubling my aunt with any news or enquiries as she was perhaps even less interested in the business of extracting copper from its various ores in a country many thousands of miles away. She received rather a large income from it directly into her account which she spent wisely on such things as my education and the maintenance of the house, and we were all extremely happy with this arrangement. It meant neither my aunt, or myself or Uncle John had to worry about a thing.

It was not lost on me that I had rather abused the privilege this had afforded me over the years and it was the shame of this realisation which had caused me to fall apart. I felt I had squandered my opportunities in life and thrown away that which had been gifted without an appreciation of the way my privilege had been gained.

It was another reason for my journey. I wished to right this wrong by changing myself, my attitudes, my beliefs, and my orientation to the world in which I found myself. I listened to Mr Kumar with increasing interest, trying to learn all I could, without making myself sound like the ignorant and spoilt child I felt myself to be. If Mr Kumar felt this way he did not show it. His politeness was exemplary and he showed nothing but respect for my position.

Within an extremely short period of less than five minutes of me quietly and carefully listening, I soon realised that Mr Kumar was clearly assuming I knew something which I did not. This critical fact concerned my father's fifty per cent share in Rondel Mining and that the entirety of it would become mine the minute I turned twenty-one next year.

Mr Kumar had been dutifully explaining the consequences of this imminent change and how he believed it would be best for us both to handle it. He was simply wanting to tie up the arrangements for the transition in the short period of time I was to be with him.

I felt embarrassed and a little stupid to be unknowledgeable of this important future event but was successful in staying quiet to hide my ignorance and he carried on in a professional way, labouring minutiae of legalities and ongoing business strategies.

That I knew nothing of this and got away by nodding with an affected neutrality was not too difficult for me. It was like the way I had felt upon my arrival. Some things are vital relevance to my soul, and these often seem to be of little importance to others. In contrast, I am equally indifferent about many of those things such as the worlds of money and power and the like, which seem to consume the lives of the vast majority.

I could tell Mr Kumar's thinking and consideration were all basically common sense and protocol and my response was calm and emotionless acceptance. It wasn't difficult for me to understand that my solicitor might have kept this information from me for some legal reasons and after a while Mr Kumar could see I had lost interest, and he changed the subject.

I'm sure Aunt Marie must have known about this situation but I had to guess that she may have had my best interests at heart. Perhaps she wanted the responsibility and possible burden of this impending inheritance to be left out of my mind for as long as possible. If I had known some years ago it would certainly have compounded my troubled recent years.

The thought came to me that once Aunt Marie knew I had decided to travel here she knew I would probably discover the nature and size of this 'gift' which my father had left for me. She would think it best for me to discover such things naturally, on my own and in my own way. She had always been like that with me.

Rondel Mining had grown considerably since he must have written this into his will. Copper production all over India had increased almost exponentially, this much I learned from Mr Kumar's speech.

The first seam my father had discovered appeared to have been just the tip of an iceberg, so to speak. The one small outcrop of azurite he had come upon was only an indication of this, a clue for a trained geologist. Concealed beneath its blueness was huge reserves of copper ore which Mr Kumar had been efficiently extracting and refining and turning into vast amounts of the reddish-pink metal for the last fifteen years. The business produced great profits and I was soon going to be an equal partner, and very wealthy because of it.

Mr Kumar must have just told himself that this was the primary reason for my visit and was going about his work without a thought to inquire about anything other. When he had finished with his enthusiastic thoughts, ideas, and plans for the development of the company he did however ask one simple question.

"As you can see, Miss Rondel, this company and its administration, has become my life's work. I have never been interested in settling down with a good woman to start a family and bring children into the world, and the mining of copper has become my life. I am very happy in my work, and I would like to ask you at this point as to the level of your involvement in the future of the company? I believe you will in fact have the controlling share in decision making and I should like to know my position. If you could clarify this matter for me, please."

I smiled as I realised now what he might be getting at.

"Mr Kumar, I can honestly say I have no intention of moving to India permanently to help you with this work. It is a place of incredible beauty. I am so glad to have come here to have seen this place, where I lived so briefly, and to have seen where my parents rest. But my future lies elsewhere.

"It seems you have achieved incredible things from such small beginnings and are continuing to do so. I am more than happy to have you make any and all decisions on behalf of our family's interest in this enterprise, just as you see fit Mr Kumar."

Mr Kumar was very happy to be made aware of my approach to this.

"Thank you for this clarification. I would be very grateful if you could inform your solicitors of the exact arrangements you wish to put in place. It's just that it needs to be put in writing so that I may legally be empowered to make the decisions I need to be able to make."

"I will see to it as soon as possible."

There was nothing about this man which gave me any

cause to doubt his trustworthiness. His goodness and sincerity alone were enough for me to feel safe to put all faith in him. There was something fatherly about him I realised later, as though he were addressing his own daughter with great respect about issues of great weight.

"I know next to nothing about copper mining. I can only imagine that it must be incredible hard physical labour for the miners themselves, that the process involves the destruction of Mother Nature to some large degree or at least a gross disfigurement of her natural beauty and that the industry produces huge amounts of pollution. I have no doubt this will have a lasting impact upon our health and that of our planet, but it is perhaps the cost of progress.

"However, I also understand that there is huge and rapidly increasing demand for the metal, most especially in the expanding electronics and telecommunications markets and that this company must provide opportunities for employment for many men and women which is vital of course for their lives and the economy of your wonderful country.

"But as I say, I'm not that interested, on a personal level, in the extraction of copper ore or its refinement and distribution to the market. You have created a business of great integrity and efficiency and I'm sure my father would have been impressed beyond belief with what you have done. But then I think you know this. I think too that you must have known him better than me in many ways."

He seemed very moved and paid me the nicest of compliments.

"You are obviously a very wise young woman Ms Rondel. You have the beauty and intelligence of your mother and the strength of character which always impressed me about your father."

Mr Kumar bowed his head and looked down at his desk before looking up again.

"He was a good friend to me, as was your mother. I have missed them both dearly since we lost them. I think of them so often. I am also always thinking of you Ms Rondel."

There was a deep moment of silence between us.

"Please, do call me Ananya. My purpose here is a deeply personal one as I am only trying to find out more about the person I was, the girl I was before I become the person I am now because I believe they are very different people. I am Ananya but I do not remember her so well myself."

"I understand you. What is it that you wish to do with your life, Ananya?"

I let out a short burst of laughter, which proved to be a turning point for us both, as the atmosphere had become quite sombre and a little tense.

"Ah, now that's an interesting question! My passion is for music, jazz music especially. I was reminded of that this afternoon, but one cannot build a life on just notes and melodies, no matter how beautiful they are!

"I am not sure yet … what I will end up doing, only that music will be a central part to it. Tomorrow I will be leaving as I hope to locate an ashram which I have heard of just nearby in the Palani Hills. I don't know how long I will stay there but I hope to discover a more meaningful purpose while there."

"It's a good idea Ananya, there is no need for someone such as you to rush into a life of business and commerce. To find the feelings and ideas which define you is vital to a happy life."

With this it felt to me that we had reached a conclusion, if not a complete resolution.

"Mr Kumar, I also had the hope that you might be able to tell me a little about myself, as you knew me, back then."

"Ah, well, we all used to call you 'Little Unique'. "

"Why?"

"You were so small, to start with, but then you became so tall, so young, so quickly and it was kind of joke."

"Oh, I see, but why 'Unique'?"

Mr Kumar was now very surprised.

"It is your name! Your name Ananya, it is Unique."

"That's very kind of you to say so."

"No, it is Unique. I'm sorry, I'm not being clear. There are obviously other people who share you name, perhaps only in India though, now I think of it, but it is Unique, your name."

"I'm sorry, you've rather lost me."

"Unique is the meaning of Ananya. Ananya means unique. It is the Hindi word for the English word unique, or perhaps you could say that the Hindi word for unique is Ananya! It is a little confusing perhaps, but do you not see? Did you not know!"

I laughed because it was not possible to hide my ignorance and I did not feel the need to try,

"I did not know it! I really didn't, all this time."

"But how could you not know such a thing?"

I was as incredulous too and we laughed, eventually looking at the look on each other's face, before he suddenly started again.

"It matters very little really Ananya. Names can be very complicated sometimes! What matters is that you are Unique, and you were always unique and once you were Little Unique and now clearly you are all grown up and Big Unique!"

I laughed again as he had become so much more animated.

"Shall we have a drink to celebrate your name?"

"That would be lovely Mr Kumar."

He then proceeded to tell me all he could about the 'Little Unique' as he said he used to call me. The wild girl who ran around everywhere, dancing and singing jazz songs. The picture he painted was an incredible one for me but more interesting still was what he had to tell me about the days after the funeral and the journey we made together back to London, when I was just six.

We had left Kodaikanal on 1st January 1946 and it had taken several days by car, ferry, and then by a series of aeroplane flights. During the entire journey he said that despite his best efforts, although I was alert and curious of my surroundings, my silence had persisted. He told me that in fact I had not said a word to anyone from the moment Indira had told me about the accident upon return home from my piano lesson. He had not witnessed this moment, but Indira had later told him that I screamed and wailed and struggled and fought with her as she tried to hold me but that I had suddenly become still and quiet and subdued.

Throughout the entire journey to London, he had told me stories, all the stories he knew in fact. These were mainly myths and legends which he had learned as a schoolboy. I remembered none of these, as I remembered nothing of the journey at all.

Then he said he was forced to recount all the anecdotes about his family and his friends which he was able to recall. Next the demand had been for the reading of stories from various newspapers he bought at certain places or found on recently vacated seats. Whenever he he had stopped telling these stories, whenever he had stopped talking at all in fact, I had apparently tugged at his coat incessantly until he was obliged to think of another.

The entire trip had taken almost five days as there were so many stops and stay-overs, using the tickets we had. We had spent only five hours in Paris however, all at the airport but of this I remembered nothing.

By the time we arrived at Aunt Marie's house in Primrose Hill, Mr Kumar said he was completely exhausted. He had a throat so sore it felt like sandpaper, he said, and his voice had become nothing more than a strained whisper.

It was only now that I began speaking again myself, being almost totally mute for more than a week. When John opened the big yellow front door and I saw him filling the doorway with his oversized body, I had clearly felt compelled to say something.

And this is the first memory I have. It is the first memory I can remember at least.

Just as Mr. Kumar had apparently run out of stories to tell me on that journey, and lost his voice in the process, so he eventually ran out of stories to tell me here.

Mr Kumar and I drank a whole bottle of sherry in his small office that evening. I began to feel dreamlike memories emerging but in content they were so vague and sparse as to be almost unintelligible. They were no more that faint clouds floating through the sky of my mind, dispersing and being blown away by winds of distance and time.

As he got up to leave, rather unsteady on my feet, Mr Kumar casually asked me something.

"Ananya, I just had an idea. Unfortunately, I have to go to Sri Lanka tomorrow and I leave early, so I will not see you in the morning."

"Oh, what a shame, I had hoped we would be spending a lot more time together. Can it be postponed by any chance?"

"No, I'm afraid not. It's been in the calendar for a long time. Had I known you were coming to visit us in Kodaikanal today, or any day in fact, I would have organised a flight to Colombo for a later date, but I'm afraid my travel plans have already been made."

"Oh, I see. I hope you have a wonderful holiday Mr Kumar, I really do. I imagine you have earned it, doing so much around here."

"Oh, it's not even a holiday I'm afraid Ananya, just a boring business trip, a conference really. It's run by the Copper Development Association."

"I'm sorry I'm not familiar with their work."

"They are a little secretive in point of fact, because of certain … er … possible interventions by external government forces, and the sums of money involved of course and the politics, etc. They are essentially a non-trading organisation however, maintained by the British copper industry, formed primarily to collect and distribute information and to develop applications and processes connected with copper and its alloys."

"Oh, it sounds very important."

"Yes, it is. They bring people in the industry together from all over the world, just once a year, there are lectures and such things. This year it is in Sri Lanka, which is not so far away, so I decided I would attend for the first time."

"Of course, you must go. I am only sorry we will not be able to spend any more time together. Is this a goodbye then, for now?"

"I am afraid so. It's a shame, it really is, but some good may come from it. I was just thinking, do you recall earlier I asked if you would mention to your solicitor in London about the changes to the arrangements to the running of the company we spoke about upon your coming of age?"

"Yes, I haven't forgotten, I will see to it personally when I return to England. I'm just not sure exactly at the moment when that will be, how long I will be staying in India."

"Yes, yes, I don't have the detailed paperwork drawn up of course, as I said, we really did have no idea you were just going to drop in like this, really the Indian Mail service is so terrible these days. However, it has just crossed my mind that I do have a basic transfer of Business Power of Attorney. I keep all sorts of standard forms in this office. I happen to have one here I think."

Mr Kumar reached into a drawer in his desk and pulled out a single sheet of foolscap paper with some printed text on it.

"My thought was that if you signed and dated this now, I could take it to the conference with me. There will be representatives from all over India there and I may be able to make some long-term decisions for the benefit of the future of the company, if I have this paperwork in order, forthwith.

"I wondered, could you just sign and date it for me? We wouldn't want to miss out on some lucrative opportunities, would we Miss Rondel?"

"No, certainly not."

I walked over to this desk, quite wobbly actually and my eyes slightly out of focus, and Mr Kumar gave me a pen.

"Oh, what a lovely pen."

"Just sign and date there at the bottom, if you please."

"Of course. Ah, what is it today? The date I mean?"

I looked up to the ceiling to try to remember.

"It is the 14th January."

"Of course it is, yes."

In that moment I noticed a small skylight in the roof. Framed within it, quite perfect as a circle within a square, was the bright full moon, beaming down from on high.

"Ah, wait a minute," I said. "I cannot sign this today."

Mr Kumar looked slightly uncomfortable and sightly annoyed in fact.

"Why ever not?"

"It is a full moon, and one should never sign one's name on a full moon!"

I put the pen down rather heavily on the desk.

"I'm sorry Ms Rondel is this er … a religious matter or some such thing? I'm afraid I don't understand."

"No, hah! It is a silly superstition in my family Mr Kumar, nothing more. I suggest you send the letter to our solicitor in London and he will deal with it forthwith!"

"But I do not quite understand still."

"Keep your papers dry, do not attempt to play the twelve-bar blues in a place of worship and NEVER sign your name on a full moon! Now if you please Mr Kumar, I am off to bed!"

I left, found my way to the building where Indira had prepared a room for me. I slept as a peaceful baby for some sixteen hours.

13

If Mirrors Could Talk

I left for the ashram after only two days. There was no doubt in my mind that I would not find anywhere else in the world with the majesty of the view from this mountain. The vista was in some way too beautiful for me, as though it had been perfected or contrived especially for my tastes.

All around it was just so pretty and charming but infused with colours that were saturated and overwhelming. I did not recognise the flowers I saw, they were attractive in that I was drawn by them enough to go close to them but upon inspection I found it hard to appreciate the structures of leaves and petals as I might have done. The shapes made by the bark of trees were alien and the immediate curiosity this brought with it was replaced by a sort of repulsion.

I felt I did not belong, and I did not like the feeling.

Although it took pride of place on the site, I had not been invited by anyone to look inside the main telescope building. It seemed to be out of bounds to me. It crossed my mind that perhaps it was not operational or that it might be temporarily closed for repairs. I realised there was no physical evidence to make me believe such a thing, only a particular psychology which kept me at a distance from it. It was as though it was guarded by an invisible shield.

I had decided to continue onwards with my journey to the ashram but before I left I walked up to the telescope building. I saw a metal door ajar and my feet took me to it. My hand reached out to open it and the momentum of my body took me through it. I found myself standing before the instrument, not dwarfed, as it was no giant, but nevertheless struck motionless by the reality of its existence and the ideas behind its purpose.

It was trained on the sun through a long slit in the roof. Not a sculpture intended to inform the senses by its looks, it did however command a great respect in the way it had been put together. Made to measure, each component served a necessary function, each element sufficient to fulfil its function but nothing more. Time had not been spent on the aesthetics of the parts from which it had been created, but assembled as they were, unified in the one way they had been designed to be, the overall impact was hard to analyse. Brass and steel, copper and zinc, chrome and some silver and gold in places too, she was bejewelled in her own way as a marvel of Victorian engineering. A queen in her own right but isolated and lonely I felt.

It was quiet in here and significantly darker, and cooler too. I was incredibly relaxed and at ease all of a sudden. I felt I belonged here. It was something like standing next to a friend in a wide, open field but here we had been put together in a safe place for a while, separate from all others to be alone together and share some few moments. I said goodbye and left.

Before leaving Kodaikanal I was able to see Indira once more and to say goodbye to her too. When we hugged, we held each other very close.

On parting she gave me a small copper mirror of the most incredible beauty, and she told me its story.

It had been my mother's. Known as an Aranmula Kannadi mirror, it had been a wedding gift from the holy man who had performed my parents' Indian wedding ceremony, just prior to arriving in Kodaikanal in the spring of 1939.

They had been married in England of course, many years previously, but this second occasion had apparently been a spontaneous event, an expression of their love for one another and taken on impulse as they had passed through a small village on their way from Bombay to the Hill Station here at Kodaikanal.

The mirror was small and circular, only six inches in diameter. Known as an Aranmula Kannadi mirror, they are made only by one extended family in the district of Aranmula and the exact metals forming the alloy from which they are made have been kept a family secret for many centuries.

Unlike normal mirrors there is no back surface to them, no second surface to give unwanted secondary reflections. They are polished over several days using a paste of rice bran and oil extracted from the seeds of marotti trees and subsequently the image they give is as pure as can be. They are rare and beautiful, unique in fact.

She thought it only right that I should have it now and was so happy that she had been able to find it, tucked away for safe keeping in Mr Kumar's study all this time, just waiting for me she had said.

I had wanted to say goodbye to him also. I wanted to look him in the eye and I did not know why I wanted to do this but perhaps thought I would be able see something I needed to see. What that might be I had no idea but anyway I had been unable to find him all day. Indira informed me that he had spontaneously decided to go away on holiday, to Sri Lanka in fact, and had taken the opportunity to leave just yesterday. I was surprised that he had not tried to look for me, to say goodbye himself. It struck me as a little rude, but perhaps he had been in somewhat of a hurry. Indira looked at me, a serious look upon her face and seemed to think carefully about what she said next.

"To be honest with you, Mr Kumar and I do not get along. He was what I call a small man."

"He is so very short I must say but he seems kind and

thoughtful and runs the company well."

"That is how he seems Ananya, but all is not as it seems. When I say small, I mean small in character and to be truthful with you I am not sure he runs your father's company as well as it might be run. I have always suspected some of the profits are siphoned off for nefarious purposes. I have said too much, I should not have. I am sorry. Please don't worry yourself about this, about what I have told you."

"Indira, you look scared, what is it?"

"Scared! I am not scared of him. He shouts and curses often, but I am not scared of him. No, it is silly really."

"Tell me."

"When your mother and father left us forever, it was so incredibly sad and then Mr Kumar took you to England to be with your aunt. When he returned, the day he returned in fact, all the rhododendron flowers died.

"They used to be everywhere here, all over the place. Throughout nearly the whole of the year they made this place smell so wonderful you cannot imagine. But they have never flowered again.

"The Solar Observatory is such a beautiful place as it is, as you have seen, but without the deep pink of the rhododendron flowers my soul is always sad. I cannot explain it. I sometimes think that it is because your mother and father died or that it is because you had to leave, and the gods have abandoned us.

"But I cannot believe this because their spirit and your spirit is always here for me and this keeps my soul as happy as it needs to be.

"No, Ananya, I feel it might be Mr Kumar, he is in charge of everything here now, not just your father's copper mining business which he continues to run from your father's old office in the house, but he took it upon himself to influence the running of the Observatory itself too. I fear it is his mere presence here which gods of the surrounding forest object to and that is why they have punished us by taking away our rhododendron blossoms."

"My god, Indira, this is terrible!"

"I know, but it is so, and I wish that it were not."

"If I can have anything to do with it, I will put in a word with these gods of yours and make sure that it gets put right!"

I shook my Aranmula Kannadi mirror in the air with defiant pride.

"I have luck on my side now, nothing can stop me. You tell these gods to watch out what they do, meddling with the ways of Nature."

Indira laughed, the best good-hearted laugh I had heard from her since I arrived.

"I wouldn't go against you Ananya!"

"Perhaps the flowers will come back while Mr Kumar is away on his business trip!"

"I can only hope! But it is not a business trip, he is merely going away on holiday for a couple of weeks. He has always wanted to go there and he bores me with it sometimes, quite often actually. Perhaps he will never come back, then I'm sure the blossoms will return. I shouldn't say such a thing … but this morning so very early he became extremely angry with me, more so than ever before."

"But why? What had you done?"

"Nothing at all! He had simply misplaced a … good luck charm, one he carries with him whenever he travels. He accused me of stealing it as he said I was the only person who knew where he kept it!"

"Is that true?"

"It's true I know he had something precious to him, which he could not find! Oh who cares! To hell with the man!"

"Well, Indira, it doesn't add up and it all smells a bit fishy if you ask me. If you don't like the man, then neither do I!"

"I hope his plane crashes into the mountain on the way to Sri Lanka! I shouldn't say such a thing … but I have wanted to for so long …!"

We laughed with a carefree happiness for a long while at the absurdities of life before crying over the abundance of beauty in the world and then laughing once again at our own silliness with each other. She was lovely and I began missing her the moment we parted.

The mirror I would treasure as the only real possession I had in the world of my mother's and Indira assured me it would bring me great good luck in my personal life, especially with men!

14

Airmail

The ashram became my home for the next nine months. It was easy for me to stay here. The location itself was breathtaking, the people I lived with were all very interesting and many were a great inspiration too. They came and went over those months; sometimes we were as many as thirty but on occasion we dwindled in number to as little as five. From many countries, it was a secluded sanctuary for all of us, for each of us, far away from whatever troubles we had individually left behind.

There was a routine of sorts too, a loose structure and once I found the rhythm of the place it felt second nature to sustain it and to live in harmony with the benefits it brought.

It was a simple way of existing but not uncomfortable and over these months I learned to appreciate the simplicities it encouraged and grew.

There were just three activities which occupied the most part of my time: cooking, the practice of yoga and the craft of making pottery.

Cooking was a daily task but quickly I found interest in so many ingredients which were previously unknown to me. I was part of the cooking group my whole time in the ashram and we traded skills and recipes from each other, from our own different cultures of origin but mainly of course from the country to which we had all decided to travel.

People came and went but often the types of cooking they brought with them became staple meals long after they had gone. This was even more the case with the Indian people I knew, many of whom lived here or came and left and then maybe returned with a freedom and regularity which had no pattern.

The complexities, subtleties and sheer variety of Indian cooking is without end and this part of my life was an endless learning experience where each day brought new ideas, tastes flavours and feelings.

The satisfaction of feeding people regularly with good food and seeing their appreciation of it in an immediate way was the foundation of the happiness which grew within me during my life in this place with these people. Because of this, I was always very popular too and this new sensation was always a surprise for me and always a most welcome one.

Yoga was also a daily activity. The Guru sometimes taught these lessons himself but other people, both men and women, were involved in the teaching of this ancient exercise. The showing and learning, and the repetition of the forms of the Asanas were not so much lessons but more akin to a way of life where there was a formal discipline which usually took place first thing in the morning but also a free sharing of knowledge which could happen at any time of day.

Breathing and meditation were my key areas of focus which illuminated my own private inner world as I realised it was this I needed to become in tune with. In yoga I found that the emotion and the spirit, the physical and the mental, sound and light, were each merely two sides of one piece of paper and that when I put them together over time these pieces of paper were just single pages in my book.

Although I became whole in my philosophy of life, these abstract ideas which were flowing from the soul of the Guru in an almost constant stream were sometimes just too much. I was not the only one who experienced this. Quite regularly, woman the same age as me, and men just as often too, would lose their bearings and direction completely. They were either just not ready for this kind of enlightenment or they were using natural hallucinogens to augment their experience and this led to breakdowns, personality collapses, identity fractures and sometimes severe illness.

I stayed clear of all that, I wanted nothing to do with it given the nature of my own journey to reach this point. I wanted to be pure in mind, body, and soul. I wanted to heal myself and natural health and cleanliness were a great part of this.

But 'purity' was a difficult idea for me, I didn't like its perfection. Increasingly I had begun to appreciate the differences between people and see the beauty in these differences too. The similarities bring us together to show us that we are one, but it is the differences which define us, which make us who we are as individuals. These qualities harmonise when looked at from a certain point of view and as part of this I had found a way to completely accept imperfection, that is what others might see as imperfection.

This thinking was the greatest part of the change in my character while living in the ashram and this in turn changed my personality. I became more outgoing in social situations and more creatively introspective when alone.

However, my identity did not change in this place during this time. The essence of my being remained unchanged as the sum of my memories and these one cannot escape. There were vital memories of mine which were absent, obscured, hidden or lost, they had not returned to me and this was still a cause of great sadness. As a reflection of this, perhaps after only a few days of arriving, I stopped using the name Ananya and became only Ana.

Making clay pots and firing them in a simply underground kiln was the greatest of therapies. This craft was fundamentally a practical one as the pots I learned to make were mainly for use in food preparation but later I began to experiment with more decorative and artistic designs and this brought huge enjoyment and peace.

The texture of the clay itself was fascinating; thick and heavy, smooth and squishy, pliable and soft. Squeezing it and shaping it, as it oozed through my fingers all wet and slippery and muddy and fun. The sound it made when you dumped it on a stone to shape it. The heavy, dank smell it gave off. The way it glistened in the afternoon sun, light bouncing off its slimy, curved watery surfaces, its forgiving nature, its limits, its possibilities, the deep, dark redness of its nature. The fire that makes it hard, the entire history of the Earth. I loved it.

I received letters from my aunt very regularly. Every month she would write with news of England, London, Primrose Hill, John and developments within the 'tiny world of fashion' as she called it. I looked forward to these letters which came with a surprising degree of reliability via a well-trodden route. The last part of the letters' journey was made by the same boy the whole time I was there and he must have grown an inch or so during this time.

He came up the hill with his bag over his shoulder and if I would spot him, he would wave. He would make his delivery and sometimes we would talk together for a while. If he had a blue airmail letter for me, I would sometimes save it for the evening and open it in a secluded spot to read alone.

One day there was a letter but from the writing of the address I could see that it was not from my aunt. I was intrigued and went down to the bank of the little river where I sat on a large stone, opened it and read the few pages from beginning to end.

I cried, caught in a numb, frozen state, staring at the water's surface as it flowed past me. There were no sobs after a while, no sounds, or sensations of any kind really. Then slowly I became aware of the feeling of these tears as they made their little streams down and over the contours of my face, changing course sometimes as they ran together, sometimes pausing, waiting, and increasing in size until they were ready to be enticed downwards again, motivated by gravity, their momentum carrying them over the texture of my sun-soaked skin.

I did not wipe them away, absorbed as I was in this feeling, absorbed I think because it was a tangible sensation and something real for me to occupy these moments. I was perfectly still until I caught my tears striking the rock between my legs on which I sat. Other tears returned to the inside of my body, via my lips and through my mouth as though a precious commodity to be recycled for future use. They were many, all these tears, but together they were the memory of my aunt.

When they had run their course and there were no more to come, the sound of the babbling stream became stronger or perhaps it was that my awareness isolated them more keenly. I began to look at parts of the brook which ran over particular rocks, around them or in-between them and I thought I could discern the origins of certain collections of harmonies among all the random white noise. They had their own music these little undulating waves, but they played for me for a while and their music became my music too.

Without thought, any intention or purpose I stood, but as soon as I did so it was clear to me where I must go. I needed to talk with the Guru, to tell him of my sad news and to seek his guidance.

I had never been intimidated by him as some here seemed to be, nor was I under any kind of his 'spell'. There were those who had warned me to be careful of 'mind control' or 'brainwashing' and other such nonsense just before I left England. These people had no knowledge of what they talked about. This kind of thinking and speaking was simply a manifestation of their fear, or of their fears I should say because I'm sure of these they had many.

It's true that there were some among us who were profoundly 'lost' in different ways, but that was why they had come here no doubt. I had been just the same but if nothing else this was a place where people changed. I had changed so that I could not recognise myself when I looked within, and the Guru was just skilled at subtly guiding these changes. The truth was the interactions I'd had with him during my time living among this community were rare and brief.

He was for me simply a man. Sometimes I felt like a pupil in a school who occasionally says hello to a certain teacher, a teacher who acknowledges you and sometimes remembers your name but who always teaches you in a way which seems independent of who you are. He was impersonal and neutral and almost invisible for me. I had only spoken in depth with him on three occasions.

The first time was when I arrived. He interrogated me for a long time I think, but I was so shell-shocked and disorientated that I have no recollection of his questions or indeed my answers.

The second was when I fell ill for some time with malaria, and I remember him sitting with me for days. I was hallucinating with the fevers, and he talked and told me stories through the night. I have no recollection of what I told him, although I know I spoke more in these days than in my whole life put together. This memory is vivid but more visual than verbal and I recall that week or so as one might a period of intense weather, a heatwave or an enduring snowstorm. It was to be survived and it seems my mind was not interested or capable of making memories.

The third time was just a few weeks ago when he helped me while I was cooking. We ate together and had a long conversation about food, diet, and energy. Of this I remember a great deal of practical details, including cooking techniques, recipes, and specific ingredients.

I found him easily. I could see him meditating in his little hut and paused for a short moment to think better of disturbing him. It was as though the pause I made caused him to finish his meditation in that instant and to immediately open his eyes. He could not have heard me for I was still some thirty feet away. Yet he saw me instantly and beckoned me towards him. I could not even call my pause a real pause, it was more of a change in the pace of my heart.

He must have noticed that I had been crying because he was gentle and soft from the start as he bade me to sit by his side. We were in his hut, half facing each other and half looking at the door. It was a lovely day, the morning showed people becoming slowly busy as their sleep faded and the tasks and ideas of the afternoon lay waiting ahead. We watched the community wake up as we spoke and of course we looked at each other from time to time.

"I have had some horribly sad news, via a letter from England."

I held up the letter, which I suddenly remembered I was holding. He took it from me as I moved it towards him, and I found I was able to let go of it easily. He placed it behind him without looking at it.

"My aunt has died. She was my only living relative and I think I must return to see to her affairs."

"Yes, you must go Unique."

He was the only person to call me this. I had arrived as Ananya. When he addressed me on the few occasions he had, he called me Unique, and this seemed natural to me. I had called myself Ana since I had been here and this is how I was known to everyone, except to him. We sat in silence for a while.

"You must go Unique because although this is a very sad day it is also beautiful too. You will have a good journey home because your memories will be full of all the beauty that is here now and all the beauty you have experienced since you arrived. You will be the guardian of this beauty to transport you to the next place. When you arrive there the beauty will be with you and you will find more beauty still where you find yourself."

I looked up. He was crying, but he was smiling too.

"I fear that I have not finished what I have started here. That my time here with you is incomplete."

"Time is never complete but it never matters because you are complete, and you can be everywhere. There are no boundaries to a flower. The flower is part of the Earth. It is on the Earth, and it is in the Earth. It has roots so it can be part of the water, but it is also part of the air and part of the sun. You are a flower, Ananya, and you need have no boundaries either. Go and be a flower everywhere and love will be everywhere within you."

He raised both his hands upwards. I stood, ducking my head as I exited the hut, turned, and bowed with my hands together over my heart.

"Thank you."

I walked away and was perhaps more than forty feet away when I heard him shout out after me.

"Unique! Remember there are many sad things in life but there are also many things which are very funny!"

When I turned around, he was walking away from his hut and I watched him disappearing into the forest.

15

The Philosophy Of Being Art

My name is Arthur Armstrong. I've just turned twenty-one years of age. Among other responsibilities here at the Atomic Weapons Research Establishment I am the bursar of the Social Club and we'd been using the main site canteen once a week on Saturday evenings to show a motion picture.

So far we've seen *Vertigo*, *Touch of Evil* and *Cat On a Hot Tin Roof*, all in Technicolour and pretty good sound too. The reaction to an old 1930s black and white silent short featuring Charlie Chaplin's antics was a complete revelation to me and all others, people were in fits.

I'd rigged up the rather bulky Bell and Howell 35mm projector with the help of one of the first year apprentices right at the back of the canteen because we could get a bigger image with a certain lens. I had been tasked with ordering and buying this machine myself and it had arrived more than a month ago from the States along with some power units for the ongoing ATLAS installation work.

For sound we were hooked up by a home-made amplifier which Roger Stevens in Instruments had been working on in his spare time, and we were using the two 'Tannoy' loudspeakers we'd invested in last year for a PA system. In fact, they were slightly low impedance for the job and consequently a little too loud if anything and the bass speakers were distorting at very low frequencies. I needed to get Stevens to toy around with that, or do it myself.

Freddie Dunbar, who worked on the perimeter gate with security, had a girlfriend who had just got a job at The Gaumont picture house. Until just recently it was The Pavilion, of course, but with new owners came the name change and then staff changes too. Jane, Freddie's girl, had got lucky and was now an usherette, she had the hat, the outfit, the torch and everything. She also doubled up with the ice creams at the intermission and Freddie was happy because she let him and his mates in for free through the fire escape at the back.

Jane was a friendly lass and had been able to persuade the projectionist at The Gaumont to lend her the reels of their latest releases the day after the run had finished. She then gave them to Freddie, Freddie gave them to me, and I ran them through the Bell and Howell in the canteen on the Saturday night before handing them back to The Gaumont, via Freddie and Jane. I believe their resident projectionist then sent them back to the Rank distributor in London via some special courier of some sort. It was a funny arrangement and the process was being further greased by some funds garnered from the sales we made on the Saturday at the bar.

We could drink and smoke and, with it being a free for all, it was starting to get slightly rowdy. All and sundry were welcome, so it was quite a mix. As apprentices we were 127 in total on the site ranging in age from seventeen to twenty-four. There were fresh school leavers, as I had been seven years ago, all the way up to some of the PhD lot and a few from Weapons. After the rather sparsely populated first showing, word soon got around and at the last event there was standing room only.

It has proven to be a great way of unwinding and relieving the tensions of everyday life here at the Establishment with those of every grade letting their hair down a little. Technicians stand next to the top chaps and it's become quite an occasion.

Earlier today in B7:A, we had been using the projector for its originally intended purpose and there had been feelings on show which couldn't have been more contrasting or more serious. These feelings in me were becoming too much.

The films which I'm about to show down here in room B7:A will be silent and in black and white.

There are only fourteen of us currently in this room, including myself, and we are all in suits for the occasion. Some of us are smoking and I have just readied the reels. We are just about ready to go.

I had the job of projectionist because I was the only one who knew how to operate the new Bell and Howell 173. The room was full, the chairs were close together and the atmosphere was one of nervous excitement. It was a kind of preparation for intense concentration I felt.

The first floor of building B7 was a modest research library. We kept scientific journals up there, textbooks, data sheets, the microfiche machine, newspapers, all that kind of stuff. The ground floor was mostly used for the storage of office materials and consumables and was often referred to as 'The Stationery Cupboard'.

In this room, B7:A, we were surrounded by a large number of huge rolls of architectural blueprint paper, stacked five units high. As apprentices we seemed to get through these at an alarming rate. Mostly they were used for technical drawings and due to the nature of our work and the way it was carried out there were always a very large number of these to be drafted and processed.

Anyone on site who wanted to make any item, from a specialised bolt for a weapon casing to a cadmium copper gasket for the experimental reactor, had to draw it, submit it and then wait, usually about two days or so to get the official approval. It would be returned with a stamp and the clearance level and only then could you think about even switching on a lathe. So there was rather a lot of this paper and I felt a little claustrophobic to be truthful, with the stacked rolls of it leaning inwards up high it seemed. The room was windowless.

It was a Tuesday morning. Outside it was gloomy and overcast but the projector didn't seem so friendly now, its current purpose not to entertain but to inform. I'd helped to set it up down here where the screen was considerably smaller, the room was windowless, pitch black with the room lights out in fact and the seating was not ideal. We were only a few but by necessity the chairs were tightly pushed together.

These were to be silent, black and white films but I felt the contrast with the likes of Mr Chaplin's efforts would be extreme and make for an entirely different mood. The subject matter could not be more opposite.

We had known these reels were on their way for some time now and their arrival from a government department in the States had been anticipated for several months. I had realised the budget for the Bell and Howell was clearly greater than necessary for the purposes of entertainment when its purchase had been requested of me.

Like everything else here, this was a business based on a long-term plan with plenty of money to spend on long-term investments in the search for permanent solutions. It was the business of war, defence one would rather say, it was at least the prevention of war which was the ultimate goal. We had been entrusted to be Keepers of the Peace which had been won by a continuous development of our deterrent. It was hard work, the weapons we designed were so designed so that we might never have to go to war again. That was the idea.

I had been to the cinema with my father to watch the first footage of the Hiroshima Atomic Bomb explosion as presented by Pathé News. It was 1946 and I was seven years of age. We walked from our house to the local cinema, I remember it mainly because he held my hand for the duration of the thirty-minute walk, something he had not done before. In his other hand was his pipe, the Old Holborn a constant background to my childhood. His Harris tweed long coat flapped a little in the wind I remember. It too had an evocative odour, especially when damp.

I saw the explosion as recorded in black and white from the Enola Gay shortly after it had released its payload. I cannot tell you my emotions or feelings or state of my mind, I cannot remember these so I can only imagine. Perhaps that image had been permanently burned onto my innocent retinas.

One cannot erase such a vision, all who have seen it cannot help but recall the seeming impossibility of its scale and newness of the dark beauty it forces into one's soul. It certainly must have affected me on some primeval level for it had brought me all the way from that cinema to this place, a journey which had begun to confuse me of late. I had been inspired by fear and destruction but now however, perhaps only due to the natural balance and harmony of life, there was a seed which yearned for love and creation. It had begun to grow only recently, and its source was a mystery to me, but it grew.

The group of fourteen of us were about to see almost all the original footage, three hours of it in fact when spliced together with additional American test footage we had yet to see.

When I flicked the room's light switch we were absorbed by the darkness for a few seconds as my battery-operated torch failed for a few moments. I shook it quite vigorously for a while and it flickered into life.

Locating the power switch for the projector, its powerful bulb illuminated not only the screen but the room too. It was bright white for a few seconds as the leader ran through the gate, then various American standard markings flicked in front of us.

These alien symbols and marks were unknown entities, familiar as we were with UK standards, and they gave me the impression that we were being let into yet another secret, as we often were. That this one originated from our US friends gave some kind of strange thrill that our 'special relationship' was still alive and well.

Images began to appear. I took my seat at the back. The special feeling of elitism was mixed with a heavy emotion of responsibility as we were all perfectly quiet for this education. I changed reels seven times, and it was only during these brief interludes that subdued conversation came to the surface among the entranced audience members. This would quickly dissolve as the next reel rolled to reveal its rare memories. How few were those who had seen this light? I felt unable to reconcile the blinding after-flash we witnessed with the feeble 90 W tungsten projector bulb.

We were the guardians of these artefacts, ours a timeless duty to protect this record, this memory, to ensure that the forces which had motivated the use of the weapon in the first place could never live again. Watching these images with all that I knew in my mind and my heart, I had started to feel for some reason that we were equal to the task. That the nature of the reason I felt this way eluded me did not seem important. Clearly at some point rationality breaks down and the images we saw were the proof.

As an engineer I began to think on a technical level about this film. To record these events must have been quite a responsibility for those making the preceding decisions concerning lenses and film stock. There would have been considerations and discussions over damping mechanisms to minimise the effect of the plane's vibrations.

These practical thoughts had helped me to turn away from imaginations of the horror occurring tens of thousands of feet below the tops of these mushroom clouds. Such footage of the aftermath was available but was not included in these reels.

The sound of the projector was comforting to me as I associated it with our recent Saturday movie screenings. It was a relatively quiet machine but the regularity of the sound of the perforations of the film running through the sprockets became rhythmic for me, hypnotic even. This sound overwhelmed the images, overtook them, superseded them, usurped them.

I became somehow disengaged, divorced and pleasantly distanced from them. I was able to dissociate my awareness of what I was looking at from the feelings the images were making inside me. I began to recall and reimagine the stories of the films we had seen in the canteen, the faces of the actors and even some of the dialogue.

Then my attempts at a dreamlike distraction would be violently refocused to what was before my eyes in the present moment. This was not fiction, it was not even a documentary film. There was no narration, no structured story, no meaning. It was bare, raw evidence and a deadly, sombre, sober show of power. It left me feeling profoundly numb.

When the final reel came suddenly to an end, the film flapping around the take-up spool, I must have been in a daze of sorts. Someone else threw the room's light switch. There was an instant murmur which grew and morphed into a heated discussion which carried on as everyone began leaving B7:A.

I stayed behind for a while, staring at the powerful bulb of the Bell and Howell which glowed a warm orange now and then dimmed slowly for quite some time, before fading completely.

With this experience I knew something had changed, I had changed.

16

Secret Springs

I'm currently in my fifth and final year as an apprentice at the Atomic Weapons Research Establishment here in Aldermaston, which is in Berkshire, England.

The village itself has a population of about one thousand but the numbers of us at the research centre, located just nearby, is an official secret. I suspect there are as many of us within the wire fences surrounding these grounds as there are people in the village. We are of course not on the map, as our location is also officially a secret.

There was so much going on here at the time. It was 1961. We all had trouble digesting the fact that the Cold War had been escalating in its own way all the time, ever since the end of World War II and even now seemed to be intensifying. The idea that Soviet nuclear weapons, of which there were a surprisingly huge number apparently, could find their way to a land base close to the States was a growing concern.

There were rumours on site of the Soviets wanting East Germany to build a huge wall that would split Berlin in two. Spying was apparently rife all over Europe and rarely we knew if the rumours we heard had any basis at all.

In this quiet little part of England, we simply continued to keep our heads down, keep researching new ways to make bigger bombs and missiles that could kill greater numbers of people with greater speed and accuracy and believing that this was the only way there was of keeping the peace.

I had to convince myself on a daily basis that this was what I believed, that it was the truth, and that it was the best way to keep going, to keep working at it. But lately I had been having some doubts about my work and my career path in general. No longer, as sure as I had been five years ago about the direction in life which it might take me, I had begun to wonder whether I wanted to continue walking along the path I had set out upon when not much more than a schoolboy.

The film footage we had screened in B7 the other day had compounded the feelings of uncertainty I had been having, feelings which I had already been discovering within myself which seemed to have other origins. However, the stark, cold, naked images we viewed had stayed with me, at the front of my mind, and the feelings they induced I carried like a heavy cold which couldn't be shaken off.

Nuclear deterrence as a philosophy was at this moment a hot discussion in the press. Certainly, the scale of nuclear proliferation on all sides had become a serious concern for many in the public and government alike. None of us working in the industry could fail to ignore this although it was rarely spoken of.

When I joined, I had originally wanted to specialise in weapons, but I was very young and clearly I'd grown to have less fervour in this area. The work with ATLAS was fascinating and I felt sure that computing was the way forward.

At my yearly review with the head of the Apprenticeship Programme I told him that The Weapons Department was perhaps not 'my thing' anymore and had expressed my greater interest in pursuing further the work with ATLAS. There had been a long pause and then a very negative reaction to my enthusiasm. I was told quite firmly in a patronising tone that mechanical engineers are trained to work with mechanical machines. Computing, he said, required a more 'academic' orientation and that I should stick to less 'esoteric' ideas for my future plans in life. I had protested and mentioned my excellence with mathematics and he became quite angry with me saying I would be 'wasting tax-payers money'.

The following week I was asked to look into something so banal as to make my life seem rather meaningless: springs, copper alloy springs to be exact. I just got on with it, as one had to do, without questioning my place or purpose.

In many very real ways, I had become an official secret myself, a hidden number at the very least. We could not talk of what we did here to anyone outside of this place. There was always going be a part of me which would remain secluded from regular people behind a dark shadow. It made me increasingly sad that I might be forever locked in, my soul inaccessible to anyone without the right code.

Upon my heart, however, I believe there is no such lock. My heart is free and strong and it has always been so, but by continuing to live this life I know it will remain forever unshared and in some kind of an eclipse from the heart of another. And of the ideas which have been growing within me here of late, I can speak to no one. What would I say? What could anyone here say to me in reply?

Four years of the apprenticeship followed by three in the job are enough for me and this journey has nearly reached its end. There are friends of mine who will be taking up new contracts here shortly, but I must surely leave. It's time to give my heart the freedom it needs, time to search for someone who understands me and who also has a heart which is seeking a new home.

To compound my increasingly conflicted emotions on the benefits of this approach to life, I was increasing nonplussed with the work itself. Having signed up for the 'Big Stuff' and having spent so many years carefully training and working hard with all aspects of mechanical engineering. Now though, after a full five years I was in fact often engaged in quite mundane projects.

We used a lot of springs on site for many machines. Some springs were on the extremely tiny side only a few tens of an inch in length and all ranged greatly in form and functions differing to all others. Some were immense, one I was involved with was more than twenty feet long and ten inches in diameter.

Springs have different kinds of springiness and, depending on what type of material they have been fabricated from, the frequency of their use, their maintenance, whether they have been fitted correctly and whether they have been abused or damaged in any way, they do tend to break on occasion.

Someone had decided that, given the number of springs being used on site and the incomprehensible regularity of their snapping, bending, or malfunctioning in any way, someone should look into an alternative supplier for our springs or even evaluate the possibility of manufacturing all of our springs on site. Many of our machines were specialist, bespoke one-offs so it stood to reason that we should make up our own springs and be better off for it in the long run.

I was chosen for this, I don't know why, I think it might have been a good project for a first year. I was already busy drawing up the schedule for the new ATLAS computer installation, which was clearly of far greater priority, and although I complained a little, I soon just got on with it as everybody was used to doing.

It surprised me how quickly I became particularly interested in various copper alloy springs, this being due to the remarkable modulus of elasticity some of these alloys possess. Furthermore, their elastic drift and recovery qualities were quite incredible. It was a bit of an eye-opener for me and I couldn't quite understand how I had overlooked such a thing all this time.

I soon became even more fascinated and with all things related to copper, not just springs fabricated from its alloys.

I couldn't explain my feelings about this as it was quite an explosion of curiosity I must say. When I tried relating my newfound interest to various other engineers their reaction was one of amusement and some even mocked my attempts to share my enthusiasm of this marvellous and versatile metal.

I began keeping my ideas to myself. I shall not even sketch them out now, for fear of further jibes. It's not too much fun when otherwise polite people poo-poo one's passions.

The jointing of copper, and its many alloys, was intriguing to me; soft soldering, brazing, and welding techniques were activities I would investigate to some depth, often in my spare time and in tucked away locations.

I don't imagine that others could see how the exploration of a metal, and its alloys, could be thought of as being fun in any way at all. It wasn't exactly fun for me either but rather more of an intense distraction. The copper seemed to require my focus and attention and I was happy and prepared to devote my time to it. In return for my efforts, the copper started to reveal her nature as she slowly and teasingly gave up some of her secrets.

In a way, it was a symbiotic relationship, a secret affair perhaps which I was having 'on the side', privately and away from ideas of destruction and the weapons of war. I found some much-needed peace and quiet too, as I worked alone in far corners of rarely used workspaces.

Maybe you could say that I was 'playing'. I have always played on my own, being an only child, and the friends I attract tend to be loners of a sort too, people who perhaps also play on their own. I am not sad in any way at all, I am in fact a happy soul, I have to say.

Sometimes I think that others look upon people like me and use the word 'sad' incorrectly to describe our behaviour. I used to worry that their opinions had great value, more than my own, but I have come to learn that their opinions have little weight or foundation at all, they are just words and ones which they use improperly in any case.

I have been told, by an educated medical man while I was at school, that I am afflicted with a medical condition called dyslexia. Honestly, I don't know exactly what it really means, only that words and numbers can be a problem for people with this condition. I am very good at mathematics though, both my mental arithmetic and on the page and my vocabulary is perfectly adequate for the life I lead. It is only spelling and pronunciation with which I sometimes struggle.

I am left-handed, which marks me out as 'odd' but mostly by people who are right-handed. They like to tell me such things that the word 'sinister' has its root meaning in the word 'sinistral' which means 'left' in Latin. I already know this as I went to a minor London public school where Latin was compulsory.

If this teasing makes them feel clever about themselves then so be it, I can easily tolerate it. Besides, when I tell them that I am in fact ambidextrous in certain sports such as snooker and tennis, they soon become quite quiet. This label is one which seems to impress these sorts of people. I don't tell them that I am not very good at either snooker or tennis.

However, I learned to keep my love of copper to myself. I would have liked to have shared these new thoughts with someone else at that time but in a way their personal exploration gave me a secret inner contentment. This happiness was quite a comfort considering the change in career direction I was already privately considering, perhaps planning would be a better term for this activity.

17

The Name Of Armstrong

It's stupid. My name is Arthur Armstrong and the car I own is called an Armstrong Siddeley Sapphire. It was my father who bought the car in the first instance but he sold it to me earlier this year for a nominal sum as he was quite happy to run the Morris Eight down in London.

I drove it up here to Aldermaston earlier this year and it desperately needed an oil change and some new plugs which I could easily do myself at the weekend. It was grand thing which might stand up well next to a Bentley or even a Rolls Royce, a very good motor vehicle indeed. I'd liked it ever since my father bought it, brand new in 1953.

He had taken me with him to the showroom in Twickenham as I recall when I was only fourteen, where he'd picked out the model he wanted. It had a straight six 3.4 litre engine and looked very similar to the smaller Rolls Royce, I remember thinking at the time, only a little shorter and narrower. It was a creamy-beige and quite regal in its attitude, more than adequate for the accountant of Cordings and Co., the men's outfitters in Piccadilly which my father had helped to run before and after the war.

He'd been stationed in India with Army Signals and Ciphers throughout the war, his actual activities never fully explained to me, and was away from England for the most part of my childhood. My memories of him only really begin at our house in Kew, just near the Botanical Gardens. However, it was with the Armstrong that I have created my enduring image of his life, his tastes and his style.

I'd admired the thing from day one, it was majestic. It rolled along with Mama and Papa upfront and me in the back gazing through the windows as the sights of London scrolled through my vision. My father would often talk of its merits, he was proud of it, of us and the life he had been able to make for us. When I gained my place as an apprentice at Aldermaston and spoke to him of my need for a vehicle, he had bought for me the gift of a pre-war Morris Eight. It needed some attention, but I was glad of the opportunity to begin my self-taught education in car maintenance with this car. It was quite a present for my seventeenth birthday.

However, he really loved that Morris Eight, especially when I had it running smoothly. He proposed that he drive it as it was perhaps more suitable for the busy London traffic, and that I have the Armstrong. When I had saved some money after a year or so of my apprenticeship, he sold it to me for less than half its value. I think he wanted me to realise that such a status symbol and piece of engineering excellence was more than just a car and that I should not take its excellence or indeed its class for granted.

Having just checked the spark plug gaps and finished the oil change, I was looking at it now, parked as it was on the far side of the site. It had presence. The Sphinx hood ornament was known as its 'Symbol of Silence', its large engine did run quietly but for me it was the exotic Egyptian mystery of this forward-looking and ancient mythologic beast which piqued my imagination. It could take me anywhere, including Reading of course.

I'm not sure why people sometimes give inanimate objects names, but what with mechanical engineering being my thing, this motor car should have a name. There had been one clear front runner from the moment it had become part of our family, but I had always kept it to myself. The naming of boats is commonplace and indeed I believe that it is unlucky to go to sea in a ship without a name. That it is often the name of a lady, a woman, a girl, or a muse of some sort was puzzling for me.

The Armstrong Siddeley Sapphire didn't feel particularly feminine. With its bold square bonnet and V-shaped grill, it sat like a proud and confident man. The name I had in mind was Louis, as in Louis Armstrong. It was a slightly sentimental choice as my mother used to sing along, out of tune I might add to the iconic American jazz singer in the war years when it was just the two of us in the house.

I just tapped the Sphinx one day and said, "Louis it is" before walking back to the main buildings and towards the canteen.

Because I had felt myself growing away from the community here I think I was subconsciously on the lookout for something, anything really, which would help to decide exactly what it was that I could do as an alternative. This was especially difficult because I did not feel like talking to anyone on site about my ideas.

One small event occurred which was to accelerate this movement and strengthen my resolve to act upon it.

I was in the library, the one on the first floor of B7, and had been investigating the process of producing high conductivity copper.

High conductivity copper, as supplied commercially, can have a conductivity approaching one hundred and two per cent. It's hard to believe, I know, but it is the truth. I checked in *Copper Data*, a small book published by the Copper Development Association which had become my bible of sorts. One hundred and two per cent!

I thought that's enough for the day. I sat back and was just about to leave the library when I saw the most recent edition of the AWRE newsletter magazine. I picked it up and flicked through it casually. Usually this publication, which is thrown together by a few anonymous second-year apprentices, contains some interview with the top brass or government officials and a few advertisements. Many of these ads are often for women's fashion labels which is quite strange. The population of employees on site is almost entirely male, save for cleaning staff and a few secretaries. I don't know why engineering does not attract more women or perhaps why they are not employed here.

But the ads do give us men something to think about and this was probably why I picked the newsletter up in the first place. It also was the other main reason for me wanting to get out of this place. I wanted to meet these women, in person, and not just when they were wearing clothes! I know there were others like me who felt this way, but the difference was that I was actually going to do something about it.

On the last page at the bottom was a very small ad, words only, in a rectangular box which read:

Ivor Ranjanisthan, Metal Smith.

Lessons in Silver Smithing, for Beginners and Advanced pupils alike.

Reading Technical College, Upper Mottly Road, Reading.

Every Wednesday, 7pm. £1,3s per evening.

Please bring you own metal.

Copper work also taught.

It seemed quite expensive but there was no question about it, I was definitely going. I had access to as much high conductivity annealed copper as I could possibly need right here, and no one would ever miss a few pounds of it from Stores. The promise and excitement of this new adventure was incredible, and it would take place only twenty miles from here by car. It would be a solo sortie into the unknown, Reading on a Wednesday night, the Armstrong meant escape and the beginnings of a new life.

18

A Silent Sphinx

Tomorrow was Wednesday and I had already loaded Louis up with various sized pieces of high conductivity copper sheeting and some cable too. The boot was very large and there was plenty of room for more should I need it. He was ready to go.

Wednesday afternoon and I downed tools. I shaved, my moustache needing a trim anyway. I put on some casual clothes, corduroy turn-ups and a Viyella shirt which looked reasonably clean. The Armstrong has 'suicide' front doors which open the 'wrong way', being hinged in the middle of the car. This means you get used to approaching it from the front to facilitate entry. The Sphinx was shining, I hopped in, it started up first time, those sporting gaps being just right now.

At the gatehouse at the exit of the site, I had to stop to be let out. Freddie was on duty and mentioned the next film that would be coming my way.

"*Spartacus* for next Saturday Mr Armstrong, hope you approve? Mr Kubrick's most recent effort, I believe, Kirk Douglas starring."

"That is correct."

"A good choice, Freddie."

"Well, Mr Armstrong, there was no choice, it was that or nothing!"

"It's an excellent choice then!"

"Gong, anywhere special?"

"Reading."

"Have a good one, watch out for the motorcyclists in the centre of town, they're maniacs!"

"Thanks Freddie."

He opened the gate and Louis and I sailed through, bound for Reading with all its charms and mysteries, the A4 all the way.

Louis and I floated to Reading. I parked outside the Technical College in its new car park and although I was a little early I decided to go in straightaway to investigate. I presented myself at a small reception where I registered for the night and was offered a discount if I signed there and then for all ten weeks. I didn't hesitate and handed over a cheque for £10. More than a week's wages.

With directions, I arrived at a door with 'Nolan Workshop' written above it and I went in. There were seven work surfaces, raised wooden tables, and as I scanned the room a tall, thin man in a grey flannel suit emerged from some shadows to my left. He had wisps of grey hair on a balding dark-skinned head and sported a long silver-grey beard, which seemed to become more silver the further down one looked. It ended in the middle of his chest in a sharp point where it was so silver as to shine.

He walked towards me and we shook hands. Looking into his eyes, they flickered with a blinking sparkle but this could have been due to a dodgy fluorescent tube above us. I noticed more silver hair coming from his ears. These hairs grew upwards, straight up, some two or three inches in fact and as I spoke they lent to him a squirrel-like appearance I thought. As he spoke to me, I imagined that they were aerials of some sort.

"Hi, I'm here for the metalworking course."

"At least I'm in the right place then," he said and I smiled.

"So you want to be a silversmith then?"

"Actually, I'm more interested in copper."

His eyes it up even more, the flicker in them becoming brighter and more regular.

"Ah! A man after my own heart. Copper is the super metal

I believe and overlooked by so many who see only interest in the glitz and glamour of silver and gold. I'm so happy I have found you! Did you bring metal?"

"Yes, yes I did."

"Well, let's waste no more time. Where is it? Let me see."

"It's in my car, just outside."

"Let's go!"

He pulled a blue bobble hat from his coat pocket and put it on, I'm not sure why, as it was quite mild this evening. We walked outside to my car at some pace as he led the way through the corridors of the building.

"Is this your car?"

He went straight for the hood ornament and ran one hand over it.

"Yes, yes it is."

"My, my. Very nice. I have never seen an Egyptian motor vehicle before."

"Oh no, it's not Egyptian, it's British. That is simply the bonnet mascot, the symbol of the marque, it's called 'The Silent Sphinx,' because their engines are so quiet."

"Oh, I see, like the Silver Lady of Rolls Royce, the Spirit of Ecstasy ... Did you know she was originally just called 'The Whisper'?"

"No, I didn't."

"I wonder which of the two has the quieter engine, The Whisper or The Silent Sphinx?"

"It's a good question."

"Perhaps it was designed in Egypt? Mmm … Yes, I think so. Very Egyptian lines. What a work of art! What's it called?"

"It's an Armstrong Siddeley Sapphire."

"No, not its model, what is its name? It does have a name, doesn't it?"

I was a little shocked and my answer took a few seconds.

"It's called Louis, he's called Louis."

"A good name for a motor car. Is it your name?"

"No, I'm Arthur, Arthur Armstrong."

"No, I mean did you name it yourself?"

"Oh yes, I'm sorry I misunderstood."

"But you have named yourself after the car then, the model that is?"

"No, my name was Armstrong before I bought the car. I bought the car from my father."

"Ah, I see. So it was in fact he who named himself by the name of the model of this car."

"No, no, you misunderstand me. He was also already called Armstrong, before he bought the car. It is our family name. His name is Robert Armstrong."

"Oh, I see, I apologise, now I am beginning to understand. He bought the car because it had the same name as himself."

"No, no, I don't think so. I think that he just liked it because it is a very fine car."

He looked at me quizzically for a few moments as if to ascertain the type of man he was dealing with. He nodded slowly …

"Well, I think it highly likely that the name of the car had something to do with his decision to purchase it, and if so I think we can say that he was very lucky indeed to find a car which bore his name, and indeed that you should also have this name. Very lucky indeed, wouldn't you say?"

It seemed important to him that I agreed with him on this point,

"Well, yes, I suppose so, if you put it that way, yes, very lucky indeed."

He was greatly relieved now and was suddenly very enthusiastic again.

"That's that then. Now let's have a look at the copper you have brought with you."

I opened the boot. A bright streetlight which had just come on seemed to pick out the edges of some of the pieces of copper I had gathered together from Stores, and they glinted within the wooden box I had put them in. The man, who later told me he was from Sri Lanka, was incredulous.

"What kind of copper do we have here?"

"It's HC, high conductivity copper. It's been deoxidised."

He looked up from the boot and made eye contact with me, wearing a serious expression.

"What is its purity?"

"Ninety-nine point nine nine per cent," I stated.

His look became more intrigued than even before. And I continued.

"Its electrical conductivity can approach one hundred and two per cent."

He waited a few more seconds, then with some deep curiosity enquired of me, "What is its modulus of elasticity?"

"I'm not sure, but I can find out."

"If you could I would be very ..."

I pulled out *Copper Data* from my jacket pocket and quickly found the correct table in the appendices.

"17.2 x 10 to the 6 pounds per square inch. As for its malleability, the process of removing oxygen from the copper has no significant effect. Essentially it is as bendy as regular copper."

His face hadn't changed but his tone was subtly different now, more respectful but also a little cautious perhaps.

"Do you work for the government?"

My hesitation was only a few seconds. In this time I closed *Copper Data* and returned it to my inside jacket pocket as I was composing my answer to his question. I wasn't sure exactly what I was going to say but it would certainly include reference to the Official Secrets Act, something I had been required to sign more than six years previously. My hesitation was enough for him and before I could speak he spoke himself.

"Don't tell me, I don't want to know, I don't need to know. I've heard enough."

But suddenly I couldn't help myself.

"I also have access to some rather exotic copper alloys including cadmium copper, chromium copper, tellurium copper, and naturally silver copper too."

"I think you should stop there. I imagine I can guess where you have travelled from this evening, and that possibly you are not at liberty to divulge the nature of your profession. You've probably told me too much already. Let's pretend we didn't have this conversation and get this copper inside."

I concurred with a nod of the head as I felt we had formed a bond of sorts. I lifted the box from the boot, and we went back inside. As we walked through the labyrinthine corridors, he told me a little more about his origins in Sri Lanka. I knew a little about this country because of its proximity to India and I had a strong feeling my father may have visited it once as a soldier.

On returning to the workshop, there were already three more people in attendance. One more was to arrive in the next few minutes, at which time our teacher addressed the group as he handed out protective aprons.

"So we have so much to learn together ... and so little time. The course was advertised primarily as silversmithing and I can see that some of you have brought with you some small amounts of silver with you this evening. However, if you don't mind too much there will be a slight change in emphasis of this course. Due to some extreme good fortune and the generosity of Mr Arthur Armstrong here and his kind employers also I believe, I am going to introduce you to this ancient and wonderful craft using another, perhaps more humble metal.

Nevertheless, it is one with which you are going to be able to learn all you will ever need to know.

"There is a timeless Sri Lankan which says if you can master copper, you can master life!"

He slid the box of my copper samples along the surface of the table which he now stood behind, facing us, at the front of the room.

"Along with metal work another complimentary passion of mine is everything to do with music. This evening we will be initiating your education in life by making a musical instrument – copper cymbals!"

And that is what we did. After three hours of hard work involving, melting, cutting, annealing, brazing, hammering and polishing, each of us walked away with a large pair of cymbals.

When we had completed our metal work, to varying standards, leather straps were added for handles which our teacher had made as we worked on our copper. The cymbals were approximately sixteen inches in diameter and we made a fair cacophony with them as we tried them out as a group at the end of play.

My education had begun.

The other four in our group were as excited as me. We didn't have a great deal of spare time to talk to each other as we worked but when we did it was pleasant, light-hearted chat, polite humorous exchanges which helped to keep us ticking along nicely.

During later lessons I came to know these people more closely as we also began going afterwards to a nearby pub. It was our diversity which struck me most, five unique people brought together by copper. There was both a butcher and baker, if you can believe it, but no candlestick maker although we often joked that perhaps one week, we should have a crack at making some candlesticks. The other two were a light aircraft flying instructor and a lady librarian. Then of course there was me, an atomic weapons engineer, well, potentially at least.

This unification of random specialisations by virtue of an even more esoteric pursuit started me thinking more about my future and my place in the world. There was clearly so much more out there than I knew and the idea that I might find ways of exploring these areas and the people involved in them was genuinely exciting to me.

Louis and I drove home quietly but now there was music within me and this was not just the amateur clash of my newly made cymbals. These rested proudly, with promise and great potential, on the passenger seat. I was genuinely shocked at their power when I had to stop suddenly at some traffic lights just coming out of Reading. They slid off the seat and into the footwell, their notes cascading and colliding, resounding and reverberating around the spacious interior of the Sapphire.

After I had collected myself and the sound in my ears had dissipated, I pulled away from the lights. It was late, way past 10pm, it was dark and there was next to no traffic. Turning on the AM radio I found some reasonable reception to a station and no other than Mr Louis Armstrong burst into life with 'On the Sunny Side of the Street'. Not recalling having heard it before, I thought it might be one of his more recent numbers.

Louis and I strolled through the night at a sedate pace, unobstructed by worries. As he hit a long, high note at the end I wondered from what kind of metal his trumpet might be made.

19

The Singing Bowl

The course led up to a series of classes in which our teacher instructed us and guided us through the practical steps of making a 'singing bowl'. This is a type of bell in fact, an inverted one, which is played with a wooden mallet or baton. Some of these bowls are struck with the baton, sometimes they have water in them, and a note is made. However, one which can 'sing', an example of which we were to make from copper, is known as 'friction idiophone'.

One uses a smooth piece of wood known as a baton, which is placed in contact with the outer rim of the bowl and moved around its diameter. The vibrations made within the bowl make a resonating sound and the volume of the continuous note created depends upon the speed and the pressure of the wooden baton on the bowl.

We learned all this from our curious teacher in theory classes before we were allowed to attempt the manufacture of our own bowls. Suffice it to say this man was somewhat of an expert and had learned his ancient craft from his grandfather, who had also taught his father and his brother and his two cousins.

He was most interested in using some of my high conductivity copper for the job as he was intrigued as to the sound characteristics the heightened purity might lend to the performance of the bowl. I was only too happy to oblige as stores had an overabundance of supplies and I was able to sign out enough for our whole group. In the space on the form entitled 'Intended Use of Item or Items' I had written simply 'Acoustic

Research'. I had received no queries and the Armstrong's boot space was ample for the transportation.

We melted our copper in a small furnace, somewhere along some winding corridors on the other side of the building in the pottery and ceramics department. The Sri Lankan way was to add various other metals in small quantities so in effect our bowl would be formed of a unique alloy. He would however not divulge the specific nature of these additional elements, informing us with some ceremony that the ingredients were a sacred and symbolic enhancement to the process and their identities were a family secret which had been kept close to their descendants for over four hundred years.

We then poured our molten magic into stone bowls, about eight inches in diameter. The red-hot liquid glistened and spluttered like primeval lava as it was poured and there were rapid tiny sparks too, which jumped crazily all over the place.

The fire precautions practised in this academic institution were not of the standard to which I had been made accustomed in my job. I was myself a little more cautious than the others who I felt were somewhat slapdash in their attitude towards this.

One older lady managed to catch her woollen scarf alight on one corner but fortunately I was nearby and able to douse the flames with my thermos flask of tea which I had brought with me before the blaze was able to grow any bigger. I was slightly perturbed as she said I had 'ruined her chemise' with my actions and had not thought to thank me one jot for my quick thinking.

When it had cooled, we were each left with a hemisphere of solid metal. It was only when that had cooled sufficiently to be able to upturn the stone moulds and handle these that I realised how similar they were to the uranium hemispheres we used as the fissile material in the heart of nuclear weapon.

Of course, uranium is more than twice as dense as copper so it would have been twice as heavy for the same size. Needless to say, I had never held a piece of uranium in my hands.

I had some difficulty processing this comparison which lodged itself in my mind. This was due I think to the extreme differences in the intended purpose of two seemingly similar pieces of metal; one to kill tens of thousands or the other to make a pleasant sound.

I busied myself with the process, which was now all about hammering and re-heating. Three people would complete this phase in about an hour using a large pair of tongs and with each person wielding a six-pound sledgehammer. We got through a great deal of water mixed with Sri Lankan mountain salt as we wetted the bowls between re-heating. The saltwater created large amounts of dark smoke and the flames of our furnace turned a deep blue.

By this time, we had disabled the smoke detectors in the room as they were sounding continuously. I was so involved and absorbed in the work that this misdemeanour bothered me very little.

It took me six hours over three weeks for us to complete our rudimentary bowls. We had all received immense help from the master, who appeared to be abnormally strong for his size, with a stamina to match.

The results were mixed. I was quite proud of my effort and as the work continued, utilising progressively smaller, and then some really very fine hammers, our bowls began to look quite impressive, elegant even.

The final phase was to use a milling machine to smooth the top edge and give the bowl its final form. I was familiar with this lathe-type device and was able to assist others in its safe operation.

With a tungsten carbide tool run over both the inner and

outer surfaces, the bowls were suddenly bright and shiny and true. A last filing of the top edge made sure it was smooth to the feel of our fingertips.

The polishing took very little time indeed after this but brought out the colour of the alloy which was certainly recognisable as the pinkish, reddish hue familiar to anyone who has polished copper, but the secret composition of the additional metals had now made our bowls glint with a golden silver glow too.

I was so happy as I drove home again late at night. The radio was playing, and I may even have been singing along. This contented state was rudely terminated however when I hit a pothole just outside of Aldermaston. They were everywhere on this stretch of road. A massive clunk at the front of the car pulled at the steering wheel and I veered sharply towards the centre of the road.

It was a sudden shock and there was a burst of adrenaline within, but I didn't feel in great danger as I was probably doing less than 30mph in a residential area. There was no other traffic, the brakes worked fine, and I was able to bring the Armstrong to rest quickly and safely at the side of the road on a muddy verge near a few houses.

It was bloody annoying as I just started to think about a quiet late pint and something to eat before going to bed. I was almost home, maybe only less than a mile away and it was exceptionally cold. There was not a soul about.

The sound and vibration had come from the front offside, and I checked there first. A connecting rod in the suspension had either come loose or broken and was hanging down onto the road. It was dark but I was fairly near a streetlight and I thought I'd better have a closer look to see what the damage was. I thought maybe I could rig up a makeshift repair and limp home.

Without a torch I couldn't be sure how bad the damage was without taking the wheel off and as I could just about see what I was doing it seemed to be the best option.

I needed a block of wood to get the car jack on as it would only have sunk into the soft ground. Right by the car was a large skip, full of both an old bathroom and a kitchen by the looks of it. There was also a huge pile of old clothes dumped on top. I lifted these away and managed to find a slab a substantial piece of pine which would be just fine for the job in hand.

However, when I got the car up and the wheel off, I could see the damage was quite nasty, the connecting arm had broken in two and the Armstrong would be going nowhere further tonight.

I put the wheel back on, lowered the jack and put it in the boot. It was really very cold now indeed and I was wearing only a thin jumper. I thought for a minute assessing my options. I'd have to walk home and come back tomorrow.

Maybe Roger Stevens would give me a tow but then on second thoughts I was going to need to get the car on the back of a lorry to move it anywhere without ruining the suspension completely. Potholes. You'd think that a civilised country of fair wealth would be able to maintain its roads to a higher standard … It's 1960 for god's sake!

I looked up the road, the streetlights stopped in a hundred yards or so and it was blackness ahead, my hands were freezing.

In the skip I found a pair of old garden gloves and then what looked to be a brand-new coat. I put the coat on. It was a perfect fit, so warm and long enough to come down to my thighs. I fastened the hooks it had at the front and was so glad of it, the transformation in my mood was tremendous.

The gardening gloves I now discarded as they were too large and cold – the leather was stiff and several of the fingers were missing on one hand. Instead I put my hands in the pockets of my new coat, where a fur lining greeted them, comforting them after their battle with the jack and tyre lever.

I wanted the bowl, there was no way I was going to leave it alone in the car all night. With it under my arm, I wrapped it in a blanket and walked away smiling, glancing back only once to see the sorry Sapphire all lopsided and sad. I should think about buying something more modern perhaps when I graduated from the Establishment.

The course had finished. I got home, I went to bed, I woke up.

It was a sunny spring morning and with its freshness I hadn't even yet thought about what I might do with my car.

Taking the bowl outside and removing it from its protection, the reflections of the surrounding woodland, the blue of the sky and the white of the clouds were mesmerising. I was hypnotised for long moments, simply regarding this object as I turned it and looked at it from all sides. I could not quite bring myself to believe that I had made it with my own hands.

We had also made a small mahogany baton with which to play a note from it. This was itself little more than a wooden cylinder about five inches in length which we had made once during part of the bowls' cooling periods. I could not get the bowl to sing as it should on that occasion, and I failed to sustain any kind of note on this morning either. Only two in the class had been able to do so and the teacher had said this was often the case with a first bowl.

I was disappointed I have to say but the object was so beautiful in this light as to compensate for my feelings. I wondered whether I might be able to refer to it as sculpture. I smiled to myself as I thought it was certainly a 'Work of Art'. Wrapping it in a soft towel, I placed it under my bed.

20

Can I Get Some Potato Chips?

That day there was an important meeting with a visitor from the States. A man called Jon Chrysler who was ex-IBM and had come to consult on the ATLAS installation. I was to be in attendance, and I was running late.

The meeting was fine, a couple of hours as we got straight into some technical details regarding its power cabling requirements and its cooling needs. He would be here only a few days and we needed to pick his brain on a whole load of stuff before he had to get back for the start of the new semester at Caltech and his regular job as professor in their Computing Faculty.

He was clearly jet-lagged, and I feel we grilled him quite intensively but then he was getting paid a lot for his specialist knowledge. I was assigned to keep him company at lunch and took him to a local pub rather than the canteen as I felt he might like to see a small authentic piece of England on his first visit here.

"It's Arthur right? As in King Arthur I guess?"

"Yes, that's right, but we're not related …"

"I'm just joshing with you. So, tell me Arthur, you're clearly wired in pretty tight to the nuclear weapons programme here, how do you see your future unfolding? Within the context of the relentless expansion of the Arms Race that is."

"Er, well I'm not sure I do see it, unfolding I mean. Not how I thought it might anyway. I'm currently weighing up my options. What would you like to drink?"

"Oh, I've been told to try a pint of 'bitter'. Will be that be

OK? I hear you guys drink it warm, I'm not too sure about that though, can I get a cold one?"

"Ah, probably not. I'll get you some Stones, see how you get on with that. You'll soon forget about it being warm, you know because it tastes so bad."

"Hey, that's funny Arthur. I like you already, I've been told about the British sense of humour. Hey, can I get some potato chips too?"

"Excuse me?"

"Potato chips … Just something to munch on, anything really, I'm famished."

"Ah, well we can order a proper meal here."

"Sounds great, a good idea by the way."

"Oh, I eat here all the time."

"No, I mean weighing up your options."

"Oh yes."

"What are they?"

"Sorry?"

"Your options, what areas are you looking into, I mean what's on the table for you right now?"

"You know Jon, to be honest, I'm kind of lost, to tell you the truth, vis-à-vis the whole, you know 'What shall I do with my life?' question."

"Oh, I see. Well, that's good too. I was like that for years at IBM until I started teaching. I can tell you I'm fairly sorted now, what with Brenda and the house and my kids and all. Brandon and Elise, they're just starting out at college, can you believe that? Would you like to see a picture of them, I've got a picture of them here somewhere."

John took a photo from his jacket pocket of his teenage children and his wife. Brenda was young and stunning and Brandon was wearing an 'Indians' cap. Elise had on a jumper with the words 'Indiana Wild Cats'. The three of them had perfect smiles with even more perfect teeth in them.

"Twins. They love their Indians those two."

He put the photo back.

"You got kids Arthur?"

"No, I'm single, currently."

"Ah, living the bachelor dream. I remember those days, just about. You want a wife, kids, the whole shooting match?"

"Er, yes, yes I do I think."

"Let me tell you a secret Arthur, just between you and me … thinking about it ain't going to get you anywhere. You just got to go out there and grab it! With you own two hands! You get me?"

"You're right Jon. You're right."

"Say. Did you know there's a US company opening up somewhere round here? They're building some kind of research centre or production plant or something. I think it might not be far from here? Some city called Bayzing Stook or something?"

"That would be Basingstoke."

"That's it, Basingstoke! It's a huge pharmaceutical company by the name of Elie Lillie or something. I bet you they are looking for high-class engineers right now. Bet they'd pay top dollar for a guy like you, Arthur. You could do worse than check them out if you're thinking of getting out of the nuclear game."

"That sounds intriguing, it really does, I'd like to hear more about it certainly."

"Yeah, I was reading about in a magazine on the flight over here. Their research centre headquarters, a production plant too. It's gonna to be a 'springboard into Europe', that's what I think they called it. Ah here's our beers! Which one's mine?"

"Er, that one."

"Great, let's see what we've got."

John drank a large gulp from the pint of Stones, removing the whole of its foamy top inch in the process.

"My god! You weren't joking! That truly is some foul-tasting brew! And you drink this all the time!"

"It's an acquired taste I suppose."

"Yeah I suppose. At least it's nice and warm!"

"You get used to it."

"I'm going to try, I'll say that much. So Arthur, what's the scene like around here as far as the feminine side of the species goes? You get much action?"

Jon and I talked for a couple of hours, during which time he tried another couple of pints of different kinds of beer. He didn't have another meeting until tomorrow and after we left the pub we walked back. I think he went straight to his lodgings and fell asleep all through the rest of the afternoon and through the night to the morning.

He was a big, friendly guy. Very intelligent indeed and it was hard sometimes to see how this went together with his loose, casual style. When I commented on this before he left all he said was, "Yeah people say I'm kinda goofy, but what do people know eh?"

"Thank you for all your advice and ideas Jon, you've given me a lot to think about."

"Hey, don't worry about it, Art! I reckon you'll be just fine, you'll figure something out, mark my words. Hey what's this about a protest march tomorrow? I've only just heard about it. It's going to be big I've heard."

"I know, it was on the news on the radio last night. They think there will be hundreds of them, if not thousands."

"What's the deal?"

"They're all coming here! By train mainly I've heard and then they'll probably shout a lot outside the perimeter fence, wave a lot of placards, that kind of thing."

"Sounds interesting, don't you think. Do you think there's any danger of it getting nasty?"

"No, no, I don't think so. The police will be out and about but it's a peace march. The CND, the Campaign for Nuclear Disarmament are organising it, this will be the second year they've run the thing. There will probably be a lot more protesters though this year, I'm sure."

"I might pop along for a bit. I don't have anything to do tomorrow and my flight's not for another day after that. Will there be TV cameras there? I'd like to see how your media cover this kind of show."

"Maybe … Maybe."

"You gonna check it out?"

"No, I don't think so. I'll be on the other side of the fence. I have quite a few things to take care of. There's this report I must get in by Friday. That one I was talking about the other day, about the copper alloy spring manufacturing proposal."

"Oh, I recall, yes, the springs. You might miss out on some drama. You never know those, hippies and commies can get a bit lively when you get enough of them together."

"Maybe I'll see you tomorrow, around and about at some point anyway."

"Cool."

Jon gave the two-finger peace salute. "They say the times are a changin' Art, you know they could be right …"

"We'll see. Jon, we'll see."

We exchanged addresses in case are paths didn't cross the next day and promised to stay in touch.

21

Music In A Memory

Having lived in the ashram for almost a year, I have just returned from India. I went there to find out who I was, and who I am, but I have had to return suddenly because my Aunt Marie has died. I feel horribly alone.

It's just me in the house. John has gone out for the afternoon to sign some papers at the solicitor's office in town and then he's going to stock up on food for us both. We realised today that we've eaten very little in the last week with all the stress and arrangements for the funeral which was only two days ago. We're holding each other together but the shock of Aunt Marie dying has hit us hard now and we suddenly find ourselves with a lot of spare time. It's really beginning to set in.

The abrupt news of the trauma has clearly left us both in a profound confusion. I am also quite obviously experiencing what I believe is referred to as 'reverse culture shock'. On a superficial level my strawberry blonde hair has gone wild and I have noticed that my freckles are nowhere to be seen now as the dark tan I acquired in India has engulfed them all. A year in the Indian sun has made my skin so dark that I have several times been mistaken for a foreigner here in recent days. John says I look just as I did when he first saw me, standing on the doorstep when I was no taller than a tenor saxophone.

I am concerned with the prospect of selling this house, No. 29 Meadowbank, Primrose Hill, NW3. It's a beautiful house, it always has been, and I am lucky to have such incredible memories I have made here. These memories are strong, and I will never fade. There are breath-taking views over Primrose Hill Park and perhaps I am a fool to be even thinking of selling it.

After nearly twenty years in England, John is going to go back to the USA for the first time. A reunion with his brother is the main force driving him there. His brother is a few years younger than him and lives in San Francisco.

He simply cannot bear to be here another day. To be in this house, as beautiful as his memories are for him here also, he cannot live among them knowing Aunt Marie is gone. I have never seen such a large man broken into so many pieces as he.

It kills him to leave me alone like this but his brother is in fact his only family and I have helped him reach this difficult conclusion and encouraged him to go. Strangely I feel competent to handle the pain and grief I am experiencing, perhaps my time at the ashram has made me stronger than I know. I'm struggling though, and we support each other so in many ways. He just wants to 'go home'. He keeps saying it.

I have been in almost continuous dialogue with Mr Short, our family solicitor since the time my parents were married back in 1934. I believe he was a friend of my father's from university in Manchester. He is an agreeable man of some considerable humour who was able to contact me swiftly upon Aunt Marie's passing. Since I returned, he has been doing everything humanly possible to make my life more bearable. He helped organise the funeral and is dealing with all financial matters.

Mr Short will soon help me place the house with an estate agent and I have no doubt it will sell quickly. I know I could live here quite easily but I have a desire and an inner passion to make a new start. Mr Short has said this is the best decision I can make, he has a lot of experience with this kind of thing, and I know I am doing what's right, it's just painfully hard to do.

The will is going to be read in a week or so, at his offices in Piccadilly. He has mentioned it several times now, to prepare me I think for information I know I will be receiving which is going to be difficult to digest.

I turned twenty-one at the ashram just a month ago and I imagine there's going to be a great deal of money involved in my future. It might be that this is going to make the journey I have ahead of me easier in many ways, but I know it will desperately complicate it in so many others. I am trying not to think about it at all as I know I am going to be alone with these matters for a long time now.

This is a new life for me, horribly new. Fate has dealt me a fearful blow but has then given me an opportunity to choose to make my life anew. I will take this opportunity to a new place, I simply don't know where it will be yet.

The deciding factor in this decision is, as always for me in all things, music. There is no music here anymore. John has always been a musician and he and Marie had such good music together. Their relationship was a continuous improvisation around contrasting themes. There was harmonisation, sometimes there was discord, but there was always melody and rhythm. I hadn't imagined that it might end in the middle of a song.

It was only while in India that I began to realise that my inner world, where I spend so much of my time, is a place so very different from that experienced by most other people. The music I heard there, the tabla drums, the sitar of the Guru and the sounds of all manner of instruments I had never even laid eyes on before, came together in a heady mix. Together with the yoga I practised daily, and the insights gained through regular meditation, there was most definitely a shift in my consciousness, and my awareness of my own nature. Music is all encompassing for me, it unifies my senses, it defines me and is my only way of explaining the world to myself. How people can live their life without it I do not understand.

This realisation is so hard to describe and only a few seem to understand me. When I try explaining it to just anyone, they look at me as though I'm crazy or I'm just making something up. The music within me and the music I play is all a result of the way I experience the world, and apparently it always has been. Now I have concluded that I don't need to explain it to myself, any more than I need to explain it to anyone else. The music itself is explanation enough.

Now the music created by the three of us in this house has died, so has mine. I have no doubt it will return but it won't be here. I cannot evolve their music and I cannot build on my memories of it here either. This house is their music, but it is completed and finished now and I must somehow build a house of my own, and make my own music.

John has a huge number of records here. His collection of vinyl is almost exclusively jazz from the 30s, 40s and 50s. His brother has been sending these over from the States all the time I have been living here. It was the way they corresponded with each other. Now John is going back, he is giving me this entire collection which fills the shelves on a whole wall of one small room. It will take a lifetime to listen to them all.

Along with the records I think the only thing I will take from this house is the piano. It is a fine Bluthner, a baby upright grand. I learned everything I know about playing music on this piano. It has a deep resonant sound, warm and pure. Listening to those records, being inspired by them, doing my best to emulate the artists who made them and playing the notes I found within myself was all made possible with companionship of this piano. John and I used to play together all the time as he's an excellent saxophonist with a unique and original touch. Hours would go by, and Aunt Marie would smile and listen and dance. Our souls are worn into those eighty-eight black and white keys.

Miyu is my only other real friend, true and trusted from university days. She visited me this morning, and I was overjoyed to see her standing there in her cool funny clothes. Her mother is English, and her father is Japanese. She looks like no one else in the world and the sound of her voice is unique too, so delicate and soft but high pitched on occasion too. She was devastated when John had told her the news as Aunt Marie had a huge soft spot for her.

She is so smart and empathetic and I love her so much. I'm just so lucky to have someone who knows me at my core. I had forgotten about her resilience, her power even. She is tiny and quiet, but her physical presence disguises the ferocity of her spirit. Being half Japanese, the painfully delicate and beautiful look of her fragile face conceal a wild soul and a heart of pure gold.

Miyu has been here all afternoon but has just left. She is going to visit again tomorrow, I can't wait to get out of here and go and do something fun together. Until then she has inspired me to write, and to write now, to order my thoughts and perhaps if I can, my feelings also. She is a wonderful person, so exotic and fresh and has helped me decide to start putting down what I can remember of my Aunt Marie's life, and my life with her. It will be part of the grieving process, a catharsis she tells me, and something to confront head-on what I am going through. It is a way to avoid ignoring my circumstances, something she has told me will not be possible in any case. Better to do this now because although the suffering may be more intense, acceptance will come more easily and I will be able to find contentment again all the sooner.

I am not attempting this with a sense of nostalgia or for posterity's sake but to recall what I can, while I can. However, it is with great sadness that I do this, and I think it is an act most probably motivated by fear more than anything, not least the fear that these memories will slip away from me, as those of my parents disappeared and indeed those of myself as a child.

All I have written so far on the first line of the first page of the large notebook full of only blank pages, is a title:' The Problems of Being Unique.' It seems apt, if perhaps a little self-absorbed.

Sitting at the kitchen table, I am however very present. As I look at my surroundings for clues, my feeling is one of profound stillness. I am not depressed, I'm not sure you could say I am 'sad' either, not really, not as most people think of this word. Perhaps I am numb, still in shock at the tragedy and absurdity of the loss in my life. To lose my parents as a child, to lose my aunt when I am only twenty-one years of age, and for the only man who has ever been able to really understand me to be leaving me. Yes, I am alone. Mostly I feel quiet inside, the music has stopped, but I have faith it will start again and that when it does, both it and I will be strong.

I see the prism my mother gave me, which is at this moment sitting on a windowsill in the hall. The sunlight was shining though it for a minute just a while ago, throwing its rainbow across the far wall. A cloud has passed between it and the sun now, so it's merely a piece of inert glass, unfilled by its multicoloured magic. Nevertheless, it triggers me. The silence here might be troublesome for someone in my situation, but it creates a physical stillness which seems to help me start writing.

The first thing I think of has nothing to do with Marie or my life here. What I wish to describe is all that I can of a solitary memory which I have hitherto kept locked inside, since I was that child in fact. It is perhaps the very last memory I formed for myself before I was told of the accident which took my parents' lives. It will be hard for me because words have always felt limiting for me and my grasp of the subtleties of the English language is not my strongest skill. It is also a brave decision for me as I feel very strongly that I must do it justice.

Less of a memory, it is more a collection of vivid impressions composed of dreamy sensations which even now are always shifting and remaking themselves into new patterns. Since the events of the day they were formed, I have been reshuffling the world of this sensory space as a kind of frequent distraction. I have played with its shapes and moods, I have focused on its moments, and I have altered them but still I cannot share their content or meaning, not even now some fifteen years since I was that child aged six.

Clearly this one memory has acquired an almost untouchable and precious status because I have never expressed it before in words, either spoken or written. I have never thought that I would be able to, but then I feel I have never really tried. To do so now is my way of beginning to share the spirit of the girl within it in a literal way so that she can become less abstract and more defined to myself and to anyone else who might care to know her. The girl in the memory is me of course and this is my way of giving her a different kind of status, one with a permanently beautiful soul.

My greatest frustration is that I have been unable to introduce her to anyone, to present her to those I love. And now, in attempting to convey this one memory in words, spoken or written, I find myself at a complete loss. I am a piano player and in general I am confident and competent enough to express most of my feelings through the music of this instrument. It's range in this regard has no limit for me. But this memory, or whatever it is, seems to be written in my soul in a language I am no longer able to speak.

Kodaikanal's beauty is also now a part of me. As I have my recent fresh memories of its nature and its happy people to draw upon, I once again try to reimagine Ananya. Following my visit to the paradise where she began her life, I am now more certain than ever that the memory I wish to express is more of a fusion of visions and sounds but that it does indeed represent a very real event.

The day after my sixth birthday was 27th December 1945, it was a Wednesday. It was the day my parents died together in the landslide at the site of the copper mine, and it was the day I lost the chance to know them, and indeed to remember them.

I have come to understand from one piece of information told to me by Indira, my nanny, that the truth of the memory which fascinates me is one which I may have formed while sleepwalking outside in the forest in the very early morning of that day and that this is when the memory I want to write down was created. I had apparently walked in my sleep on two occasions previously, so the idea does seem credible.

That I have reformed this memory – and reimagined it over and repeatedly during the fifteen years since it was made – means to me that it has evolved to be more than a recollection. It doesn't seem right to call it a story either, but without doubt it is a key part of my inner workings and I am not sure that I wish to label it at all.

I was so happy in Kodaikanal, and then at the ashram, and so sad to leave, and in truth it has prepared me well to deal with what is before. However, I am further away from Ananya than ever before. She has always had the most central place in my heart, but an eclipse which does not wish to pass has forever hidden her joy.

I want to see her. I want to meet her, somehow. I want to make a place where she can talk to me. I am her, but she has always been missing. I have always hoped she would come back to me and bring with her all the other missing memories I must have once had. I only hope that she is not lost.

When Miyu arrives the next day, the three of us – John, Miyu and I – are together for the first time since Aunt Marie died. We are the oddest ensemble, but we have always harmonised so well with each other and now it is no different. Tears come and go easily and smiles have changed slightly, but humour is in far greater abundance than any of us might have imagined. We are each quite special I would say as individuals, each of us alone, but then as a trio too.

John and Miyu and I played music together sometimes, often in fact. We are all colour and notes and rhythm and light. I am jazz through and through, but Miyu studied classical piano, and our styles could not be more dissimilar. She is highly trained, I am self-taught, with a huge input from John of course. His sax is sublime, and he plays drums and any percussion he can lay his huge hands upon. His influences from living near New Orleans are vast and varied and he can bring them all together at the drop of a hat. We jam, we improvise, we lose ourselves, we lose track of time. We play.

Our music is within us, and it is not just a part of our lives, it is the essence of them. For myself it is the colour in my life and without it the world would be a set of monochrome shadows and bland noise. It's empty and sad here now and we just can't even bring ourselves to play music or listen to records or even the radio.

As Ana I search for Ananya within myself, not only for her sake but for mine too. I believe she can help me from feeling so remote, a feeling which has suffused every new memory I have been able to make since coming to England. It occurs to me that perhaps I will find her outside of me, outside of the life I have now.

She is quiet, but her music is playing somewhere.

22

Where There Are Wills

The day of the reading of the will came, and went eventually, fortunately, thankfully.

I had been dreading it and so had asked Miyu to come along for moral support. John and I walked there from the nearest tube which was Oxford Street and met Miyu outside the offices of Bahnell, Heally and Short but when we arrived at David's office door, unfortunately he took me to one side and had to quietly inform me that Miyu would not be able to sit in on the actual reading. I felt stupid because I should have asked.

"How long do you think we'll be, all told?"

"Oh, probably more than an hour or so I expect Ananya. There is rather a lot to get through."

I apologised to Miyu and suggested that she should go and look around the shops, which she was more than happy to do because she is, among many other things, a fashion fiend, and an icon for me in this respect too.

I'd assumed that there would be others there, without having given it any thought at all, but it was just myself and John and David in his small, beautiful office tucked away in a grand old London building, surrounded on all sides by oak panelling and paintings of illustrious men in wigs.

There were plenty of leather chairs. I sat and ran my fingers over the round dome studs which were as worn as the dark green leather which had clearly held tightly to the substantial wooden frame for many a year. I felt privileged, older and serious. John sprawled out on a chaise longue, taking it all in.

He felt at home wherever he went and never stood on

ceremony or was in the least bit aware of the impact his American manners had on anyone. In turn, I couldn't care less either. It always made me laugh the way he rubbed the back up of some people we met over the years. Indeed, historically his casual retorts to protestations of the most English kind were usually so fast and apparently even more offensive to the person who had made the mistake of objecting to his behaviour, that they were mostly terminal to any further conversation. I won't say that he swore a great amount, but his language was so creative and contained reference to such words that English men and women were often struck dumb and had to walk away, offended, mute and confused.

David found John to be the most big-hearted man who contrasted his own small frame and delicate sensibilities so well as to make them quite a pair. They had even spent nights drinking together, with and without Marie, although I have no idea how their dialogue was when I was not around. Here we were, all aware of the sombre business which had to be processed, and John's relaxed manner was simply a good way of attempting to deal with it.

David himself was wearing a broad pinstripe suit, which looked thick and heavy and warm. A white shirt had a perfectly starched collar and, perhaps for my benefit, a bright jazzy orange and green tie brought together in a huge slightly off-centre Windsor knot around his slight neck. His appearance brightened my mood no end and seemed to summon up the jovial spirit of Marie within us all. This wouldn't be so bad I decided.

I had cobbled together some relatively formal clothes which I felt were suitable for the occasion. I was trying for an 'autumnal' look and although I thought I had met with some success, my jacket felt tight around my arms and the matching tweed trousers itched around my ankles. I wasn't wearing any socks, and these little brown brogues were digging in too.

"Would either of you like a cup of tea? I can ask my secretary to bring a pot in, she's very good like that."

"No, I'm fine, really I am, let's just proceed shall we?"

"Don't worry about me David, you know I don't care for tea so much. Let's just, well, 'skip the formalities' and so on shall we?"

"Of course, of course. I know this is emotional for us all but Ananya especially. I just had these words I wanted to say to you before we begin.

"I want to advise perhaps just suggest that you try to separate the personal side of this from the more er … financial aspect, whatever it is we are going to discover here."

He tapped the large envelope on his desk.

"Thank you, David, that is good advice. I know that will not be easy, for us all, I must say but you're right, it is the best way to proceed, you're right. Your approach is always very professional and clear, I know how much Marie appreciated this."

I could see David beginning to well up, and to cut short any upsetting scenes I buoyed him in a stronger tone.

"Come on David, let's just get on with this and get it over with shall we."

"Yes, of course, here we go then."

He had been standing but now he sat and picked up the envelope, opened it carefully with a long, sharp letter opener and removed the contents. This was a large single piece of paper, folded into four. He began to read.

The Last Will and Testament of Marie Gallard.

29 Meadowbank, Primrose Hill,

London NW3.

I am a woman of relative humble origins. Even though they were French, I do not believe my family background suffered from a great deal of conceit or arrogance and it is purely by good fortune and the generosity of my remaining good that I have found myself living in a beautiful place in London for the most part of my life, entertained daily by a tremendous view with the delights of the drama of the constantly changing British weather.

Being here, living with the only man I have ever deemed worthy of my love, a man who is the only man who has ever known how to love me I might add, means I could not have been happier. But then of course I have been delighted to have in fact been made happier than I could have imagined by the arrival of my beautiful niece. These two people have lit up my life with their humour and of course their music.

I refer to the incredible John Jackson of San Francisco and the unique Ananya Rondel who hails from India. With their being my only relatives, I have decided that should my death precede theirs, by whatever cause, I would like to leave my house and its contents to them both jointly and in equal distribution. We have all lived there with much happiness and should they wish to live there together, and perhaps with others in the future, well it makes me smile as I write.

If either or both should wish to sell the property for whatever reasons they may have, individually or together the monies raised from the sale should be split between them half and half. And that will be that.

John deserves everything he gets, and he will know that by me saying this he will know I mean it in the nice way its meant, as well as the funny way.

The same division also applies to the assessed value of the few financial assets in my name as regards stocks and shares and their corresponding dividends.

Ananya should keep the piano. She should play it often and maintain it and practise, much more often than she does. John cannot play for toffee and Ananya is so incredibly gifted and talented so that I often think she has been touched with a gift of rare genius. She should practise more often however, there is nothing more shameful than wasted talent.

The passing of Ananya's parents, my sister Sophie and her fine husband Callum, was a tragedy of such terrible shock for me but I naturally fear that for Ananya the hardship was horribly compounded by her abrupt relocation. The sudden transition from what is apparently an idyll of incomparable beauty to the dark grey, misty fogs and miserable people of old London Town must have been horrific. I have never liked the folk of this city to be truthful, that is except for a few good people who live in and around the Primrose Hill area.

Her parents' estate was left to me in its entirety and their generosity during their life continued after their death. We live like minor royalty I sometimes think. John and Ananya take this a little too much for granted but I have not the wherewithal to chastise them for their omissions of gratitude to the Good Lord above.

Clearly their situation is not what one might describe as 'normal', not at all, and they should count their blessings more often, at least once a day I would suggest.

On their passing, a maintenance was provided for Ananya which has always been more than ample, and I have in fact held some of this for her as her needs and wants are thankfully inexpensive, but certainly the money has enabled her to have the best education money can buy.

Experience is by far the greater teacher in my opinion and Ananya and John could learn so much more from each other should they so wish.

Upon my death, her parents' estate will pass in its entirety to Ananya, this is my wish and I know it would have been her parents too. We have always been a small family, but family is paramount and the idea of selling off the company Callum founded during the war is unthinkable. It is a family business, and my wish is for it to stay as such.

As I understand it, our family has a controlling fifty-one per cent share in Rondel Mining. Callum's specific wishes for Ananya are contained within his own will. Our solicitor David Short, who must be reading this now if I am deceased, has always attended to these matters and I trust he will continue to do so as his judgement and professionalism is beyond question.

He should however look in a mirror more often, to straighten his tie, as it is often askew, to the left usually and gives him the unbearable air of a man who is inattentive to details. This is unfortunate as in his work this not the case, but appearances account for over ninety per cent of the impression we make of each other.

I leave you with no regrets or complaints. Any criticism of the state of the contemporary fashion industry would take more time than I have available to spare. Fashion should pull its socks up in my opinion. As for the government, well it should govern, should it not! Or at least try to.

The English are such a dour lot overall and could learn to have a trifle more bohemian fun in their choices. They could learn a thing or two from the panache and flair of the Europeans but of course they will not swallow their pride long enough to do so.

Au revoir it is then, and bonne chance!

Ms Marie Gallard

P.S. Ananya, the money you inherit, neither be frivolous nor stingy with it, both philosophies look terribly silly on a wealthy woman. Aim high, and NEVER dress down because you will ALWAYS be disappointed with yourself. And remember grey will never go out of fashion, because grey has never BEEN in fashion.

P.P.S. John there is a little something special hidden for you behind the boiler immersion tank in the airing cupboard upstairs.

P.P.P.S. David, your company and yourself of course will be dealing with probate of my unfortunate legacy but I would like to put in writing here than an extra amount, equal to your company's fee for this work, be deducted from the final valuation of my estate and added to your personal bank account. That's all folks!

David stopped reading, he was quite flushed in his cheeks and looked at me and then John in turn.

"Well, I think that's all relatively straightforward. Ah … How do you feel?"

David looked up at us to make eye contact for the first time to see us sitting quietly.

"If you have any questions, I might be able to answer …"

We looked at each other.

"Me? I'm OK, I suppose." I really didn't quite know what I was supposed to be feeling, given the unprecedented and perfectly unpredictable nature of the human experience as it is lived and not having any relevant frames of reference with which to compare my situation. I looked at John and shrugged my shoulders.

John shrugged back.

"I'm just fine. Kind of strange to hear her words like that though. It felt like she was here one last time, just a little, it was nice really. I do have one question though and it's sort of a dumb one really. I feel stupid asking it, er … here, and er … now but maybe it's the best place for it."

David quickly put him at his ease,

"Don't worry John, there's nothing stupid with anything that arises from this kind of thing. I have done this many times and heard all manner of things. It's all a bit confusing and the technicalities and formalities can be difficult, if it is a legal matter I can."

"Oh no, I just wanted to ask. I mean er … money is a bit

tight at the moment and we, well we have a lot of bills stacking up and well I just wondered how long it might be before we'd be able to get some, er, cash flow so to speak? It's just I don't have a bank account, as such, you see. Marie handled all that you see, and it worked well, she kind of made sure I wasn't wanting for money for certain things, clothes and the like and I, I'm just, not sure, you see I'm running I bit short and er …"

John had worked himself into a tight spot and was now nervous and unsure of himself in a way I'd never seen before. It was clear that this was causing him distress. He was no longer relaxed nor his usual self but sitting up, muttering his last few words into the ground as he hung his head.

I got up and walked over to him, then sat down next to him.

"John, don't worry about a thing. I didn't know. I'll get you some money. We don't have to worry, I'm just sorry, I just hadn't thought about it."

John was now working hard with pride to hold back his tears.

"Well, I didn't want to say, you see, it sounded, well I thought I'd sound disrespectful or …"

"Stop, don't worry anymore."

David came to my aid.

"Ah Mr Jackson, I understand you concerns here. It is quite often a problem in these situations, the necessity for accessibility to monies forthcoming. I'm afraid, to answer your question, which is not in any way unusual, probate often does not clear for many months, sometimes it can even take years."

John was recomposing himself and I could see he was doing so by concentrating.

"I can easily arrange for a type of loan in the meantime if it would help your financial situation. It would not be difficult as I would not hesitate to vouch for your credentials and suitability."

"David, thank you, but really please don't worry at all. I don't think we'll be wanting to get into all the fuss of a loan at this point, would we John? We're quite flush now, you realise!"

I laughed and pushed him gently on his shoulder. He wobbled back in his chair and laughed a little too, wiping any tears that may have been in his eyes with the back of one of his huge hands. I loved his hands, long large fingers wrapped loose in their dark skin with large veins running all over the backs. His pink palms all smooth, he put one to my face and stroked it gently, moving away my long hair which had fallen across one eye. He laughed a little too.

"Neither a lender or a borrower be. My father told me that."

David gave us this moment but then kept things moving along, because there was more.

"Now, Ananya, I need to read to you your father's will, as written by him on, let me see now … the 5th March 1944. You would have been five then. Are you all right with this?"

"I think so, ready as I'll ever be I suppose."

"Unlike your Marie's will, which we have all just seen for the first time, I have read this before, shortly after you arrived here. In fact, it was brought in transit with you personally by your guardian at the time. I have reviewed it just recently, to re-familiarise myself with it and it might be hard for you to digest it fully right now. Nevertheless, I have to read it to you and now is the best time."

"David, please, just read."

"Yes, of course."

The Will of Callum Rondel.

Managing Director of Rondel Mining (India)

'The House,' Kodaikanal Observatory, Palani Hills, India.

Upon my death I hereby bequeath my entire estate to Sophie Rondel my beloved wife. In the event of my death, she should inherit ownership and control of Rondel Mining, all my personal assets and powers of my financial instruments. If her death should precede mine and it be that I have made no amendments to this will at the time of my own death, my estate should be left in its entirety to Ms Marie Gallard, Sophie's younger sister, currently residing at 29, Meadowbank, Primrose Hill, London, England.

Marie lives in the house but currently the deeds are in my name, and these deeds are currently held with my solicitor Mr David Short at the offices of Bahnell, Heally and Short in London.

Marie is to inherit the house legally upon my death and the deeds transferred into her name. If Sophie shall become deceased within a year of my death and shall not have written a will herself, at the time of Sophie's passing I should wish Marie to inherit my entire estate.

Our daughter Ananya, who is the love of our lives and the diamond in our marriage, should come into her inheritance at the age of twenty-one. If I should become deceased before this time, Sophie Rondel, or agents representing her interests, would administrate my wishes as they see fit with regard to Ananya's future. Until such a time, I would wish for Marie to have control over financial matters for Ananya including such provisions of an allowance.

In the event of there being no family to inherit our family business, my business partner, Mr Niral Kumar should be granted full control of the company and its assets. I have discussed this with him and he has agreed to the responsibility.

My personal assets, however, I would wish to be donated in the form of a charitable trust to the University of Manchester Institute of Science and Technology where Sophie and I met. In particular, these monies I wish to be used primarily for research into the use of copper cable to create a permanent telegraph connection to the United States of America.

The properties of copper have fascinated me throughout my entire life, for reasons I have never been able to define. I have no recall as to the origins of what some may call an obsession, only that I do not remember a time when it was not with me.

If the problems of energy loss and amplification of signal at certain intervals along the cable be solved, I can think of no better use of copper. Transatlantic trade, and the stability of the global economic and political situation, would be vastly improved and the safety of the world at large would be ensured into the future with this development. Indeed, it is my sincerest belief that copper will enable civilisation to make its next quantum leap into the future.

However, I should also wish for thirty per cent of these monies to be set aside for astronomical research. The future hopes and dreams of humankind rest on such work. I can imagine a time when all civilised people in the world will have not only access to their own personal telescope but that within fifty years a man, or indeed a woman, may step onto the surface of the moon and we will finally be able to ascertain from what it is composed.

I write this will being of sound mind so that I should not die intestate whereby I might forfeit my right to control the future consequences of the wealth I have acquired in life.

Mr Callum Rondel, MA Cantab, PhD

23

Futures In Copper

David stopped and looked up, just as before, and John and I sat quietly, much as before. This type of writing and speech was not familiar to me, and I was numb as to the full of meaning of it, something I realised David was fully aware of. He was in his stride now and I suddenly understood him more deeply as a person.

Not only was he a good solicitor, a partner in a prestigious firm in the capital of England, but because of his early friendship with my parents and then his involvement with my aunt and now me, his interest was deeply personal. That was not all. I could see now exactly why it was that he loved his work so much. He he was a husband and a father, he had a family, but this job defined him and here was an example of why.

He was a facilitator and administrator, a man who processed the wishes of others for a living and made his living by doing it well. In addition, here I could see that he was also a kind of storyteller, or at the very least a researcher, a man who gathered the facts of the lives of others, as dictated by their financial and legal actions, and then who made sense of these events.

He placed the vital defining elements of lives into a comprehensible order. It was a very specific point of view, but he was fully engaged in his style. He spoke these stories to himself so that he could understand them and so perform his job to the best of his abilities. He then spoke these stories to us, and to many other people like us, translating the esoteric words and concepts of his world into a language which we could understand.

That was it, he was a translator, a researcher, a compiler, a collator, an editor, a detective even. This was the case under his consideration now and he was giving it his full treatment. He was passionate about what he did and for much of the time in that office I was in fact thinking of him, and his life, rather me and mine. It was a most helpful distraction.

"As you might imagine, we had rather a lot of problems with this document when it landed on our desk back in 1945. It is not the most clearly drafted will and I would have advised him to clarify himself on a number of points had he passed it to me while he was alive.

"Also, the peculiarities of the Indian legal system and the fact of your parents dying at the exact same time complicated matters no end. This will became a bit of a challenge for us, Ananya, and it took several years to ensure that your aunt received full control, but we were successful.

"However, if I may continue. There is something else I'm afraid Ananya and I'm afraid it is rather serious. There has been another development while you were away. I did not want to trouble you with it earlier, because I wanted to give you the chance to recover. But I can leave it no longer and feel it is best to broach all of this all at once and together. I hope you will forgive me for burdening you in this way."

"Please, go ahead David, what has to be done has to be done."

"It is about your father's business partner. The man who has been running Rondel Mining with such an experienced hand and so successfully. He is a man by the name of Mr Niral Kumar."

"Yes, I know Mr Kumar, I met him when I visited Kodaikanal. I think I know what this is about David, I remember now. While I was there, we talked of the impending inheritance of my father's share of the company upon coming of age at twenty-one. He spoke in detail about how it would be expedient for us all if he was to take control of all decision making.

"I too have been meaning to tell you all about this since I returned but I have simply not had the space in my mind. I shall be happy to discuss the signing of any papers regarding the powers he requires."

"Ananya, let me stop you."

"No, let me finish, while I can remember, because it is important to me, to the company too I believe. What I wish to say about Mr Niral Kumar concerns his very suitability to continue in his role at the company. You see, while I was visiting it became apparent that he is not liked by many of the staff at the Observatory. Moreover, I know for a fact he was dishonest with me on at least two occasions and for reasons I simply could not comprehend. I was informed that his being at the Observatory is a problem. From his offices at the Observatory, he rules the company and indeed much of the Observatory itself, it seems, with an iron fist. I heard he spoke with great vehemence to one of the more sensitive staff at the Observatory. I was even made aware that his mere physical presence there has negatively affected the abilities of certain local flora in the area to blossom as they once did. I believe him to be a most peculiar man indeed and I think perhaps that he might be somehow removed from his role completely if at all possible."

"Ananya, I must stop you there. What you are saying is of great interest but the news I have for you is not about the matters of which you speak. They may have had great relevance at the time but now they are of no importance, I fear. You see, Mr Kumar is no longer with us. He was killed, shortly after you must have visited with him in Kodaikanal in point of fact."

"Oh my god! Really?"

I put my hand up to my face, covering my mouth.

"How? I mean how was he killed?"

"It was a horrible accident a terrible confluence of unfortunate circumstances apparently. He was on a business flight to Sri Lanka … the aeroplane crashed."

"That's terrible David …"

"Yes, I know. The aeroplane in which he was a passenger was caught in a freak storm over the mountains and it crashed into the side of one, killing all aboard. The plane has only just been found after almost a year up there."

"That must have been just the next day after I spoke with him, I know he was planning to make a flight to Sri Lanka then. Do you have the date of the accident?"

"Yes, yes, I have it here. It was reported in all the local and national papers at the time. I thought you might have heard about it while you were away."

"I can't quite believe it is the truth."

"However, it is. In his will, which he was thoughtful enough to write some years earlier, he stated that he wished his assets to be left to an organisation called … the CDA, the Copper Development Association. Are you familiar with their work?"

"No, I'm not David. I … wait, Mr Kumar mentioned them, it is trade organisation of some sort I think."

"Well then you know a lot more than I do, Ananya, I have been trying to find information concerning the activities of this body and have yet to meet with any success at all.

"I have found mention of it, here and there, but it is somewhat of a … phantom … There is no record of it at a Companies House for example. You see why I am concerned Ananya?"

John, who had obviously been listening intently, suddenly came into the discussion with great interest.

"Mr Short, are you trying to tell us that this, this Copper

Development Association, now has control over Rondel Mining?"

"Ha! Good heavens no John, not at all, not at all."

David was having a good laugh at this idea when he realised he had left our faces in a confused, bemused and frozen state.

"Good Lord no! No, the will of the late Mr Kumar has proven to be somewhat of a red herring if truth be told. Because of a technical legality within the drafting of his will, another horribly unfortunate occurrence when one considers his wishes, it has meant that none of the contents of it can apply."

John was incredulous.

"None of it?!"

"No, none of it, that is why after so many months of hard work we have been able to dismiss it as a red herring vis-à-vis ours and your interests this end. There was a default clause in the papers that your father and Mr Kumar drew up when founding the company of Rondel Mining. The clause stipulated that in certain circumstances, and the death of both founding members by any act of God being one of these, that ownership of the mine, and all profits obtained from its operation should be transferred to the institution of the Kodaikanal Observatory itself."

John seemed relieved but still not entirely satisfied.

"So, are you saying that now the Observatory owns the mine?"

"I believe that this clause would have been added, very judiciously I might add, in consultation with your mother, as a kind of insurance perhaps, to benefit solar research in the event of some unforeseen tragic occurrence. She clearly had the foresight to understand that mining can be a dangerous enterprise.

"However, now the situation is such that another man, a man who is entirely unknown to me, a man by the name of…

Anish Patel, has assumed complete control of Rondel Mining. All I know of him is that he owns nothing of the mine for himself. He draws an extremely modest monthly income. His wage is little more than that of a cook or a cleaner, a fact I was able to glean from a copy of the Observatory's latest financial report which I was able to cross reference with the most recent tax audit submitted by Rondel Mining. This man, Ananya, this stranger, is making all the vital decisions to do with the running of the company. He answers to no one, he is his own sole agent, and he is out there, just making it all up as he goes along. It is a tense situation, and you can see why I am vexed by it, Ananya. I require your input, your local knowledge and your assistance to rectify matters."

"What did you say this man's name is? Was it Anish, Anish Patel?"

"Yes, that is he."

"I believe I met him when I visited. Yes, I remember it now. It was only for a few minutes he spoke with me just as I was leaving. He seemed an incredibly kind and thoughtful soul and he spoke directly to me, looking deep into my eyes. He said he knew my parents … but only very briefly, having met them not long before the accident. He said that he was involved with the surveying of the mine and the land on which my father had made his explorations and discovery. He said that he had something of great importance that he wanted to tell me. He told me my mother and father died in an instant, that they were listening to music, and they would have felt no pain, no pain at all, he was very clear about that. He said they died in each other's arms."

I felt myself to have entered into a deep meditative state as I recalled these few minutes of conversation, for when I snapped out of it both John and David were staring at me, in a kind of meditative gaze themselves. It was only their fixed stillness which prompted me to snap out of my own trance-like moment.

"That was it, that was all he said. I spoke with him for a minute, no longer and his name was most definitely Anish Patel. Must say I dismissed him as a gardener and had not thought of him once until just now."

"I have found from national records that he is in fact trained as a chartered surveyor, so your account verifies my scant knowledge. Apparently, from company records I asked to be copied and sent here, he started working with Kumar very soon after the accident and he has been employed the whole of the time from those early days. I have had one single correspondence with him, a letter in which he says simply that he has been Mr Kumar's 'right-hand man' as he put it for the last ten years and that we need not worry about a thing as he knows the company workings inside and out and that it is in 'good shape' as he phrased it. I have thought to travel to Kodaikanal myself, Ananya, to meet with him and his legal representatives to try to untangle this mess.

"This is a personal letter to you, Ananya, from him. I have had it in my possession for over six months now but of course I did not open it as it is specifically addressed as a personal correspondence to you. In fact, if I were to have opened, it anything contained within it would be of no use in court because of such a transgression. I am giving it to you now and would like you to attend to this matter as soon as you can, Ananya, as a priority."

I took the letter from him as he handed it to me across the wide desk.

"Thank you, David, I will see to it straight away".

"As I say Ananya, he has been running the company entirely on his own. I have to say though, I think he is doing quite well, really very well indeed actually. In this last year, profits are up thirty-two per cent and dividends by twenty-six per cent. So just to clarify, Ananya. You are the sole owner of the company now, we have established that fact conclusively through our legal investigations, there can be no doubt about that. It's just that we don't have any idea whatsoever who this Mr Anish Patel is … we just don't know Ananya."

We all sat motionless for a few moments. It was John who broke the silence.

"Sole owner you say?"

"Sole owner, we have no need to worry about that as I said. Ah, also there is another letter here which arrived just recently. It is also from Kodaikanal but in a different hand. The name of the sender is an 'Indira Samsara'. Do you know her?"

"Indira, yes! She is the most wonderful woman. She works at the Observatory. She was my nanny when I lived there as a child. She is an incredible lady."

With Indira's letter in my hand, I wanted to read it there and then, but I decided I would save it until I was alone, and somewhere special. I had renewed energy and vigour, I stood up and held out my hand which David took and shook.

"David, we should be going now. I will get back to you with my thoughts on everything we have covered her today. After I have read these letters and John and I have had time to talk further about the house. John, shall we?"

"Yep, let's go, come on. You need to get some rest Ananya, your head must be spinning."

David took us to the door and saw us out.

"Take all the time you need to adjust to all of this. I know it's a lot and whenever you are ready, simply call me and we can arrange another meeting to address your plans and thoughts for the future."

John shook hands with David too.

"David, as always you are a gentleman."

"Thank you, Mr Jackson, I do what I can. I'm sure we will

be meeting again soon and if you have any questions at all regarding anything large or small, I will be more than willing to assist at the drop of a hat."

We left the building and as we walked outside onto the pavement, John casually said, "Well, you own you own little copper mine now little lady. Not sure I'd know how to handle that myself. Are you going to be OK?"

"I am, I am. I think I need some time on my own right now though, John. I'm going to go for a walk, maybe through Hyde Park, you know just sort of … move forward a bit."

"You do that, good idea. So long as you're OK."

We hugged and parted and as we did so John turned and called back, "Say, what exactly is a 'red herring'?"

24

Wonderings

I wasn't OK at all, but I was walking and the inner rhythm this gave me was calming. It created a reassuring logic which enabled me to think in streams of reason and truth, but these were always interrupted by fuzzy abstract pools of irrational colours and patterns which made little sense and wound their way towards numerous dead ends.

There was this fact of me being the only one of my family now living and this further fact of me owning a prosperous copper mine in a remote and beautiful location in India. It was a place I knew now, an area of intense colour and magic and a place which was both old and new to me.

The realisation of my age, twenty-one years only, barely more than a teenager in my own eyes, but now with responsibilities and experiences of someone double this.

The knowledge of this information was huge, yet completely contained within these small, simple facts. My understanding of them was perfectly clear and I could accept them in a rational way. What I couldn't accept were the brutal feelings which accompanied them. The contrasting effect of intense emotions in flux with my cold analysis of myself led me to conclude that I was in shock. The accumulated events of my short life were too condensed for me to process in the moment. If I wasn't walking, I don't know how I would have coped.

There was nervous tension in my solar plexus and guts which was inching its way around my rib cage. As I entered the large open space of Hyde Park, this tension relaxed somewhat but I was constantly aware of it. Breathing techniques learned through yoga came to me now and the muscles around my shoulders and neck I could loosen by swinging my arms. My stride was longer too, on the grass, and on passing benches and other opportunities for rest l told myself not to sit. There was a real fear of the feelings which a stationary body might induce within me. It was best to continue walking, walking was change, a moving viewpoint which gave the possibility of finding peace.

I did not feel a whole person. Not having rested in mind, body or since I read that letter at the ashram. I thought of the two letters in my pocket now, their edges digging into my midriff a little within my coat. The prospect of the further information that they would contain and the idea that the rest of my life could be a relentless succession of dealing with such information made my steps slower, heavier and my mood low. I would open the letter later when it felt right.

Later that evening, John would ask me where I had been on my walk and I knew already I would not be able to tell him with much accuracy. Time was passing but I was not aware of how much. I was already through this part of the park and somewhere else, among buildings now which I did not recognise.

I saw a postman emptying a post box on a comer. But which corner was this? His red van was parked at an angle on the pavement and faced a small public space. This was a small and beautiful area, a rectangle the size of half a tennis court maybe and full of flora. It was a dense island of trees and bushes and shrubs and flowers.

I stopped for the first time and stared at it. It was enclosed by iron railings, four or five feet tall. They have those in near Gloucester Road, don't they? Where was I? Was I nearer home now in fact, nearer Primrose Hill? I did not feel lost or scared, my thoughts were only that I was like this island of nature, hemmed in and claustrophobic, surrounded by metal and then the bricks and stones of the buildings all around this place. The postman looked at me and smiled. I was quite close to him I realised.

"Hi," I said.

"Hello," he replied, and went back to filling his sack with letters.

It was the shortest exchange possible, but it changed everything and I walked on, suddenly knowing exactly where I wanted to go.

I had often made these types of exploration before. They were wandering journeys, nothing more or less. That they had no defined purpose or route plan meant very little, that was the point in fact, to follow one's nose to let spontaneity and the unfolding events of the exploration colour the direction of the next steps.

Such walks I had made from a very early age but I had not to my recollection felt lost even once. I might decide to leave the house on a whim, at any time of day, from sunrise to sunset, and sometimes at night too.

Aunt Marie was troubled with it at first of course, my wanderings around Primrose Hill, but later, as I grew older, she came to see that it was something natural for me, and part of my being. "All animals know their own habitats," I told her, and taught her about the behaviour of bats and cats, fish and birds, migrations, and ways to find one's way home. With maps and compasses in mind, their local environment in their memories. Humans were no different, I told her, and she came to believe that at least for me this was true.

I thought of walking all the way back to India, to visit with the Guru and explain to him my feelings. He would understand and he would say something simple and humorous which would make me feel happy and whole and I would be content and calm.

I would give all my money to him because he would be the only person who would know what to do with it to benefit the maximum number who needed it. This is all simply the circle of life and death – Samsara. Growth and evolution followed by revolution and re-evolution. It would be easy at the ashram.

There would also be the possibility of forgetting while there, the bliss of letting go of all which has come before so that one can see oneself in the mirror of the world. Without the illusion and delusions of the person we have been taught to see, the persons we are expected to be, we can be ourselves.

However, I said no to this idea. It would be walking backwards, would it not?

I am Ananya, but if I am as unique as my Guru says I am, and these feelings are the feelings of uniqueness, then I do not wish to be her. I will be who I was at the ashram, but I will be here where I am now, I will be her here. I am 'Ana'. She is my creation and so she is the person I have chosen to become and to be in life.

I found myself at the place I had decided to come to. I was standing next to a huge piece of public sculpture. I arrested my locomotion, my train of thought reaching its destination. There was a magic here for me, a subtle power contained with the alloys from which this sculpture had been cast.

I was right up close to it, only inches away. I saw its texture in the folds of the clay from what it had first been shaped. These folds, once soft and pliable, were now solid and permanent for all eternity. Fat and thick, they were folded, and smooth and wavy and ridged.

I could do nothing else but put my hands on them, first my right hand and then my left. Then I leant the whole of the side of my face on it too, my cheek meeting the cold, hard, dark metal in a kiss of visceral relief. I smiled for the first time in a while.

A few moments of the sensation were enough for me, it was quite intense, and it was all I needed. I sat and read the letters.

Anish Patel's letter was a short note to inform me of the death of Mr Kuma. He also mention his plans for the long-term future of the mine and his reassurance that all was in order. He reminded me of our brief chance encounter as I had been leaving Kodaikanal and apologised for any 'peculiar feelings' he might have caused by his 'hastily improvised introduction upon our surprised and serendipitous crossing of paths'. He also wished me a belated happy birthday and hoped with all his heart that I would return once more again one day soon.

It was a beautifully written letter, flawless in its composition and grammar and penned with calligraphy in a dark azure blue ink.

Indira's letter was far longer and full of humour and misspellings and mistakes. The significant elements of it were twofold. The first was that upon the death of Mr Kumar the rhododendrons had blossomed and bloomed, and that their colours and scents filled the surrounding gardens of the Observatory with love and harmony. Her second piece of related news was that she was now in a deep and loving personal relationship with the man who had taken over the running of Rondel Mining, a 'beautiful soul by the name of Anish Patel'.

I smiled with some acknowledgement of the poetry of life and was ready to go home. I felt truly ready to search for Home too, as a concept. This was not to be simply a new physical location which I would seek, but a new home within. I did not know where it was or how I would get there but I knew there would be a man there for me too, that he was in the future and that when I found it and him, I would not need to seek anymore for I would belong. This no longer felt like hope, but more like something I would manifest and would simply come to pass.

As I walked, I thought I needed a name for it, for this new place I would call my home. I did not know how this placename would sound until I heard it for the first time of course, but even a child learns to say that they do not know what they are looking for but that they will recognise it when they see it, so it shall be with the place where I am going. There were no fears or doubts anymore.

The sculpture, which had become the starting point from which I was setting out on my search, was a huge piece of work in bronze by the artist Barbara Hepworth entitled 'Meridian'. It had been commissioned by State House and placed outside their buildings at High Holborn just a year ago. Now, for me, it had become the origin of a new walk, and a new idea, the idea of a new life. The first stop on this fresh walk would be back at the house in Primrose Hill where there was so much to talk of with John and I fairly floated all the way there as a butterfly on a breeze.

25

Change Always Changes

The little yellow door looked a little different now. It was still yellow and lovely but the setting sun had warmed its colour, now more orange and a little pink also.

I was in and greeted by John who was sitting in the main hall at the table. In front of him on the table was a canvas duffle bag a couple of feet long. It sat squat and open and looked maybe like an army issue item. John had a coffee mug in his hand. As I came in and took of my coat, he said, "Hi, how are you are you? Are you OK?"

"Fine, fine. You?"

"I've just been sitting here, thinking for a while. Do you want a cup of tea?"

"A big glass of water would be good, I just need to sit down, my feet are fairly killing me."

"How far have you walked on your stroll?"

"Not sure, I've been walking all day though, might be a record actually, covered a lot of ground today."

John came from the kitchen with some water for me and we both sat at the table. I was quiet, recovering from the transition of outside to in, and movement to stillness. John was quiet too. Always comfortable with our silences, we just sat. Eventually I got curious and started to pull open the bag to see what was inside.

"What's this?"

But it was clear what it was as soon as I looked. It was full of cash.

"John! This bag is full of cash! What is it?"

"Well, it's a bag full of cash ..."

"I know! That's what I said, that's what I'm saying, I can see what it is but ... why is it ...?"

"You know in her will Marie said to look behind the boiler upstairs? Well, I did, and there it was, stuffed down in the corner under some blankets."

"What's if for? I mean, what are you going to do with it? You can't just leave it on the table like this. What if someone comes round?"

"I've been sitting here about two hours now thinking those same kinds of things."

"Wow, it looks like a lot of money, I've never seen that much money before, not all in one place all together like this. How much is there?"

"I don't know. I started counting it, I got to several thousand then I stopped, and I realised. This is just cash, it's just paper."

"It's not 'just' cash John, and it's certainly not just paper either. It looks like it's just been stolen from a bank, in a heist or something, like in a film, like it's a prop. Are you sure it's real?"

I picked some out of the bag. A lot of it was in bundles of crumpled used ten-pound notes, rolled up and held with elastic bands. Some of it was loose and there was a fair amount of what appeared to be untouched brand-new stacks wrapped in little paper sleeves. It was one of these which I held now.

"Oh, it's real all right, I checked that. I've been holding it up to the light, it's got watermarks and everything. I think this is Marie's way of telling us that there is a lot more money in your family than you might have been aware. I think, after today at the will, this is the tip of the iceberg, small change you might say."

"Whoa, I'm not sure I can deal with all this, it's a bit 'in your face' isn't it?"

"It is, it is. It's right there all right, right there in front of our faces. Drink some more of your water, I bet you haven't had anything to eat or drink all day."

"I mean I've been thinking about the mine and the money all day, but this just brings it home, doesn't it?"

"Don't it just. I mean we've never wanted for anything, but I think your aunt has made sure that it wasn't going to go to your head. You, know, not given you an idea of the … scale … of the situation if you like. I mean, she was still paying me two shillings a week to mow the lawn just a few months ago. She's kept us honest, so she has."

"Mmm, that's probably it."

"We've got to do some serious talking and some serious thinking little lady, if we don't want this to get too big for the two of us to handle."

"That is true."

"Don't get me wrong, with this kind of money we can have a real good time for the rest of our lives, but we've got to watch it don't get too good, you know what I mean."

"I do. I can't believe I hadn't thought about this situation before. You know, ages ago."

"Like I said, your Aunt Marie has kept us honest all these years, in the dark and innocent as well, you might say. To get through this all we've got to do is just see the facts as they are, accept them for what they are, recognise them as such, accept them and get on with living. And you know that ain't going to be as easy as this little pile of cash might want to make you believe. That's how I figure it."

"You're right, I've come to some similar ideas of my own, along my walk, without thinking about the money side of it that is. I want to talk to you about all that too."

"It's good you've been walking and thinking and it's good I've been sitting and thinking. I've put all my thinking into three boxes for us. We've got this little old house which we're sitting in, which ain't so little. You've got your little copper mine to play with, and apparently that ain't so little either, then we've got our futures. My thoughts are that our futures needn't be so little neither."

"Three boxes, that's what it all comes down to ..."

"Yep, oh, and a little ole US army issue kit bag full of paper. So that's three boxes and a bag by my reckoning."

"I'm going to put some music on, can't do this without some sounds. What do you think? I was thinking Coltrane or maybe Dizzy?"

"Go with Coltrane. Coltrane will do it for us."

I put on the turntable and turned the amplifier up, quite a lot. The needle came down heavy and the crackle was loud and when the music arrived it blew everything away, our worries, our melancholy, our blues, our shock and then our reserve and restraint too. We threw the money around and before we knew it, we were on the table dancing and laughing and shouting out loud. It was an extreme release, an uncontrolled celebration of Marie's life and our life in this house.

When the music stopped, we had to stop too. We had to come back down to earth, we had to climb down off the table, and we had to tidy up all that cash. John made some coffee, and we ate and talked all night. I wrote it all down and we made our plans, right there and then.

Life goes on, but sometimes life must start again. We both wanted to start over, and we both had this opportunity now to do it right and to do it in style. We knew what we were doing, we were serious in these hours, right the way through the night we sat there, discussing, imagining and writing endless lists and action plans. It was nothing less than a revolution of our souls and as the sun came up and a new day began, we started our lives anew.

The sun was a great big, fat jolly friend breaking through

the morning mist on Primrose Hill that day. We saw it peak its head up over the horizon and throw its energy into our dark little cave with its incredible view.

The new light switched us and our plans into gear. We went outside and walked to the local bakery together, bought a large loaf of brown bread and had scrambled eggs on toast for breakfast. Then we crashed, just like the unfortunate Mr Kumar's plane had done into the side of that snowy mountain. Only for us, we had the good luck to be able to live again afterwards, a type of reincarnation for John and I both.

I slept for twelve hours and rose around 8pm. John was up and about as the sun was going down.

In the weeks which came after that day, we remembered Aunt Marie in all our words and thoughts and most vitally our deeds but, although she was in our hearts, the hard work was to learn to live without her.

We were selling the house, that was agreed from the start. John was making his new life with his only family, his brother in San Francisco. It was the hardest decision for him to make but I encouraged him to do it when it became clear how close he and his brother had been before the war, how he never been back there and how he had sacrificed his entire American life to be with the love of his life in England. Now Marie was not here, I fairly insisted he return, at the very least for an extremely long holiday.

When I told him that I thought I would be able to afford the flight to visit him, that I had always wanted to drive across the Golden Gate Bridge in a huge open-top American car and that he could of course come back to England anytime he wished, he looked at me and laughed.

"Funny what money can do."

He was in regular contact now with his brother on the telephone. They were busy catching up and making plans. The long-distance calls cost a fortune, but I didn't tell John quite how much because I really didn't care.

I began teaching him to write. He found it so incredibly frustrating, and it made him mad and angry all the time because he said it made him feel like "the dumb stupid kid he had always been at school". He suffered badly with dyslexia I suspected, although didn't wish to go make an amateur diagnosis or even to talk with him about the condition. John is by no means dumb or stupid and it was his perseverance which I found so impressive. He was brave and learned to be patient with himself and to control his outbursts of self-denigration.

It was when he wrote to his brother for the first time when it all fell into place for him. He received a beautifully written reply within only two weeks. Daniel was 'the intelligent one' between the two, John told me. He had graduated from high school and taken a degree in sociology at San Francisco State. He currently worked for the local municipal offices in social work.

That first night when we set our ideas and our dreams for the future, he said that before the war he and his brother had talked about setting up a music school in their neighbourhood. It was their pipe dream together and it was all they were interested in when war broke out and they were called up to fight. Now the idea was alive again, and with the necessary ingredient of money having made itself available, the dream had begun to evolve into reality quite quickly.

When I asked John if Daniel played an instrument he said, "Well, he can read music, he knows music, he can theorise about music, and he can tell you a lot more about the history of jazz than just about anyone. But between me and you, although he likes to play, and he thinks he's pretty good too, I must tell you, he ain't got a lick on me when it comes to blowin' the horn! But you know he puts the effort in, he practises a lot and all that, he does try …"

His confidence grew with reading and writing, and he wrote more and more to his brother, every day it seemed. Most of all he wanted to know what he called "the better words, the one's you use from time to time". He said that when I used these "better words" they "squeeze all the ideas into just a few notes". I knew exactly what he meant and I did something good. I bought him a pocket Oxford dictionary, a small leather-bound edition.

He always kept it on him and the words he found in that dictionary set him free. He'd just needed someone to spend the time with him and to be motivated by something bigger than he thought was possible. By the time we had an offer on the house, which was in record time with David's help, that little dictionary was so well thumbed, the pages were all creased, corners of so many folded over, and each and every new word he looked up was underlined, with a red pencil he kept sharp and tied to the book with a piece of string.

We both knew how hard it was going to be when the time came to separate ourselves from each other, but it was the way … We had to live our lives, and this was how it was to be done. Neither of us were religious, there was life, then there was more life and then at the end of it there was no life.

Marie's heart was still beating within us, we moved to its rhythms, and it carried us along our paths.

26

The Big Silver-Blue Cat

My plans for moving away from London were initially met with shock from David, but when I had explained my idea to him he began to understand.

I needed to begin again. I wanted a brand-new life and here in London I was always going to be held back by the past. No amount of money would fill the space left by Aunt Marie and I wanted to find my own ways of expanding my soul.

I wanted to make a brand-new home and I wanted a brand-new house in which to live. This was 1961. The future was now.

David brought together as much literature as he could for me and he supplied me with advertising brochures concerning new housing developments and the references of various architects. I wanted to remain in the south of England, as I did not want to lose touch with London completely, largely for matters of convenience and practicality, but I did want to be far enough away so that I would not constantly feel its pull.

I drove to some of the places he suggested in Essex, Surrey and Kent and one day Marie's old Jag which was always on its last legs finally gave up the ghost one afternoon on a steep incline in Ewshot. In spite of John's best efforts, we decided it was a write-off and the need for a new car arose.

Now, the Morris Mini-Minor had arrived in 1954 and by now everyone of any taste who didn't already have one certainly wanted one or was at the very least talking about wanting one. It seemed to be the best place to start.

Miyu said she thought it was 'the very thing' for me and all the rage. She felt it was the only thing in fact as now that all the famous people had them and there was such a 'buzz' around them I shouldn't even think about not getting one, or two.

I think that they appealed to her so much, largely because she was so small, and it appealed to her Japanese ideas about aesthetics. I wasn't so sure, but I wanted to go for a test drive and one day we found ourselves driving down to Brighton in a little light blue Cooper. They let us have it for the day when Miyu said we were thinking of having one each.

It was such a fun day. Miyu was beside herself with love for the thing and we look it in turns driving. It was a huge amount of fun but for myself however I decided I needed something a little more … grand. Not that the Mini didn't have class and the jazz and everything but I owned a copper mine in India and I had all this money and my thoughts were that I had to start spending it on something.

I did some research and talked with a few chaps who were 'in the know' about these things, and then I talked with David who was a bit of car nut himself. He owned a reasonably good condition Bentley. It was as a throwaway remark I believe that he said, "Of course, the new Jag is the business, any man in his right mind would have one of those."

"And what about any woman?" I asked.

"I'm not being old-fashioned Ananya, but really it's a man's car, they are quite a beast I've been told and oh so very sporty. I really don't think you'd get on with something so powerful and fast."

"I'm going simply by the name of Ana nowadays," I said.

I made a few phone calls and once again Miyu came with me on another test drive.

We took the train to Richmond and arrived at the Jaguar dealership in the early morning. The salesman, a man in his forties, sporting a combover, initially thought we were merely 'window shoppers' and had said something a little sexist I thought. I didn't quite catch what it was, but I must say I took a dislike to him from the outset and he to me.

When I informed him that it was I who had called ahead to book the test drive, he was taken aback. "I do apologise ma'am. On the phone I had thought you were older, I mean less young … if you will excuse me."

He was a trifle embarrassed at the situation and I feel this may have been something to do with the new mini-skirts both Miyu and I were wearing.

"That's OK," I said.

I had developed a very mature and more adult manner. It was an approach and a behaviour which Miyu referred to as my 'Mrs Style'. She said it was contrived and pretentious and I should watch myself or else I might get stuck with it and think it was the 'real me'. We laughed about it as it was clearly a self-conscious act on my behalf but I took what she said seriously nonetheless. The Jaguar representative was, unfortunately for him, just my next victim.

I was in love with the car itself already, even before I'd even climbed in. We had the keys to an opalescent Silver-Blue Jaguar 'E' Type Roadster. It was a convertible with a 3.8 litre engine, all shiny with its chrome bumpers and sumptuous with its dark blue leather seats.

A long, low car, obviously altogether different from the Mini, it looked fast, sleek, cool and deliriously beautiful. A big cat, sitting on its haunches ready to be released into the jungles of the southeast of England.

This car was their 'flagship' demonstration model which he told us was new but had already been 'run in'. We were told it had less than a few thousand miles on the clock and that these had been taken at a sedate pace at engine speeds less than 3000 rpm. I must admit I was not sure as to what that meant.

I had to reassure the men on several occasions that I would

be careful with her but once I had completed some paperwork and left my passport with him, we pulled out onto the main road and were away.

I was in heaven instantly and drove safely with passion and purpose, moving through the gears with some ease. I could hardly see the end of the bonnet though it was so long.

With Miyu in the passenger seat, we drove with the convertible roof down, wind blowing our large hair all over the shop! It was such a problem in fact that after only a few miles I had to stop to tie a scarf around my head. Miyu decided not to follow suit. We walked round the car as it was parked and admired it from all angles. There was no doubt in me that I would be buying one but I did not tell Miyu this yet.

The car flew, reaching Hampshire in no time at all, and Miyu looked like a wild thing! Her long, thick black hair, usually so neatly brushed and hanging straight halfway down her back, blew around the whole of her half of the topless cockpit in a mad swirl. It was now a tussled, confused chaos almost as big as her and her smile, usually small and tight lipped if there at all, was nothing short of a permanent grin.

I felt I had tamed this Jaguar. She responded quickly to my every small instruction. And as we pulled up at the site of the property development I had arranged to visit as part of this little excursion, this automobile and I were as one, woman and machine in perfect unison and harmony. Miyu told me that she thought I'd 'become myself'.

27

A Roof Over Your Head

The property developer's 'offices' were not quite as I had imagined they would be. In fact, there was only one 'office' and it was a kind of a temporary metal 'hut' really, the resident of which came out to meet us as we arrived.

He turned out to be a lovely man, a bit rough around the edges and there was nothing about him that reminded me of London. He was more of a farmer type. I think he mistook us for famous actresses or pop singers or aristocracy even – because of the car probably – and Miyu and I enjoyed playing up to this. He offered us a mug of tea and we sat outside his office on deckchairs, eating Garibaldi biscuits as we discussed the possibility of conducting business.

He was building twenty-nine houses here in total, with just four already under construction. Effectively we sat in a huge field with some twenty or so builders not so far away who occasionally seemed to be doing some building work.

We were shown plans, lots of plans drawn up on huge pieces of paper which blew in the wind as much as Miyu's hair. We discussed plot sizes and budgets, building materials, customisable features, and timeframes.

I loved the view, the field was flat but slightly elevated and I could see trees around us and in the distance too, mostly beeches but some large oaks too.

We were given a guided tour around the whole site, a good walk around the perimeter, and met a few of the builders who were so polite as to be unbelievable. It may have been that they too had mistaken us for visiting minor royalty or some such thing.

He said I could be moved before the end of the year into my own luxury custom-built house and I could choose any plot I wished. There was only one for me and it was just where we were now standing. It was the best view and as I scanned it, I saw the moon low near the horizon to the east. It was not full, it was new, and I shook hands with the man there and then.

He said I would be house number one on plot number one. I have never seen such a happy man but asked kindly whether I could be house number twenty-nine instead. He scratched his head.

"I don't see why not, if that's what you want but then we'll have to change the number of the plot too …"

"Can that be done?"

"It is my building site, I suppose. Certainly it can be done!"

With that he took a large red marker pen from his pocket and wrote 'Plot 29' on the plans of the house which he had been holding and were flapping around in stiff wind.

"That good enough?"

"That's great, lucky number you see."

"Ah, I see, a bit superstitious like me. Here, you can keep this."

He handed me the plans.

"Thank you. The beginning of something unique I think."

"Indeed. Ah, if I'm not being too rude, while we are at this juncture of the negotiations, might I enquire about the nature of your intended financing for the purchase of land and building? I'm not trying to be funny, it's just that I have had one customer prior to you earlier this month whose deposit cheque bounced and when I made enquiries it turned out he was wanted by the Law, for tax evasion can you believe it. Ah, he was a gentleman who was from London also. So I … er …"

"Oh I can assure you, Mr Bagley, we are not criminals or fugitives from the law in any way, shape or form."

"No, of course not, Ms Rondel, but you can understand my concerns?"

"I own a small mine, Mr Bagley, and, well, it's doing rather well at the moment."

"Oh, that's nice. Coal, is it? Wales perhaps?"

"No, copper, in India. My father found some copper there during World War II."

"Oh, that's nice, to find copper that is, in India."

"Yes, sadly he passed away shortly afterwards."

"Oh, I'm sorry about that. Still, long time ago now, lucky that the mine is still in your family I suppose ..."

"Yes, yes it, a lot comes down to luck I would say in this life, wouldn't you say Mr Bagley?"

"Lady Luck is always a winner! I've always said that."

"It's lovely having met you, Mr Bagley. I'll arrange to get a banker's draft to you for my deposit very soon and you won't have any trouble with it bouncing!"

"Lovely to meet with you here today. I think everything will turn out right, just you see. Lovely day to buy a new house too."

"A bit windy though!" Miyu piped up for the first time.

She hadn't said anything until this point but Mr Bagley was obviously fascinated by her, being slightly mesmerised by her unconventional looks and indeed her mad unruly hairstyle.

"It was a pleasure to meet you too. I'm sorry, I didn't register your name. I am terrible with names."

"It is Miyu, it is Japanese meaning beauty, gentleness and superiority."

"That is lovely, that really is. I wish my name meant something a little bit like that!"

"Miyu Yamaha. As in the motorcycle manufacturer."

"I know that name. It's a pleasure to meet you Ms Yamaha."

"You are very kind Mr Bagley. Where does the name Bagley originate from?"

"I am a gentleman of Romany descent. Of Royal descent I have been told. But I haven't got a pink clue what Bagley means. It might be something to do with carrying a Bag, or something like that I suppose. It owes me nothing though, and I've done quite well by it over the years."

"Well, I think it's a lovely name, Mr. Bagley."

"Thank you very much."

We drove away in the Jaguar all smiles, with the builders looking on.

I now owned not only a copper mine but also a sizeable plot of land just near the expanding town of Basingstoke in the county of Hampshire where a new house would be built for me by the lovely Mr Bagley. When we arrived at good speed back at the Jaguar Dealership in Richmond I bought the E-type too.

As we drove back to Primrose Hill, Miyu asked, "So does this mean you are going to buy me that Mini now?"

"Possibly, but I thought maybe you were more into your motorbikes these days, er, Ms Yamaha ..."

28

Molten Streams Merging

I'd decided to go outside the perimeter fence and take a good look at the protest. I don't know what possessed me. I was just moving the singing bowl in its protective blanket from under my bed to the other side of the room. I was about to open it to have a look when I saw the coat I had found in the skip.

On my way in, earlier that morning, I'd seen some of the keener protesters already beginning to gather by the gates. Some of them were wearing coats just like this one and I'd asked myself some questions.

I was wearing my suit, as per usual and it occurred to me that perhaps the differences between those on the one side of the debate, the argument, the whole issue of nuclear disarmament might be primarily superficial. What if these people merely looked so very different from us on the other side of the fence and that in fact our values were fundamentally similar.

Surely we all want the same thing at the end of the day? Isn't it just that we're lacking the understanding to communicate it to each other effectively from our different viewpoints, backgrounds and ideologies?

I picked up the coat, I believe the style to be known as a 'kaftan' and mine was rather a handsome example I thought in comparison to some I had seen earlier that morning. Putting it on, I looked into my long wall mirror. It was a good fit.

As I say, I don't know what came over me but before I knew it I had put on a pair of loose fitting bell-bottomed trousers and tousled my hair about a little and then I suddenly stopped.

How was I going to get out of the Establishment looking like this? What if someone recognised me as I walked through the site to the main gates to exit into the protest? Clearly, I needed to disguise myself further.

I had the perfect solution and, throwing on a huge poncho-style waterproof over my kaftan, I picked up my wallet and a small haversack and left with some purpose and curiosity.

The poncho proved to be overkill and I ditched it as soon as I was off the grounds and out into the growing crowd.

I was wearing a kaftan, I was mingling with a bunch of noisy agitators and very quickly I felt integrated and one of them. With my disguise a success, I was no longer one of 'us', I was one of 'them', and I was starting to enjoy myself. Maybe as, one of them, I was becoming one of us?

Although I did not know it at the time, something else momentous was about to happen. I was about to meet the woman I would fall in love with, marry, have children with and live with for the rest of my natural life … eventually.

I don't remember exactly just how we came to be pushed up against each other in that thronging mass of bearded, bespectacled, sandal-clad peaceniks. I don't remember our first words to each other or even at what point I learnt her name and she mine. So dazed was I by the impact of the event I was now a part of, that she was in those initial minutes mingled up in an incredible whirlwind of overwhelming sensations and impressions.

I do however remember very clearly indeed the instance of the second time Ana Rondel met me because it was such a surprise and a shock and a very pleasant one of course, but there was absolutely nothing about it which added up.

Until that moment I had resigned myself to accepting that for rest of my life she would always only ever be a most beautiful memory.

The memory I had of her was of a young woman in whose

company I had been lucky enough to spend a few glorious days earlier that year. She was a lady who had entranced me with her intelligence, her drop-dead good looks, and her spirited outlook on life. However, in the months we were apart, between that day of the protest march and the day at the traffic lights, I had had to swallow the pill which said that our destinies were not meant to be intertwined.

On that day in Aldermaston, with me in my kaftan, Ana was with two friends. One of them, who was called John, she sometimes referred to as her uncle, on several occasions in fact. This was confusing for me as he was a huge African American. I didn't ask the questions I might have done because I didn't want to appear nosey or interrogative.

I was in disguise and essentially undercover and this created some problems of a unique nature. I had to conjure up an impromptu alter-ego, a central heating engineer from Bromley called Louis.

It was the best I could do on the spot so as not to reveal I was in fact involved in the design and manufacture of the very nuclear weapons and indeed warheads which this group was passionately suggesting should be reduced in number. I would not have been perceived as part of the solution I decided, only a major part of the problem, if not the actual problem personified.

The problem with my pretence became one of stamina and consistency. This came to be such a problem because at some point during that day I had made the decision to continue with the march all the way from Aldermaston to London.

This wasn't such a hard decision to make in fact. In fact, it wasn't really a single decision at all. To begin with, I was swept along with the body of the crowd to such a point that after half a day of shouting and walking I eventually found myself a long way from home.

I kept justifying my continuation with the walk by telling myself that it was 'research' and that the information I was gleaning from the 'other side' was invaluable to progress on all fronts.

Still, I kept up my act and I was so fascinated by Ana and really enjoying myself more than at any other time in my life, that the justifications I needed to just keep walking became less and less necessary.

There were times when I wanted to 'let the cat out of the bag' so to speak but it just wasn't called for. I was accepted, I felt welcome even, and, in a bizarre way, I felt that this was where I belonged.

The first night I shared a tent with John, then day two we were lucky to find some rather lovely bed and breakfast locations. I was in the groove and digging the scene.

My ruse was sufficiently robust to be entirely believable as I was also able to converse freely with Ana about copper piping and in particular the novel use of small-bore copper piping as a mainstay in the design of modern central heating systems. Louis was an entirely credible heating engineer.

I have to say I was intrigued at the time as to why Ana was so fascinated by me when I talked on this subject but when I later learned she would soon be moving into new accommodation in the Basingstoke area and that she was currently looking into her central heating options, my curiosity as to her interest was satiated.

When I began talking of copper alloys and their improved qualities for use in the domestic market, Ana was smitten. This was followed by quite a passionate interrogation which I really could not find an explanation for.

There was one point when she was following up on something I'd been saying about the properties of beryllium copper alloys at elevated temperatures, how it affects their tensile strength. Soon she had me talking about the modulus of elasticity of chromium copper. I had to be on my guard not to let slip the origins of my advanced knowledge, which was quite difficult at times as I occasionally strayed into realms which were classified.

Now, I don't remember a great deal at all about the next four days and there are probably several good reasons for this.

I smoked cigarettes, I was generally a 'Kensitas Club' or occasionally a 'Players' man, if need be, but of course it was not possible to find an outlet along the march route to buy cigarettes. As a direct consequence of this I found myself cadging roll-up cigarettes from various other folk along the walk. The contents of many of these roll-ups I believe were most probably augmented with marijuana. My short- and long-term memory is usually crystal clear, so this is the only explanation I have for my poor recall of the events, happenings and indeed geographical path of the route itself.

Ana and I got on like a house on fire, we really did. She told me that she thought I was free in my mind but not yet so in my soul and I said that I thought this was true. I said to her that I thought her soul was free but that perhaps her mind was not yet as free as she wished it to be. She nodded and said, "You might have a point there, but none of that really matters much, your heart needs to be free first before anything good can happen." We said lots of stuff like this to each other.

John and I also clicked right from the start too and our conversations ranged over so many varied subjects. We spoke at length of the English involvement in American history, The Founding Fathers, American Independence, the Boston Tea Party, the Slave trade and more currently the Vietnam War and the Black Civil Rights movement. We spoke of the way the Second World War had started and how the US had been relatively late entrants but had been able to help end it so decisively with the use of the Atomic Bomb.

The Cold War, nuclear warfare, and the possibility of 'Mutually Assured Destruction' was something I knew rather a lot about. A bit too much for the likes of Ana's other friend, Miyu, who was a university pal from their London School of Economics days.

Miyu was a very well-educated young woman who was half Japanese. Her English was perfect, being brought up in the UK, and she insisted on remarking that I was incredibly well spoken for a heating engineer. I said I was from good stock, but her suspicions were not quenched. After quizzing me about the bombing of Hiroshima and Nagasaki, she was incredibly impressed with my knowledge, having an uncanny ability to prise certain facts from my classified mind.

She thought that perhaps I 'knew too much' and once asked me directly if I was a spy. I managed to laugh this off and changed the subject, quickly turning the tables asking her about her background and trying to change the dynamic so that she was on the spot for a while.

Her story was so sad. Her father was one of the first to be interned in England, on the Isle of Man in fact. He was living in England with Miyu's English mother several years before the war began. He was a pianist studying music in Glasgow but he had been rounded up as with all 'enemy aliens' and kept imprisoned for six years, even though he was not a soldier for the entire duration of the war.

He was able to stay in England, but it was only then that he was reunited with his English partner and they had married and had Miyu just a short while later. Her father was still alive and living in London but her mother, she told me, had drowned in the Woolwich Ferry disaster of 1949.

Later I discovered that none of this was true in the slightest, except for the part about her father being a pianist. He was a motorcycle mechanic by the name of Tomoya Suzuki, although I'm not sure that can be trusted either. Apparently, he had stowed away on a cargo boat a couple of days before Pearl Harbour and managed to make it all the way to Liverpool. Once there, he had evaded being interned by moving to Ireland where he worked illegally fixing cars and motorbikes for the IRA. However, he earned the most part of his money playing the piano in various pubs in Dublin. There was no Woolwich Ferry disaster, in 1949, or in any other year for that matter.

I felt with Miyu that I was always on the verge of being unmasked and having my own cover story blown. I think she had enough evidence to do it too, from her private investigations and interrogations. However, I believe she held back because she could see there was something special happening between Ana and me.

Ana was of course a piano teacher, or so she said. I had no reason to disbelieve her story, and it struck me that she would make the most perfect piano teacher for almost anyone. I was thinking of signing up for lessons myself upon finally reaching London as a way to 'get in' with her and her 'crowd'.

It was her occupation which coloured my perception of her. She was so strange in so many ways, and I suppose as a group we were a very rum bunch of disparate individuals who were all very odd and peculiar in our ways. Perhaps it is these ways which make us unique.

As a piano teacher, Ana had a certain integrity and wholeness, the wholesome aura of someone who wished only to teach, to bring her passion and joy to others. But of course, she was not a piano teacher at all. And this was something I was to find out only a few months later, a few months after our next encounter at the traffic lights near the Black Dam roundabout.

In that short space of time, I became good friends with

Ana, Miyu, and John. This was quite an achievement given that three of us were charlatans and being completely dishonest about the truth of who we were. Only John had an ounce of credibility in hindsight, and it may have been that he saw through us all. He did laugh a lot for those four days.

We arrived at our destination in Trafalgar Square, hundreds of us, met by thousands more. There were television crews and a lot of police too, some on horseback.

Everything was just fine, and I had just popped into a cafe to see if I could get a pencil and some paper so that we could all write our contact details down.

As I came out, I saw a scuffle not fifty yards away. John, Ana and Miyu were being bundled into the back of a police van with a load of other demonstrators and I was too late after running over there to find out even what had happened. The van drove off at speed. I was left holding the paper and pencil.

Because we had parted so unceremoniously in these circumstances and there really was no piece of information which I could use to track any of them down, I sadly accepted that we were fated to become as estranged to each other as we had been for our entire lives previously. In some ways it was as though we had never met at all. I was thoroughly upset and disappointed, angry in fact. I even said something very rude to one of the policeman who I had seen manhandling my new friends, friends whom I decided were now lost to me for all time.

29

At The Lights

I had not forgotten them at all though, my new friends. Ana, in particular, was on my mind often, but several months after that crazy spontaneous adventure, the memory of her was quickly becoming something like a lost dream which I had imagined while sleeping in a previous life.

Miraculously, however, I was looking at her now, right now! She was there, next to me, at the set of traffic lights near the bypass just before the Black Dam roundabout in Basingstoke! I did an enormous double-take.

I'd only just finished being interviewed for a job within the engineering department of this huge American pharmaceutical company, at their brand-new headquarters, and I hadn't the slightest idea whether they had any real interest in my specific skillset. I was hopeful but they were keeping their cards close to their chests, and it would be weeks before I would discover that I'd actually got the job.

When I was informed by letter that they were offering me the position of assistant head of engineering at the Main Capsule Plant, I was of course over the moon. The salary was incredible, far more than my meagre government pay at Aldermaston, and it was what they called 'flexitime' too. This meant I had a great deal of control over my working hours and if that wasn't enough, the whole thing came wrapped up in a package which included private medical care. The Americans were in town, they were doing things differently and I for one was going to make the most of it. Naturally, I accepted the offer immediately.

It was seeing Ana again though, at the traffic lights near the Black Dam roundabout of all places, which had really got a hold of me. I couldn't get her off my mind. She had told me on the march that she was about to move to Basingstoke, and it had come into my consciousness the day before when John Chrysler had mentioned it in connection with the new pharmaceutical plant.

Basingstoke was only twelve miles from Aldermaston, but I had only been there twice before. On both those occasions I'd become horribly lost because of the ubiquity of its countless roundabouts. They all look the same and the signposting is awful. I'd steered clear of the place because of this until Chrysler had mentioned the job opportunity there, and then Ana had spoken about it too.

The name had a certain ring to it … Basingstoke, perhaps it was the place to be … a new town with a great deal of inward investment, and, at the time she talked of it, the prospect of meeting up with the girl of my dreams. These hopes had of course been cruelly dashed by our rude parting in the shadow of Nelson's Column. But they had then been given a new lease of life … only to be dashed once again.

What were the chances of running into each other again like that? It was infuriating, maddening even because I had not been able to talk with her on this second occasion and the idea that we might just bump into each other once more seemed so unlikely as to be impossible. The jubilation of landing the job was tinged with a kind of distraught pessimism.

It was an extremely hot day in the July of 1961, when Ana pulled up on my left in a brand-new convertible E-Type Jaguar. It was light blue with a kind of silvery sheen to it. These cars had only just hit the market and were causing a bit of a stir. I was fairly surprised because when we'd first met, during the 'Ban the Bomb' march on Easter weekend just a few months ago, she was dressed in an authentic Indian sari and had told me that she was a 'horribly poor piano teacher'.

She was wearing some kind of chiffon blouse now, with an orange and white scarf tied around her neck and sporting what looked to be a pair of Polaroid sunglasses.

In the passenger seat next to her was someone so very small I could barely see her head and initially I mistook her to be a child. Then I saw that she was smoking a cigarette in a cool, relaxed style and I recognised her to be Ana's friend, Miyu, a young Japanese woman. I'd talked with them both, extensively, during the four-day, fifty-two-mile walk from Aldermaston to London's Trafalgar Square and there was no doubting it was them.

Bizarrely, my first thought was that Ana's eyewear could be a pair of American issue Ray Bans, as they looked to be the exact same pair that her other friend, John, had been wearing throughout the whole protest. This despite it being gloomy and overcast for all four days.

John was an African American ex-GI, perhaps forty years of age and we had all got on very well indeed and talked about all kinds of things together as there had been little else to do, except march, which was just the same as walking really. Of course, we shouted some slogans every now and then also.

John was not in the car at that moment, clearly. The E-Type is a two-seater sports car and was therefore at capacity but he was conspicuous by his absence in any case as he is almost six and half feet tall. The trio were a tight group and I had been welcomed into their company and made to feel very happy the whole time.

The couple of characters currently sitting in the idling Jag next to me were my age, twenty, or at least that is what they had said.

Ana rearranged her hair in the wing mirror and then

glanced at me as I was trying desperately and unsuccessfully to open my window. It was baking inside my three-wheeled BMW-designed Isetta Bubble Car and the window was jammed and stuck. It wasn't even my car, I'd borrowed it from Stanley Owens, a friend who was kind enough to lend it to me while my car was being repaired, and the design of its window was really getting to me in the heat in the confined cabin. I had started to lose my patience with it and was beginning to use some considerable brute force.

I must have been making rather a noise to be heard over the rumble of Ana's V12 as it sat purring loudly at the red lights. Perhaps she was mainly intrigued by my peculiar motor vehicle, as many people were, because she didn't recognise me at first. My moustache had developed into quite a beard since she last saw me and that may have had something to do with it.

Nevertheless, when I eventually got the damn thing open, unfortunately breaking off the catch as I did so and releasing a few rare expletives in the process, I looked up to see her looking straight at me, looking at her.

We stared at each, or rather I gazed, and she observed for an extremely long moment before recognition suddenly swept across her face. There had been a definite affinity between us the first time, almost four months previously now and this returned to us both within seconds. Unfortunately, it was not long enough to communicate with each other effectively.

A nasty fat man in an oily white vest who sat behind us in a large Ford low-loader began leaning on his horn. This not only startled us both into action as the lights were now green, but it also negated our attempts to hear each other as the man behind continuously leant on the horn. It was entirely unnecessary.

I began fumbling with the gear shift, which was sticky and awkward to engage at the best of times, and I had to look down at it to get it out of reverse. When I looked up again, Ana had obviously felt obliged to pull away as the idiot in the Ford had felt the need to operate his horn almost continuously. I imagine he did not care for drivers of Isettas or indeed E-Types and his impatience may have been justified as it was possible, he had been made to wait for much longer than I had at first thought.

Eventually I was able to begin moving off, but Ana was already more than fifty feet ahead of me by this time and accelerating away at a good old rate of knots in her expensive, high-performance roadster.

I had suspected that I loved her the first time we had met but our ways had parted in London in such a way that although I had thought about her a great deal on my path to getting my new job, I had resigned myself to accept that we would sadly never meet again.

To have seen her once more in this way made it clear to me that, yes, I had obviously fallen utterly in love with her right from the outset. This second rendezvous, if you can call it that, was statistically so unlikely I felt that it simply could not happen a further time. For a moment I was heartbroken.

However, her geographical proximity in this instance started me crazily speculating about the nature of statistics. If the locus of our positions had coincided for this second time, and indeed so far away from the end of the first event, then surely the possibility of a further intersection, a third encounter, was in fact now significantly greater!

I was full of hope as I drove the Isetta home from work at moderate speeds and resolved with determination to keep my eyes peeled for her from this very moment onwards. She wouldn't be hard to spot in that Jaguar and if I did see her at any time, I would do everything I could in my powers in the endeavour to intercept her.

30

Modern Central Heating Systems

Having left AWRE I'd moved my very few belongings to the small two-room flat which I'd rented near some small shops in a residential area of Old Basing. It wasn't much but I was quite happy to call it home for a while until I'd had a chance to settle in and look around the area at the type of property that I might be able to afford with my vastly improved salary and a small mortgage.

There was a great deal of new building going on around here, part of the government's New Towns project, which was a post-war effort to make room for the baby boom and take overspill from London. Affordable housing was the aim but I wasn't so sure about some of the places being built in places like Hatfield. This was good, I liked it around here and a few new bungalows had taken my eye already. It was the property ladder for me because the dream and the financial side of it made a lot of sense.

Another option, perhaps more affordable for me, had me thinking about finding a small house somewhere in need of some renovation, a small front and rear garden in a quiet residential area maybe. A place I could work on at weekends, perhaps with an option for some DIY building, maybe the possibility of an extension or an annex. I was handy with most tools and fancied attempting to make a good investment and some return on my modest savings. It was exciting stuff.

Here I was on a little cul-de-sac just off a minor B-road just off a slightly larger A-road. The whole of Basingstoke was my playground, Hampshire and beyond ... Great neighbours too, good people, very important … nice neighbours.

The Isetta was parked outside right in front of the flat. The Armstrong was still in the garage. The pothole I had hit had meant a complete overhaul of the front suspension was required. I would have liked to have tried this myself, but you really needed a garage with a lift, or a pit and I had neither available to me.

Finding myself with some pleasant free time, I'd been tinkering with the Isetta's little BMW engine to try to get some more power out of it. It was not difficult to work after I'd invested in some metric spanners. Making the mixture a bit richer and slightly advancing the timing made quite a difference. Then I found you could remove a section of the small exhaust system to great effect. She was a fair bit noisier now of course.

I was stopped by a traffic policeman with his new 'speed gun' coming down the hill near Eastrop Lane while taking the turn at the bottom a little faster than I ought to have done. Was I aware of the sound I was making? Did my 'vehicle' have a hole in its exhaust? Did I need a special licence for it? How much had it cost me? Was it safe?

I told him that the cabin of these BMWs is extremely well sealed and soundproofed will an innovative double rubber seal, "Clever bunch, those Germans" and that it was "as quiet as a church inside". I don't think he believed me, but his curiosity and my chit-chat got me off the hook.

He was also slightly concerned about the way I had negotiated the corner.

"Did you realise your vehicle was in contact with the road on only two of its three wheels throughout the apex of the turn?"

I told him she handled much like a motorbike and that one didn't notice these things after a while. He raised an eyebrow, once again.

Still the Isetta is considerably quicker now with these modifications. Stanley Owens has said that he has no need for it currently and I can keep it until the Sapphire is seaworthy again. It's just as well because I think the repairs might take a while and I'm quite enjoying the novelty of this little car. It's fun, life should have some fun in it, and a lot of people stop me to talk about it, which is good in a new town.

I might be able to get a few more horsepower out of it too if I alter the geometry of the front axle slightly. The extra speed might give me a fighting chance if I see that Jag again, and its driver of course. I was sure I'd spot her and when I did, I wanted to be able to give her a run for her money.

It was only a week or so before I got my chance, and I'd done that little fix with the axle geometry by this time too.

I was near a new building development on the outskirts of Basing. I say Basing, it was nearer Nately Scures really, out in the sticks. It was all fields and forests out that way.

Slowing down as I passed, I peered down the makeshift entrance to this site, thinking that maybe they were putting up some new bungalows there. Quite suddenly a large car pulled out right in front of me, I braked hard and came to an immediate stop but there had been no warning, and I was shocked out of my little daydream. It was the opalescent silver-blue Jaguar, performing what I can only call a reckless manoeuvre. The carefree driver had a nonchalant style and obviously no concern or forethought whatsoever for the possibility of any oncoming traffic.

I leant on the Isetta's horn in protest, it was not a particular strong sound, more of a tiny 'beep' really which apparently went unnoticed. As the luxury British sports car sped away, leaving me in the wake of its characteristic roar, I opened my own throttle, determined to give the indifferent driver a run for their money. This time, the racer in question was driving solo.

My nippy German bubble car responded eagerly.

Within less than half a mile I had closed on the long low-slung Jaguar and was up on the tail of its dual exhaust pipes. The driver's hair was blowing around all over the place, no scarf to hold it in place on this occasion. I couldn't see her face, but I knew this must be Ana, there was something about her casual driving style which made me sure of it.

How would I get her to see me? I tried swerving around a bit, thinking she might catch me in her rear-view mirror and see me waving from within the bubble, but this ploy met with no success. I'd have to overtake and flag her down.

On the dual carriageway ahead, I gave it the full beans, my race-prepared exhaust system now roaring at previously unexperienced and slightly frightening decibels. The volume alone must have been enough to get her attention. I was parallel to her now and she glanced over at me, shot me just the one look with her Polaroid eye-protection and then, just a second later, she must have changed down and leant on her accelerator because I heard her twin carburettors open and the V12 sport roadster took off like an aeroplane.

I must have been going upwards of 50mph, but she just left me in her dust. When the cloud of leaves she blew around in her wake had cleared, all I could see was a small point of gleaming metallic paintwork way up ahead in the distance ... a vanishing point of hopes and dreams. However, I was undeterred and not easily beaten.

The next day I went back to the building site around the same time, hoping that either she was a creature of habit or had some kind of regular business to attend on a repeat basis at this place.

There was no joy, only a man sitting outside a wooden hut on a deckchair eating a sandwich and swigging from a bottle of beer. I approached and enquired after the driver of the E-Type.

He was very congenial, and this was how my conversation with Mr Frank Bagley began – an ongoing discussion which would prove to continue for many months to follow.

He was the manager, the owner too of this site, where he planned to build thirty or so new bespoke homes, twenty-nine I think to be exact, three of which looked to be already well under way.

I asked if he knew her.

"Yes, she's one of my customers."

"Her name's not Ananya Rondel by any chance is it?"

"It is, well Ana Rondel is how I know her. I thought she was an aristocrat, or an actress, or a model, or a pop star, or something when I first met her. She is a looker, isn't she? Got all my builders a bit excited, I can tell you that much. Get no work done around here at all when she's about."

"Yes, she does have a certain something about her, doesn't she?"

"You know her quite well then?"

"Oh, we met quite a while ago now, I haven't seen her for ages, I just didn't know she er … drove an E-type."

"Mmm, nice motor that, nice colour, makes a nice sound too."

"Not sure how she could afford such a car, and er … a brand-new house of quite such sizeable proportions … I didn't know she was so …"

"Loaded …"

"Well, yes I suppose so. This must all be costing quite a bit."

"Not so much as you think to build a house in this day and age, with modern building methods. We're all on schedule too, pre-sold seven already. Ms Rondel's house is going to be over there, just finished digging the foundations. Are you interested in buying a house, er … Mr …?"

"Armstrong, Arthur Armstrong. No, I am looking for a new

place at the moment but I think yours are perhaps a bit out of my price range. How much are you selling these for, if you don't mind me asking?"

"Not at all, that's the whole point. Forty grand for a standard size, up to seventy for one like Ms Rondel's, except she keeps adding what she likes to call 'little extras', so I think hers might come in at more like ninety eventually."

"Is that good value, for around here do you think? If you don't mind me asking …"

"I think it is. I try to keep the costs on materials down, that's the secret, I don't like cutting corners on quality, mind you, I'm just careful about how I spend."

"That's a pretty huge pile of copper you've got there, looks like about a tonne of 3/4" small-bore tubing. For the central heating, is it?"

"Ah, you know your pipes. Got that delivered this morning, your friend Ms Rondel was able to help us out what with all that, what with her contacts in the business and everything. Just finishing off the paperwork, that's why she was here. She's often about, my builders just down tools whenever they see that Jag. I have to tell her to push off, otherwise we'd never get anything finished around here."

"What business is that exactly? I mean when we met, she was between jobs I think."

"The copper business. You don't know her so well then … as much as you thought you did perhaps?"

"Seemingly not, she told me she was a piano teacher."

"As I understand it, she does tinkle on the ivories occasionally, but I don't think she could afford one of my houses on a piano teacher's salary. Not unless you were teaching the Sultan of Brunei's kids or something. If you've got your own little copper mine in India though, it's not so hard. Not so hard to lay your hands on a tonne of copper tubing either, good price she gave me too. Anyway, perhaps I shouldn't be telling you all of this. You're not one of those journalists from the local rag, are you?"

"Ah, no ... I'm just an er … heating engineer actually. I do a lot of small-bore copper piping work in er … big business, industrial stuff."

"Interesting … Manufacturing I expect, is it?"

"No, er … government as a matter of fact."

"Council work then?"

"Ah, no, it's funny. I'm just in the middle of a big change. I was at Aldermaston, you know, the atomic weapons place."

"Ohh … I see, top secret, hush-hush stuff."

"That's it. Anyway, I'm out of that now, I'm starting a new job down here soon, only moved a few weeks ago."

"You still a heating engineer though?"

"Oh, yes, through and through."

"That's a bit handy that is, maybe you can help me with something. These are the plans for our standard new central heating systems, standard for all these houses but we've been having a lot of a problems with the gravity feed from the immersion tanks. I expect it's a piece of cake for you, but my boys can't figure these diagrams out at all. Would you mind having a look?"

"Not at all."

I began to study Mr Bagley's plans with the idea that this might be my way to stick around for a while and make myself useful in case Ana might show up again in the near future.

I could see the solution to his problems straight away, but I didn't let on, figuring I'd make it seem far more complicated than it actually was and buy some time in case Ana put in an appearance. I thought I might be able to get in here and hang about a few days. If I couldn't catch her due to a lack of pace, perhaps my best bet was to let her come to me.

That's how I became a freelance central heating consultant. I kept at it a couple of hours every day for a few days, making myself indispensable, during which time I tried to find out more about the mysterious Ana as she was now. Mr Bagley clearly liked her and greatly appreciated her input with his needs for all things copper but he did say once that he found her to be an 'awkward customer' with regards her own house.

She was always wanting to change the plans, and Bagley's architects were pulling their hair out.

The most recent 'little alteration' she'd requested, or rather insisted upon, was for a loft room to be built onto the side of the house and up onto the roof. He had just taken delivery of a specialised skylight that had come all the way from Denmark which was to be installed into the existing structure as she was apparently set on having her own Observatory up there.

"Did you know she was a stargazer Mr Armstrong?"

"No, not at all. All she told me about anything to do with that was that she was an Aquarius."

My job was very straightforward as I had only recently learned about a lot of what Mr Bagley required when I was doing far more advanced stuff during the installation of the ATLAS computer at Aldermaston. That thing needed cooling and power and cables and insulation and all sort of things. By comparison what he asked of me was child's play.

At one point he offered me a proper job, with a decent salary. I told him my full-time job was to start soon but that maybe I could call on him for a favour if I ever needed any building services in the future.

"Certainly, no job too big or too small."

We got on very well, considering our different backgrounds.

Then one afternoon Ana showed up. I heard the rumble of the V12 from within the hut and a few moments later she walked through the door. I looked up tentatively from behind a large blueprint as she greeted Mr Bagley.

"Frank! How are you?"

"Ana!"

They were far more familiar with each other than I had expected they might be. After a few seconds he introduced me.

"And this is our specialist central heating expert, Mr Armstrong, whom I think you might already know …"

I stood up.

"Pleased to make your acquaintance again Ms Rondel."

"Louis! My god! What are you doing here?"

Mr Bagley was confused as Ana and I shook hands.

"Louis? Who's Louis?"

"Oh it's my nickname, Mr Bagley. I er … Arthur is my real name, it's just sometimes I use Louis, er casually, informally if you like, when I'm not working … If you know what I mean."

"Arthur!" Ana laughed. "No, you're not an 'Arthur', definitely not, that won't do at all. … I think I'll stick with Louis if that's all right?"

"Er, well, call me whatever you like, I really don't mind at all."

"You're a piece of work, I'll say that much for you Arthur or Louis, whatever your name is. He's chopped our central heating systems costs in half, so he has Ana, twice as efficient too. I don't know how you two know each other but he's a genius this man, nothing less than a diamond, a work of art he is, I tell you."

"Well, perhaps we should call you Art then Louis. My god, it's a bit of shock seeing you though, out of the blue like this, I can't quite get my head around it!"

The three of us stood in the hut in a small triangle in silence for far too long until suddenly we were all uncomfortable and Mr Bagley thought of something to say.

"I've been hoping you'd show up, Ms Rondel. My crew have finally got your Danish skylight fitted. Just got to replace the whole of the rest of the roof now. I was just thinking you'd like to come and have a § at it."

"Yes, why not."

"Mr Armstrong why don't you come along too. You can show Ms Rondel the magic you've made with her header tank."

"I'd love to. Ms Rondel, do you mind if I tag along?"

"Not at all, not at all."

We walked out of the hut, all three in various states of different types of cognitive disarray.

Ana looked so completely different, superficially, in the way she dressed that is. When I met her and we'd spent those four intense days together, she was all flowing sari and batik and hemp and the like, now she was wearing trousers! What's more, I think they were Harris tweed!

She looked great, I've got to say, all the builders we passed on the short walk to her house clearly thought so too. Many of them knew her by name and said something cheeky or lewd, one of them up high in some girders even whistled! What's more, Ana was lapping it up.

She had her Polaroids on, as it was such a lovely sunny day and after a while the contrast with the Ananya I'd met was just too much for me to find believable. For a while, as Mr Bagley was required to see to the needs of one of his employees, Ana and I were alone together, slightly away from anyone else.

"Are you well Ana? Piano teaching going well for you then Ana? Seems to be treating you well, very lucrative profession these days I've heard. Someone told me the Sultan of Brunei was giving his entire extended family piano lessons. That wasn't you, was it? Did you manage to land that gig?"

"I have some quite famous and quite well-heeled students as a matter of fact and yes, I am very well thank you. And yourself, Arthur?"

"I'm just fine thank you. What exactly are the heels of the shoes of these students of yours made of then? Diamonds? Or is it just copper? Heh? I would have thought buying and selling copper would have been more lucrative myself. Because of the whole capitalism and global supply and demand thing. But then if you own your own copper mine you don't even have to buy it, do you? You just dig it out of the ground. Never have guessed that teaching piano would have been able to keep up with that, just goes to show how little I know doesn't it. Boy am I stupid!"

We were walking again. Or rather Ana was walking away, and I was close by on her shoulder. I'd lost her once, twice, three times in fact! I wasn't going to let her get away from me this time. She had this aloof look about her which was so different from the girl I thought I knew, and I wanted to know what had happened. I wasn't angry as such but clearly, I'd been lied to and taken for a fool in some way. Either she wasn't what she said she was when we'd first met, or she wasn't now who she was pretending to be. She knew I knew her differently from this.

"Well, you do know a piano teacher may have many strings to their bow."

"What does that mean? I'm sorry but I don't think there are many piano teachers in the world who just happen to own copper mines as well, and in India of all places..."

"But then how many piano teachers do you know?"

"Not many!"

"How many?"

"Just one!"

"And how many of them own a copper mine?"

"Just one!"

"That's all of them then, isn't it ... Louis! Or should I call you Mr Louis Armstrong!" Ana had taken her Polaroids off and was glaring straight into my soul.

At that point, Mr Bagley returned.

"Sorry about that, the sewerage pipes we laid cut across the field, we're having to share the mains with that farmhouse there and my fellas seem to have gotten their angles and numbers a bit muddled. Pipes have all backed up from the farmhouse. You might have noticed the rather powerful odour. I'm terribly sorry, I didn't mean to interrupt, what were you talking about?"

Ana put her Polaroids back on. "Piano!"

"Ah yes, Mr Armstrong was telling me that you are also an accomplished piano teacher ..."

"Well, as I was just telling 'Arthur' here, it pays to be multidisciplined and have many strings to one's bow."

"I should say, I'm lucky I've been able to make use of his services. I mean it's not often you meet a fully qualified nuclear weapons engineer who's also a dab hand at the old central heating. Not often at all, and that he should offer his service for free too."

Ana stopped in her tracks. We were some fifty or so yards away from her plot now.

"Now, this is interesting isn't it ... A nuclear weapons engineer called Louis Armstrong, it's almost too hard to believe that it could be true."

She started walking away again and of course I followed her. Then she stopped again.

"I must say, it's very noble of you to be working for free here for our good Mr Bagley and I'm still trying to get over you being here at all! It's almost as though you were waiting for me, or following me, or something!"

"I'm sure I don't know what you're implying Ms Rondel! Mr Bagley has simply been letting me assist him with a few rudimentary central heating problems he's been having here."

Mr Bagley had just noticed the elevated volume and stress patterns in the conversation which Ana and I were currently engaged in and, ever the gentleman, found a way to dissipate them.

"Er, Mr Armstrong, I just thought, you're going to be terribly late for your orientation meeting at your drug company."

"Drugs! Has the world gone mad in the last two minutes!"

Ana was apoplectic!

"Mr Armstrong has an important meeting at his new place of work. The large American pharmaceutical plant just on the edge of town. I was just reminding him, he told me he needed to be there and er …"

"I have a position in the engineering department there, it starts on Monday. Mr Bagley is right, I need to go, I have to meet my new boss."

"This is preposterous! I have an interview there on Thursday."

"Really? You're right, that is a bit ridiculous, I didn't know we were hiring new piano teachers at the moment!"

"As I keep telling you Mr Armstrong, I have many talents. I am also a gifted secretary I can tell you … fifty-seven words per minute touch-typing, sixty-seven as an audio typist and I have shorthand too! Pitman's!"

"Then I'm sure we will most definitely meet again Ms Rondel! Now if you don't mind, I'm afraid I really must go, otherwise I may not have a job to go to on Monday at all! Goodbye and good luck in your interview Ms Rondel!"

"Goodbye Louis … Arthur … Art!"

"What was all that about …?" Mr Bagley had sat down on a bag of cement and was scratching his head.

I'd stormed off. I was all hot, bothered, confused, crazy, mad, and insanely in love with Ananya … again … or Ana … or whatever her name was!

31

The Touch Of A Touch Typist

I knew she was going to be here, or at least that she was scheduled to be here, because I had the list in front of me, and her name was on it.

Thankfully the upgrades on the BMW meant I was no more than ten minutes late for the meeting with my new boss. I've got the balance just right now, so I can stay very stable on two wheels around some of the larger roundabouts at a good speed. Having successfully navigated my orientation day I was now a fully installed and full-time employee of the pharmaceutical giant Elie Lillie.

I knew about everything on site now, from the opening times of the cafeteria to the wide variety of locations where I could park my vehicle. I knew when the cleaning ladies arrived in the morning and when the wastepaper baskets were emptied in the afternoons. I knew how late I was permitted to stay on site into the evening and I even had a credit-card-sized piece of plastic to operate the automatic gates at the entrance after hours.

Security was certainly an issue, but not on the scale I was used to. I saw a couple of anti-vivisectionists loitering around outside which was something I hadn't thought about but for the first time in my life I was working somewhere which was officially on the map.

I was very familiar with the many different types of fire extinguisher which were being used here, and where they were located. I'd been given instruction on how to use the 'Water Buffalo' which was handily stationed right outside my office.

That was the thing, I had my own office, t had my name on the door, and I had a desk and three large filing cabinets. These were all totally empty, brimming with potential, just asking to be filled. Each had its own three-number combination and I'd already committed these to memory.

I relaxed, leaning back on my spring-loaded, five-wheeled, castor-action chair and surveyed my domain through a large window. My view was a none-too-pretty though, a really quite vast expanse of concrete, but it was freshly laid concrete, a canvas on which would be placed the new capsule plant.

Hundreds of thousands of multicoloured gelatine capsules would be flying through here every hour. Their chemically diverse contents spreading the benefits of modern medicine to all corners of the UK, to Europe and beyond.

My first job was to oversee the installation of the complex ventilation systems needed for cleaning the air of this clinical environment, hermetically sealed as it would be. The experience at ATLAS was very oddly similar as precise temperature control was required and many further considerations regarding power supply to massive, specialised and very expensive machinery.

An advanced knowledge of copper cabling might be thought to be a contradiction in terms, but there is nothing straightforward about it and those in the know, well, they know about this. My specialist experience was just one element contributing to the sumptuous salary I now commanded and the reason for my allocation to this lovely new office.

The USA had come to the UK and I was now a vanguard of its proactive and efficient approach; 'Performance Excellence' it was called, and I would be doing it all on flexitime.

My immediate boss was an elderly man from Wyoming called Ray Left. He was slightly dull I must say, with little inflexion in his voice, a kind of nasal monotone in fact but he had worked for many years at Elie Lillie's headquarters in Indianapolis and he was a good man. I knew I would be OK with him, and that he would look out for me.

After our meeting, which was really just an informal 'getting to know you' style chat, Ray Left said to me, "Oh, Arthur, I may not be around to help settle you in personally when you arrive. I've got all these darn interviews to do."

"More engineers?"

"Sadly not, no, my boss, that's Fred Fairlight, you'll meet him soon I'm sure, has given me the seemingly glamorous task of interviewing no less than thirty-eight secretaries for the typing pool. Can you believe that? I've got the list here, look it runs to two pages!"

My ears pricked up. Secretaries … Ana …

"That sounds a little better than a bunch of engineers in my books Ray!"

"Ah, you'd think so, but I had to do this once before, back in the States, that's why they picked me I think, I've got experience …"

"I'm sure they'll be nice enough young ladies but we only need five … Heaven knows why I have to interview all of them. I mean thirty-eight Arthur! I figure I must give each one at least thirty minutes don't you think, to be polite. Do you think that's reasonably polite?"

"Very reasonably so, yes."

"That's nineteen hours straight Arthur! I mean I'm getting older, and I've got good stamina but a man has his limits!"

"I can help you out, no trouble. May I have a look, do you mind?"

"You could! Lord, I'd certainly owe you one Art, you don't mind me calling you Art do you? I have a cousin in Utah called Art, that's quite a coincidence, don't you think?"

"Er, yes, yes, it is. Art is fine it would be no trouble at all."

He gave me the list. "Knock yourself out. I mean they're all straight out of secretarial college, they're all similarly qualified, they will probably all be very pleasant and dress real nice, how are you supposed to choose?"

The list was in alphabetical order. I went slowly down the first page pretending to read each one but then I raced down, scanning for the 'R's. They were over on page two. There, squeezed between Elizabeth Radley and Justine Stokes was Ana Rondel.

"How about you take the top sheet and I'll tackle this lot," I said already removing the paperclip which kept them together.

"Sure, if you don't mind. Gets us down to about ten hours each. You sure you can stomach it?"

That was that.

I've just processed Elizabeth Radley. She was polite, well spoken, quicker than most as a touch typist, upwards of seventy words per minute, and that on a mechanical machine. She was keen and really quite attractive but I suspected she might not make the final shortlist.

For up next was one Ana Rondel. I'd already had a couple of 'no shows' and I was not one hundred per cent confident she would just walk through the door of my place of work, for the second time in fact. She could not possibly know what she was walking into.

My name was in large letters on the outside of my door and as I waited, I wasn't sure how she'd react to seeing it there. Would she turn around on the spot, in shock, in panic? There was simply no way she would know that it would be me interviewing her, how could she know. I thought it would spook her before I had my chance to explain everything.

My door had a self-closing mechanism, but I decided to hold it open with a fire extinguisher, and in addition I moved my chair so that I was just around the corner. With a hastily written note, all she would see was a message sellotaped to the doorframe which read, "Please speak your name clearly and wait to be called."

She was late, by seventeen minutes, but I rationalised this by convincing myself that punctuality is not a primary quality necessary to be a good secretary.

Then I heard her voice.

"Ana Rondel, here to be interviewed by assistant head of engineering Mr Arthur Armstrong for a secretarial position."

Her knowledge surprised me and put me on a back foot. She was very cool, confident and clear, but her tone was one of resigned acceptance, and perhaps a little arrogance too.

I coughed. "Please enter. Ah, please have a seat."

"Shall we just get this over with as quickly as we can Louis? Arthur, Art … I'm sorry I'm a wee bit late but I met this girl called Elizabeth on the way in, as she was going out. She wouldn't stop chatting, she was nice, I mean you should really think about hiring her, she's really very smart too, and boy could she talk, she wouldn't let me go and then when she told me about you and mentioned your name, I thought, well this is going to be fun …

"So, ask me what you're going to ask me, let's get through this, I've got an appointment at 3pm so I don't want this to go on and on … I mean this could get really awkward, it could be a real nightmare. I'd already got myself prepared for seeing you again at the building site, I felt sure we'd, you know, bump into each other there pretty soon, so perhaps it's no surprise that fate has thrown us this 'curve ball'. So, you know, when you're ready just fire away.

"I promise I'll tell the truth, the whole truth and nothing but the truth, so help me god. But I'm going to be wanting some straight answers from you too, Mr Louis Armstrong. Maybe I'll just call you 'The Great Satchmo', that was his nickname, wasn't it? Come on then, stop gawking, what are you waiting for?"

It was a nightmare. She looked stunning, her touch-typing speeds were off the chart for both dictation and audiotyping, accuracy over ninety-seven per cent, unheard of. And of course, she had shorthand, Pitman's no less. I knew I was going to give her the job and of course she did too. She's starting a week on Tuesday, as my secretary.

They say truth is stranger than fiction but to be perfect honest I simply don't know who 'they' are or why they say this. I'm not sure what the difference is any more, quite frankly … I mean how would you? In the final analysis it really doesn't bear thinking about. You just end up going round and round, in circles, like me in the BMW in and around Basingstoke, trying to find the right exit. People refer to it as 'Donut City' I've learned recently, because there are so many roundabouts that is, not donuts.

32

Uniquely Rare

I sold my aunt's house, for a pretty penny I might add. John flew to his brother and his home in the United States of America carrying his small army issue holdall and his saxophone in its case. We said our goodbyes at Heathrow among floods of tears and laughter and as he walked away, he turned and shouted, "I'll write!"

"You better!" I shouted at full volume.

Miyu wanted to come with us and as the E-Type could seat only two we took her Mini. I'd bought her the one which we had test-driven, its number plate being 684 FOU. In French 'Fou' means 'mad', which was thoroughly apt as she is a bit of a looney in general and even more so now, she has the car. She's always asking me if I want to take the E-Type out for a spin with her. "We could race each other somewhere. We could go somewhere in the middle of the night when there isn't so much traffic," she said once. God knows what she'd be like on a motorbike, I'm not sure which she'd be scarier on, a Suzuki or a Yamaha! She's a compulsive liar but her father's name really was Suzuki, and he did live in Dublin for a while where he earned the nickname 'Samurai Suzuki'. I've never known why she does it, just for kicks I guess.

John was doubled up on the back seats of the Mini, his massive body folded in half filling the space.

It had taken very little time to sell the house. I worked on my memoir most of the time and managed to finish it shortly before I moved. As a project it was therapy, I suppose. I set myself a time to do it every day, in the morning most often.

I worked some ideas through and even wrote a few pieces of music. It was a way to sort my life out and put it all into some sort of perspective.

I went to the building development site often to watch my house go up. The incredible excitement of it was that with each visit I witnessed a huge leap of progress. Bagley and his team worked with great speed, and I was fascinated by their methods.

On one occasion I arrived to find the whole place deserted, not a soul to be seen anywhere. It was as if everyone had simple downed tools and gone on holiday. Nevertheless, I still wanted to have a good look at No. 29.

I parked in the spot which would eventually be my new drive. The house was nearly complete, except there were no doors or windows in place and, as yet, no roof at all. I walked into what was the shell of a house and found myself alone. All around me were the signs that men had been working hard, but there was no one here now, except me. It was so quiet that day.

In the middle of summer on a beautiful day in the afternoon I stood in this space and took it all in. It was a work in progress and during the time I spent there, wandering around from room to room and planning my ideas for the layout of each one, I felt myself to be an ongoing work in progress too. This was my present and my future and there was nothing of the past here to hold me back.

But it was eerie, the quietness of it, the solitude, and me seemingly in a similar state of perpetually building myself into a new way of life. This newness I felt with a keen sense of being on the edge of an experience, a frontier I was forever pushing back so that I could progress without having to confront the past.

I had already dealt with so many demons in so many different forms. I had confronted the reality of my past and I had seen and felt the nature of the place which had initially shaped my soul and now I was here. It was real, but in those moments I realised how completely disconnected from the reality of life I had become.

I had reinvented my image, my personality, my character, and my entire way of life. It was so hard to tell how much of this was in reaction to forces outside of my control acting upon me and how much of it was created by me. Was I the artist of my life or was I simply being blown around by the wind which blew through it?

There was a steady breeze now moving through the house. The air was warm and close and had a smell to it of the fields and crops and wildflowers over which it had moved to find its way here. I was downstairs in what would eventually be my lounge and it passed easily through the spaces where the windows and doors would soon block its path. For now, however, it had the great freedom to move from outside to inside to outside again, passing through my house and clearing it of all ghosts.

It occurred to me that when the house was finished, and I had moved in I would not be able to experience this sensation in quite the same way again. I could have all the doors and windows open but I would be enclosed in my new home, as is everyone.

I looked up.

The vast blue sky was a pale blue page, criss-crossed with the angled lines of the timbers in the structure above. I was lost for a while, rotating and gazing, contemplating the haphazard geometry of it all and my neck became stiff. On the ground where I was standing was a large pile of heavy tarpaulin being used by the workers to cover various parts of the floor. Thrown on top of this was a further pile of heavy cotton, ground sheets for future use by the painters and decorators I imagined. They formed a kind of bed I thought, and so I lay down for a while upon it.

Flat on my back and staring straight up, I could see a few fine herringbone clouds at high altitude and there were little puffy cotton wool ones moving at quite a speed much closer to the surface of the Earth. From my reclined, relaxed point of view I watched the heavens peacefully changing.

The moon was not quite full yet but framed in a square by the rafters of the master bedroom above, its light blue back-wash background seemingly bringing out a look of transparency to its surface.

I think I might have slept for a while, I'm not sure. I was so profoundly tired, perhaps not physically but mentally and emotionally I was exhausted. I was daydreaming there for so long that I lost track of time.

After that I was increasingly able to come to terms with the immense changes which had occurred in my life. Having the house built and being a part of this process created a period of transition which saw me adjust and grow. I became stable and calm and, dare I say it, happy too.

Art and I became the best of friends during this period. There was a certain blurring of our status. Because of our work relationship we were a certain way with each other during the week, it was formal and professional, it was work. At the weekends and also on some weekday evenings we saw each other casually, increasingly often, and the distance between the roles we played out in our lives grew less and less.

We went to a local jazz club in Reading a few times, where we sometimes danced together and he was always the gentleman. It was at one of these events that I started playing the piano again, just a spot of spontaneous fooling around with a rather lovely Cavendish Grand they have there. Temptation got the better of me and I couldn't resist.

Art heard me play for the first time and I think it had a great effect on him. He couldn't get over it.

"You told me you played, but … you're so … it was just the speed of your hands, and then you were so slow and soft … I didn't know you could … you would …"

I laughed. "Well, how could you?"

Then one day the house was finished, or almost finished I should say. I moved in rather prematurely because Aunt Marie's house sold so very quickly. Bagley was fine about it but I believe I was completely uninsured for some time because the house was not yet complete. Had it burned down or some such horrible thing had happened I think I would have lost it all. It didn't, but I had to live for several weeks surrounded by workman as they finished the job. I really didn't mind at all and they didn't seem to either. We had a lot of fun and I made an enormous number of cups of tea for them all.

When the sale completed in Primrose Hill I had to clear everything from the house, including the contents of the roof with all its alcoves and strange nooks and crannies.

Time became a pressing concern and I arranged for the movers to look after everything over several days. There were three of them in the roof there at one point, stumbling around with torches in the dust. I had no idea what was up there, but it all had to come down, and I had nowhere else to put it, so it was all piled up into vans and transported to my new home.

When they had gone, I was left surrounded by what looked like the effects of a whirlwind sweeping through the sum total of my family's past, interspersed with details of my own, and thrown this history with great glee throughout the crisp new present moment of my new existence.

I was extremely happy having taken a week off to get started on the job in hand of sorting through it all. I got the record player going early on and my activities were accompanied by a continuous selection of indescribably beautiful jazz from John's collection.

The piano was the only object which had been placed, by chance I might add, in the place in which it would stay. In the living room, by the entrance to the hall it was majestic, tall, and full of potent promise.

I lifted the lid and ran my hands over the eighty-eight keys, sharps and flats, As to Gs, black and white and everything about it was just so and just right. Until I made a chord and discovered that of course it was most horribly out of tune.

Realising that I hadn't played, not for as long as I could remember and naturally effected by the trauma of its translocation, it was in desperate need of a service and an experienced tuner. Its travels from the urban landscape and lofty altitude of Primrose Hill to a yet unexplored new habitat had left it in poor shape. I felt slightly ashamed and went about enquiring from just about everyone whether they knew of someone who could help.

Funnily it was one of Bagley's men, an electrician who was fitting some light switches to my barely completed house. I say he was a man, but he was not much more than a teenager. He fitted the switches, and I tried my luck to see if he might possibly know of a piano tuner nearby.

He spoke with a pronounced stutter and was, I think, maybe of a traveller type, but the first thing he said was, "I play."

"You do?"

"I love it. Your, your p … p … piano looks lovely. Can I p … p … lay?"

"Yes, certainly, you want to play the piano …"

"I've been l … l … looking at it all day."

"Please, play as much as you like."

He put down his screwdriver and I found a nearby wooden box for him to sit on.

"It is badly out of tune as I was saying but please feel free to …"

He had already launched into a piece which I immediately recognised as Chopin. He played with a touch and a depth of feeling I had not seen before, not even with Miyu, but his technique was so unconventional as to defy any analysis.

When he finished I was in tears.

He turned to see me and was concerned,

"Are you alright, is something wr … wr … wrong?"

"No, no, nothing is wrong, you play beautifully. How long have you played?"

"Since forever I can re … mem … ber …"

"How did you, I mean who taught you to …?" I was so shocked still that I found it difficult to make my own words now and he laughed.

"My f … f … f … fa … fa … dad, he liked Mozart best."

I was silent.

"I don't like c … c … c … I prefer jazz."

He turned back to the keyboard and played something which must have been his own composition because I recognised nothing of it except for the influence of Art Tatum. He stopped suddenly in mid-flow.

"Your B flat is stuck."

Sure enough, the key was depressed and stuck down. It looked stupid all alone like that and we sat staring at it.

"Would you like my c … c … c … cousin Fred to have a look at it for you?"

"Please, yes, yes please. What is your name, I'm sorry I don't know your name."

"It's Joe, Ms R … Rondel."

"Call me Ana, Joe, just Ana."

"Ana." He smiled a huge toothy smile at me, revealing several missing teeth but a very happy soul.

A few days later, Fred showed up with his tuning fork and tools and gave my Aunt Marie's piano a full overhaul. I paid him more cash than he had asked for and he told me all about his 'clever cousin' who was the genius in the family.

The piano now has its soul back, Marie and John are here with me, and I have a new regular visitor in Joe, who comes for tea and cake every Thursday to talk of his life and play. I am learning from him and I am teaching him what I know too. It is the most incredible thing.

I saw Fred again soon afterwards in town and bought him lunch. He was very grateful for my kindness towards Joe and I told him it was my pleasure. He had been speaking with Joe and was very curious to know everything about me. Because I feel relaxed in his company I have told him much of my life story.

When we came to my own abilities and talent at the piano with improvisation, he was intensely absorbed and asked more and more questions of me. The questions became very detailed and specific, and it was like being in a doctor's surgery when the doctor is asking questions about symptoms and hunting for clues to confirm or deny a diagnosis which he suspects to be at the root of a problem.

Here though, there was nothing wrong with me. I was simply trying to find the right words to describe to him the way I played, the way I composed my music in my mind, and the strange inner language I used to do this.

I had tried to do this before with Miyu and she understood exactly what I meant but had told me that 'we are all as weird as each other, Ana', and had left it at that. Fred seemed to know what he was talking about though and his intelligent probing questions and calm casual manner found a way to make me simplify myself in a way I had not done before.

"I sort of 'see' sounds and 'hear' colours," I was eventually able to tell him.

"I think you probably have what they call 'chromesthesia'

Ms Rondel, it's a type of synaesthesia, a kind of mixing of the senses. I had a friend once, he was a piano tuner too, but he was a blind man. You get quite a few blind folks who like music who turn their hand to piano tuning as a way to make a living. Anyway, he swore blind, if you'll pardon the expression, I didn't mean it as a joke, that he said he could actually see the colours of the sounds of the notes in his mind's eye, so to speak. He could actually see the sounds and when he listened to certain music it was like a beautiful light show inside his soul. That's what he said. For you, I think you see all the colours all around you and you can hear the sounds of them inside you, in your soul. The colours and the quality of light creates a music in your soul."

"It sounds an incredible theory, Fred, it really does, it's quite a beautiful idea I think."

"Oh, it's no theory Ms Rondel, it's what they say Joe has, and I think that's probably what you've got too, and why the both of you get along so well."

I was blown away and completely dumbstruck, but Fred just carried on working as he talked. He was replacing the low frequency bass strings on the piano with ones wrapped in copper wire. They make the string heavier and give more depth and sustain to the lower notes. "Something in the genes I suppose. Me, I have 'perfect pitch', you've heard of that right?"

"Yes, I have, my friend Miyu has that too, but that's very rare is it not?"

"It is yes, and I'm very fortunate because of it. It helps me to make a good living doing what I do, but I don't know if it's as rare as the old chromesthesia though, you'd have to look it up somewhere, a book I should suspect. Quite a coincidence that you have what Joe has, don't you think?"

33

Electric Lady

I told Art all about this one day. It was a weekend actually and he'd kindly offered to help me set up my television.

It was Aunt Marie's set, which I remembered we'd bought together in the John Lewis shop in Oxford Street on a whim. It was towards the end of my time at St Pauls and I was not happy there at all. It was a school day morning, a Monday, and I'd just told her how much I hated the place and that I wasn't going to go to school that day. She'd looked at me and laughed and then asked if I wanted to go shopping instead.

It was monochrome set, a Téléavia Panoramic III, and I think Aunt Marie liked it largely because it was French. She always said that form should take precedence over function, and I have to say that I liked looking at it sometimes more often when it was switched off.

Arthur had attached the cables and we'd been watching a programme called *Z-Cars*. It was very entertaining, and Art was fairly transfixed by the television in general.

We got on fine at work, it was all very professional and American of course but there was a certain, what shall I say, blurring of job descriptions between work life and his increasing social visits which I welcomed and wished to continue.

He made me feel very safe and at ease. I was relaxed and we became great friends over these months. He was nothing but a gentleman at all times and bent over backwards to help me with anything around the house.

In particular, we watched a lot of television together; *University Challenge*, *The Twilight Zone* and *Animal Magic* – these were my favourites. Art liked the cartoons and of course the news and weather.

After asking tentatively whether it would be possible, I was able to borrow one of the spare IBM Selectrics from work. This was primarily to learn how to use the thing, but as I found a good use for it, Art said I could keep it for as long as I liked.

Merely as a practice exercise to begin with, just as some text to transcribe, I began typing up my memoir – *The Problems of Being Unique.* It was just something to do in the evenings if I couldn't find anything good to watch on any one of the three channels.

The machine had a 'Golf Ball' typing element, a metal sphere with all the letters of the alphabet, upper and lower case and all numbers and symbols and punctuation marks. You plugged it in to the mains and off you went … It was fantastic! Within minutes I was up to what must have been one hundred words per minute!

Shortly after returning from India, I'd started writing down my memories of Marie and my life on Primrose Hill. I'd started this project on the suggestion of Miyu and had stuck at it over the months of my moving house. Neither John nor even Miyu knew I spent at least an hour a day at this work, but I'd completed it, just days after arriving in my new home and it was great to now have it in this finished format.

It was something tangible, something real and artful even – a pile of freshly typed sheets of A4, in a wooden fruit box on the dining room table. I had made the stack as neat as I could, but each was curled slightly having been through the machine. Each was also now covered in black Courier type, characters and words and sentences and chapters and everything! It was my life story, at least the part of it which I could remember and meant the world to me.

There was a mini disaster one day when I opened the

French doors first thing in the morning and a huge gust of wind came in and blew my carefully stacked work all over the place! I spent several hours, it seemed, putting it all back in order as I had neglected to number the pages …

From that day on, to keep the pile flat and secure, I placed a large sheet of copper plate on top of it. This was exactly A4 in size, shiny and pinkish in places but all covered in blue-green verdigris in others, I don't know where it was from, or how it came to be so serendipitously to hand, but it was perfect for the task.

When I'd written the last words on the last page I looked at it for a few days. It gathered interest. I took it into work with the thought of seeing if I could get it bound and it sat in my desk drawer for a while. I felt proud of it every time I opened that drawer. But I knew I wanted somebody to read it and so one day, trying to be casual, I showed it to Art in his office just before my lunch hour. He was thoroughly impressed.

"Would you like me to read it?"

"I really hadn't thought about that. I've been so wrapped up with just the technical aspect of the typing itself …" I paused, he could clearly see how much this meant to me and how hard I was trying to conceal my nervousness about what he might think of it. He put me at my ease.

"I like reading. I mean I don't read a lot, I can't say that I'm 'well-read' but I like a good story. I like adventure stories mainly. You know, sort of fantastical things that happen in places far away. Does it have a good story?"

"Yes, yes, I think so. But it's not fiction you understand, it's my story, it's a real story."

"Well, those are the best, aren't they? It might take me a little while to read, I'm not a fast reader and I don't read for very long at a time because it makes me sleepy. In fact, I usually read last thing at night, to get me to drop off. It looks quite long, it might take me a month or so."

"The thing is, I only have this one copy. I wouldn't want coffee spilled on it or anything."

"Of course, of course. You could make a photocopy …! They've just installed a Xerox machine in the managing director's office, it would probably only take a couple of hours."

"Are you sure, it would be quite expensive …"

"Nonsense … the new machines work out at only four pence per copy."

"Yes, but there are 306 pages here!"

"Well, that's about 1,200 pence, 240 pence to the pound, it comes in at a nice even £5."

"As I said, it's quite expensive, wouldn't one have to account for a job of that size?"

"I'm sure I could arrange something, we could call it 'staff technical training documentation'."

"Well, I suppose, if you think that would be OK."

"I could pass it to Julie, that's Fred Fairlight's secretary this afternoon. She's very competent, and discrete of course. Plus, she's the only one who knows how to operate the thing."

"It's not going to chew up my lovely manuscript, is it?"

"I'm sure it will be fine Ana, but when it is copied, would you allow me to read it? I really would like to, very much and I am certainly not a critic of any kind."

"Yes, yes I would. That's very kind of you Art. Here, please, yes, you take it now and let me know what you think. It's a kind of memoir really."

"Oh, excellent! Wow … I could have it bound if you like. They have a new spiral binding machine which I believe can cut and bind up to four hundred pages thick, I've seen it, it's a monster!"

"Oh thank you, no. I like it just as it is … but the copy could be bound, it would make it easier for you to read, in bed."

"I'll give it my full attention. As I said, I er … do read quite slowly though, and there is rather a lot here, so it may take me a while to get to the end and er … report back."

"Take as long as you want and enjoy it. But don't leave the original on a bus or anything!"

"Roger that. Oh, Ana, that reminds me, have you had a chance to type up the risk assessment report for the water treatment plant yet?"

"No, not yet. I've been quite busy I'm afraid. I'll see to it straight away though. Thank you, Mr Armstrong. I best be getting along now."

"There's no rush really, please do it at your leisure."

"Have a good afternoon."

"Thank you, I will. Goodbye Ms Rondel, er, no need to shut the door."

34

Atlas Watches The Moon

The cover page read simply "The Problems of Being Unique, by Ananya Rondel" and was dated about a month previous to today: 16th May 1962.

I read Ana's story carefully and absorbed every detail of it, learning so much more about someone else than I had ever previously thought was possible. It did take a long time but eventually I finished and had thought of some nice things to say when I returned it to Ana the next day.

"I finished reading *The Problems of Being Unique.* I just wanted to return your manuscript."

"I thought you might have forgotten about it, sort of hoped you would have done really. Was it a load of pretentious rubbish?"

"Not at all, it's quite brilliant. I'm not an expert of course but have you thought of trying to get it published?"

"I had started to but I'm not sure if it's such a good idea or how I would go about doing that or even where to start."

"I had a friend who published something once, I could ask him about his experience."

"If you could, I'd be very appreciative. Art, would you like to come to have dinner, at my place, on Sunday?"

The look on Ana's face had changed a little. It was a nuanced difference but I was aware of it and she seemed to see this in my own look.

"Yes, that would be absolutely lovely."

"Great!"

She was instantly happy and turned to leave and walk away but then stopped suddenly.

"Is roast chicken OK?"

"Outstanding."

I had a very good day at work that day, even though I had a huge amount of unexpected paperwork to do because Gavin Stuart fell into the recently filled sewerage tank, breaking his arm during his unannounced safety inspection of the site.

Sunday was incredible. We discussed the content of Ana's book at length, and she invited me to the American Blues Festival which she wanted to see which was taking place in Manchester the next weekend.

I drove us up there in the Armstrong Siddeley Sapphire which was now back on the road and running smoothly.

We saw so many incredible musicians play. We kissed during the interval and had to find a bed and breakfast to stay in overnight. We had separate rooms, of course, but a certain amount of surreptitious late-night movement between them evolved. This involved torches, alcohol, squeaky floorboards and near misses with the elderly lady who owned and ran the place.

Driving back to Basingstoke the next morning, clearly everything had completely changed, and all after only eighteen months of having first met …

When we got back to Ana's house, the deal was sealed, so to speak, and the rest was just dotting the Is and crossing the Ts.

It was the October of 1962. Ana and I kept our liaison a secret at work, as best we could but word got around eventually, that I was soon to be moving out of my flat to somewhere more luxurious, somewhere with a little more space where I would be much happier in the company of the person who was the only one for me.

We set Christmas Day as a vague date on which I would move in and my visits to her house increased in regularity and duration, with me staying overnight quite often. We watched a lot of television, naturally.

Moving stuff around at her house one day in November, getting ready for this move, we came across a large wooden box. It was a heavily built thing of some age and looked to be custom built for some undefined purpose. It was perhaps three feet wide, four feet long but less than a foot in height.

"What is this?" I asked with some curiosity.

"I have no idea at all. I only saw it a few days ago for the first time, among all the other stuff in the spare room. It must be from the loft, in my old house, it must have been Aunt Marie's or something."

"Shall we have a look? It has a peculiar appearance to it, don't you think?"

Its hinges were made of old copper sheeting. They were covered in a rich dark blue-green patina, which only old copper can make. The steel bolt was stuck shut, but I banged it with a piece of wood I found nearby, and it freed itself.

Opening the dusty lid revealed a tightly packed array of neatly ordered cards, each perhaps four inches by six in size. I removed one.

"What is it?"

"That is called a 'punched card', Ana. I have seen them before, but not one so old as this. I think what we have here is an original Hollerith punched card, probably from the 1940s or maybe even the 1930s, I've seen one in a book before. And we have what looks to be thousands of them."

Ana had pulled one out herself and was now inspecting it.

"What are they for?"

"They're like … computer programs, very basic early instructions for a machine, a mechanical machine to perform numerical operations, adding, subtracting, multiplying dividing. Do you have any idea where these are from? Whose they were, originally, I mean?"

"Wait, these must be my mother's. Oh my god! No, really.

She worked with this guy, Aunt Marie told me about him, before the war, before she met my father. I think it was when she was doing her PhD in Manchester. He was studying the moon, predicting its position and phases into the future. My mother helped him with it. It was a big thing at the time."

"This is incredible Ana. Can I take this lot to Aldermaston? There's a guy there I know would love to have a look at these. He knows all about this kind of thing. He'll know exactly what they are. Would that be OK with you?"

"Sure, I'd love to know what they are for, take them away, look into it, that would be cool."

I loaded the box into the back of the Armstrong and after a phone call to Max Dent I took them up to AWRE and handed them over to him for his assessment.

He was quietly fascinated.

"Can I hold onto these for a while Arthur? I'll have a good look at them. I'll get back to you when I know a little more."

We had a few pints at The Hare and Hounds where I caught up on all the latest gossip and official secrets and then I drove back to Basing to start packing up my stuff, ready to move in with Ana.

I was to be made a permanent fixture there just before Christmas. We had Christmas Eve as a target but as it worked out I needed to go back to Aldermaston on that day as Max Dent had told me that he had had 'some success with your little project'.

I'd already moved a great deal of my things into Ana's house and there was not a lot of it in the first place. Already parts of my life were strewn around in her incredible house, which was still not fully finished.

Tradesman were coming and going daily it seemed. There were many ongoing 'alterations' which Mr Bagley had been asked to make. He was doing his best, but there were a lot of details which needed to be changed.

The problems were largely related to 'interior design'. I'd never heard of it before, but it seemed to be all the rage these days, at least so Ana told me. As far as I could see, it mainly involved the accumulation of materials intended to help one 'coordinate' the 'internal architecture' of 'a space' with the needs and 'aesthetic demands' of the 'human presence' within the 'habitat', with specific attention to the 'interface' between 'everyday expectations' and the requirements of one's 'modern lifestyle philosophy'.

These materials were many and varied. But once a 'look' had been settled upon, all one needed to do was choose the 'scheme' from many thousands of options. I was previously unaware of this facet of the world but now I understand, because it has been clearly explained to me, just how important it is to know the difference between seventeen available shades of lilac, and the massive psychological effect which hinges on the balance between these delicate decisions and choices. Mr Bagley has also been made aware of the vital nature of these matters.

Anyway, I'm able to drop the key to my rented flat off through the letterbox of my landlord tomorrow morning, Christmas Day. I then take the very last of my things over to Ana's. It's only ten minutes in the Armstrong, and that will be that.

I was thinking of turning up as Santa, but I couldn't find a costume at short notice.

The weather looks like it's about to turn and we might be in for a cold snap. I should be fine up to Aldermaston today, but the clouds are already completely overcast, and the temperature has already started to drop quite quickly.

Max had been using an old Burroughs Machine to decode the punched cards I had given him. He found it on site in one of the original old farm buildings which was used as a kind of depository for redundant machinery, broken equipment, spares, odds and ends, parts of cars that guys were working on, old office furniture that kind of thing. It was referred to as 'Aladdin's Cave'.

He knew it was there and he knew exactly where it was too, because he had put it there himself. Max was one of the first to be a part of the whole AWRE project and had brought this thing, this oversized cast-iron typewriter with him from Bletchley Park, where he had been stationed during the war. They had been using several of them as part of a rudimentary precursor to 'The Bombe' which was Turing's computer.

Max had resurrected the Burroughs with the help of some first-year apprentices who he ordered about like a drill sergeant. Now it sat in his study and he'd run every card through it, or rather he had given the task to several of the apprentices who had been taking it in turns, in shifts, on a continuous, twenty-four-hour basis.

Max Dent was a proper 'boffin'. He was last of the old school, and he was fascinated by the data he was finding on these punch cards, which he told me dated back to 1931.

His genius was such that he had now written a special program, in a language called ALGOL, with which he could run the data through ATLAS.

This program had only taken ATLAS a matter of nine days to process and Max had called with the exciting news that the printout of the results of his program had just been concluded. Would I like to come and have a peek at them?

We talked only briefly when I got there because unfortunately, he was called away as the Soviets had been doing some fly-bys in restricted airspace over Scotland and his presence was suddenly and urgently required elsewhere.

I was however able to take the printout away with me, having asked a strong-looking and eager apprentice to help me lift it and get it into the boot of the Armstrong.

The printout was a roll of paper, like a large toilet roll, except it weighed about 70lbs and the paper on it contained everything which had been on the punched cards plus a tabulated numerical analysis of their content, a translation of their meaning.

Before Dent was called away, he said in a rush that I should 'give it a once over' and let him know my thoughts.

What a Christmas present from the government I thought.

He turned as he left. "Naturally, you should not speak o anyone about this …"

"Naturally," I concurred.

I had loads of free time now, my visitors pass was for the whole day, and it wasn't even lunch time, so I decided to see if I could look up a few old friends.

I found Roger Stevens, from Instruments, tucked away on his own in a room where he was at his Radio Ham equipment. He was my friend who helped me set up the sound system for the Social Club Cinema and without really thinking about it, I made him jump out of his seat when I tapped him on the shoulder as I crept up from behind. He was wearing a huge pair of headphones which had large orange ear mufflers.

"Jesus! Don't do that! Arthur … Crikey … You scared the wits out of me!"

"Sorry, old boy."

"How the hell are you?"

"I'm fine, I was just tuning in to the cricket in Delhi, we're doing rather poorly I'm afraid. How are you?"

"Very well, thank you. Very well."

"What's it like, out there in the real world? I hear you got a job working some private gig with the Yanks."

"Elie Lillie, they're a pharmaceutical giant, very nice employers thank you very much, they are being very good to me, I've got my own office, with my name on the door …"

"Well, look at you!"

"How are things here? Have you kept the cinema up and running?"

"Of course old boy, we have a special showing of *White Christmas* tonight, you should stick around, come along."

"I'd love to, I really would but I've got to get back, it's about a girl, you know …"

"Oh, I see … is she pretty?"

"She is, very smart too. I'm a lucky man, I'm going to be moving in with her, tomorrow morning of all days and I've still got a lot of stuff to do. I would have loved to have stayed though."

"Hey, I think you've got your priorities just right my friend. I might be getting out of here myself soon. I met some Danish guys a few months ago at a surveillance seminar I got sent on. We talked audio stuff all night. Cool guys from a company called Bang and Olufsen. They're getting back into making Hi-Fi having had the rug pulled out from under them in the war. They need new designers, and they really liked my ideas, so it's Copenhagen a week on Friday for me, I might not come back!"

"Very pretty those Danish women, so I've heard …"

"Well, Arthur, this is what I'm saying. Here, check these out."

He handed me the headphones which had been around his neck.

"Listen to this …"

He flicked a few switches on the panel in front of him and some glorious classical music burst into life, filling my head, my mind, my body, my soul. I was completely and utterly blown away.

"Pretty good heh?"

"That is incredible!"

"That's just FM radio through a pair of modified tweeters I designed."

"The quality! It's like I'm there, or the orchestra is here … Ana would dig these to the moon and back."

"Who's Ana?"

"My secretary, the one I was telling you about. The one I'm moving in with tomorrow."

"Your secretary is your girlfriend!"

"Yes, well I knew her a while beforehand, it's a long story, it really is, she's not just my secretary …"

"Do you love her?"

"Absolutely, she's the most incredible person, she really is. I just need to show her, you know, really let her know, I know she knows, you know, you just know it when it happens you really do, but I want her to know that I know she knows. That's important in a relationship these days, don't you think?"

"Absolutely."

"God, I better go, I haven't even had time to get her any kind of Christmas present yet. I've got something in mind for her birthday on Boxing Day, but I've been racking my brain all day as to what to give her for tomorrow. I thought I might take one of those large boxes of paperclips from stores, wrap it up and give her that. What do you think?"

"Arthur, you can't do that!"

"Why not? It'll be OK, if Parsons is on duty, I'm sure he won't mind."

"No, you can't give the woman of your dreams a box of paperclips as a Christmas present …"

"Really … what, because they wouldn't have been paid for?"

"It's not exactly romantic, is it?"

"No, I suppose not."

"Give her those."

"These?"

"Yeah, you said she'd like them."

"They're pretty flash, Roger. Are you sure?"

"Hey, they're just a prototype, I've a few others I'm working on, better ones actually, take them. Let me know what she thinks of them."

"Thank you, really. Thank you. She's totally into her music, an incredible jazz pianist herself too …"

"Jazz, yeah, cool man, she sounds like a swinging cat …"

"She is man, she really is …"

35

The Big Freeze

On Christmas Day we didn't laugh much at all.

I arrived and Ana was stressed because of the dinner. Her new oven was playing up and she overcooked the turkey and burned it and was upset and angry. I didn't mind too much, I like my turkey on the dry side, a bit crispy, charred you might say.

There was nothing good on the television, not on any one of all three channels, except for the Queen's Speech at 3pm of course. She's very modern and forward-looking I feel, she talked at length about 'Telstar' quite a bit. It's the new communications satellite the Americans launched into space earlier this year. It can relay television pictures, telephone calls and telegraph images through space and gives us the first ever live transatlantic television feed.

Also, they've already got two IBM 1041 computers 'talking' to each other from two different places in America and the signal was relayed by another IBM 1041 in France! It's exciting stuff and the Queen's right on it. It's the future.

Later we opened the presents we had for each other.

Ana gave me a beautiful ceramic bowl she had made when she lived on an ashram in India before she met me. It was coloured with deep dark hues of blues and purples, mauves, magentas and vermillion. I was hypnotised by its magic.

She told me it was made in a traditional way by applying a series of underglazes and then more glazes, made from various metallic copper oxides.

I gave her the singing bowl and explained how I'd made

it just shortly before the first time we met. She was delighted with it, but I was really annoyed with myself because I couldn't find the wooden baton which went with it, so she couldn't even try it out. She consoled me and kept saying how incredible my craftsmanship was but still I was just disappointed. I knew it was somewhere.

The storm was worse than I had expected it might be and then there was a power cut. All electricity went in an instant.

It was blowing a gale. We went out to explore for a while with a bottle of champagne but that was a bit of a mistake too. We got so cold and it was no fun at all, the alcohol made it worse. I tripped over and hurt my ankle and Ana ripped her favourite coat on a piece of barbed wire as we tried to climb through it into the next field.

We tried to make the most of it but of course the heating had gone now too because it depended on the electricity, and we were really a bit miserable. On other days we might both have made more fun of the situation, but I was really tired and just wanted to sleep. It got dark early, and we went to bed.

We slept together in the same bed, as we had done often over the past couple of months, but Ana didn't sleep very well. She kept getting up in the middle of the night, which kept waking me up too.

When we woke from this disturbed sleep, I was excited because it was Ana's birthday. I wanted it to be a special day, naturally, but Ana really wasn't happy, not from the minute we got up. She was annoyed that she wasn't enjoying her birthday all morning and kept snapping at me, especially when I tried to cheer her up. I tried to keep a low profile for a while and did some odd jobs which needed doing around the house.

My first task was to get some heat into the place. I knew the system back-to-front and inside-out, as I had both designed it myself, and overseen the whole instalment. However, without electricity to power up all the new-style thermostats and timers, we were a bit stuffed.

I found a large canister of Calor gas in the garage and hooked it up to a stove burner, so we were able to have cups of tea and cook some basic food. We left the stove on low and eventually this began to provide a bit of heat with the doors closed as we isolated ourselves in the lounge.

36

Dates In A Moon Diary

While digging around for the gas cylinder, which I knew I'd seen somewhere on a previous occasion, I had to move a lot of other stuff to get at it.

One of these items was a huge leather suitcase, old with its leather all dry and cracked. It was quite heavy, and obviously full of something and as I lifted it up to get to the canister, I saw the initials 'C.R.' in large, embossed gold letters, more of a coppery colour in actual fact. I raised an eyebrow before locating the gas canister and going back into the house.

As I set up the burner, I mentioned it to Ana.

"I love that old suitcase you've got in the garage."

"What suitcase?"

"The big old leather one, was it your father's? It has his initials on the outside."

Ana looked at me.

"Really, I don't think I've seen that before. How big is it?"

"It's big, really big!"

"I definitely haven't seen that. That must have come from the Primrose Hill roof space. There's so much stuff the removal men just dropped in various places. I still haven't had a chance to look through it all, and it has his initials on it?"

"C.R. and it's full of something, it's pretty heavy."

"I want to see this."

She had me take her to it and wanted me to bring it inside.

I heaved it into the lounge. We were both wrapped up as warm as we could be with jumpers and coats and the like and Ana's mood had changed completely now. She started to become so excited, and nervous too, but I didn't realise this until she started opening it and had to stop herself. She took me by my hand.

"You do realise how strange this is for me Art?"

"I do, I do, it might be a bit of a surprise to you, whatever is in here. Of course it might just be a load of old shoes or something really … disappointing. You just don't know."

"I do know Art, it's strange, I have seen this bag before, I'm fairly certain of that, but not for probably … seventeen years, I think. I remember it from Kodaikanal. It was lodged in my memory somewhere, or it was until now, now I can see it. I think I know exactly what this is."

We opened it together. It was full of clothes but on top was a large leather-bound book, foolscap in size or maybe A4, but as thick as two inches. It sat there, like a mummy in a tomb, and when Ana removed it from the suitcase it left a perfect rectangular impression in the thick cotton dress it had been placed upon in 1945.

Ana was sitting cross-legged on the floor and placing it on her lap, opened it at its first page.

"It starts with a list. It's all dated." She read from it out loud:

Everything of Importance, From Today Onwards!

11th August 1932: Louis Armstrong plays the Nottingham Palais, and I'm there!

"That's the day they met, my parents, they met at that concert! That's what Aunt Marie told me. She must have started this diary not long afterwards."

"Maybe that's exactly the reason why she started writing it."

"Could be, could well be. It's actually quite a long list."

Ana flicked through the first few pages of it, scanning through it quickly. There's everything here … It goes all the way up to … it goes all the way to … the last date which is … my birth!

26th December 1939: Gave birth to Ananya in the Observatory. She came along early, the little rascal, with no warning at all! We love her as does everyone here of course and are calling her 'Ananya' as it is the Hindi word meaning 'Unique' but it is so funny, in the last week we have met so many local girls running around who are also called Ananya!

"That's the last on the list though, I don't get it … this must have been put in the bag just before I came to England, six years after this … But there's everything else here, leading up to me, all their time in Manchester … and then in London, in Primrose Hill … then there's a gap. Ah, this is when they must have left for India."

20th April 1939: Depart London for Karachi

25th April 1939: Arrive Karachi

26th April 1939: Karachi to Bombay by ferry

1st May: Arrive in Bombay

3rd May 1939: Callum and I made love in the grounds of The Taj Mahal Palace Gardens this afternoon. The sky was a beautiful dark orange colour.

"Honestly! What were they like!"

"In love just a little bit, I suppose."

"Yeah, I suppose a lot in love, but the following pages are all empty! Look."

Ana began to flick through them and then in a hurry went straight to the back of the notebook to the last page.

"Ah, no." She started at the end and worked forwards. "Why would you do that? Why would you start a diary at the back of a notebook? It doesn't make any sense."

"Maybe she was like you with your memoir, 'Where do you start when you can't start at the beginning?'"

"Maybe, or maybe she just wanted to put the thing she knew was the best thing last. There might be some really private things in here you know, you're not supposed to read other people's diaries."

"That's true, but this is very personal to you Ana. Perhaps you ought to read this in private without me here, so that you can be alone with your thoughts."

"That's sweet of you Art, it is and I know what you are saying, but honestly I've had enough of being alone with my thoughts for a lifetime, honestly I have. I'm going to read this very first entry out loud, from the top so to speak, if you're OK with it?"

"Well, if you want to but …"

"Look, its dated 11th August 1932. That's the concert, that's when they met. I'm going to go for it. Are you ready for this? Because I'm not sure that I am."

She began reading the diary entry in a nervous way to start but soon gained greater confidence as she found her voice.

So much has happened these last two days I must write it all down so as not to forget any of the details and so that I can enjoy the remembering of them as I write. I have already begun to feel that not to have kept a journal of any kind over the years is somewhat of an oversight. How many beautiful moments may have been left behind to dissolve in the wake of my progress?

I realise it is only by luck that I find myself putting words on these pages. They have found a home in this notebook but even this was something I came across by chance and with great fortune of timing.

I sit outside in the most ridiculous sunshine of a late November morning and think that maybe my mood has been affected by the mysterious forces of a new love. My word! What a concept! There was I believing the pull of the planets was inexplicably strong, that it was the moon which affected my emotions and that this unseasonably warm sunshine might be the only force sufficiently powerful to fill my soul with such joy. Phew!

I feel as though I have been transported to some magical exotic country where hope and happiness are as common as the earth and the air. I carry myself away now. The details I must recall to make some semblance or sense of this feeling, if such a thing can be done.

The day before yesterday was 10th August 1932, that was Wednesday. Mr John Leslie Comrie personally delivered the modified Burroughs Machine, as we'd agreed, so that I might begin work with the Hollerith cards.

He is a very intelligent and important man, Superintendent of the Nautical Almanac Office at the Greenwich Observatory in London. We will be using the Burroughs with Hollerith cards to implement his Fourier synthesis method to compute the motion of the moon between 1935 and 2000.

My job is to help him create the half-million cards needed for this enormous calculating project which he tells me will take a good six months to achieve. He has 'farmed out' the work and I am one of the lucky ones. The calculations, performed at Almanac Office itself, should then take an additional seven months to complete the work.

He came here, to my ground-floor flat, and parked on the road just outside. With the help of three other men, whom I believe were colleagues from Greenwich, it was carried into my front room, and it has been placed by the window for the good light there.

It is extremely heavy, I have no idea of the exact weight, but it is made almost entirely from cast iron, the stand and the casing at least, and they had quite a time negotiating its bulk through my shared front door and into my flat. It is however smaller than I had been led to believe, its weight clearly coming from its density, and looks somewhat like an oversized typewriter.

Mr Comrie then spent the best part of the next two hours instructing me in its operation while the other three fellows went to the ale house on the corner to recover from their exertions.

He has left me with a large wooden box of the blank Hollerith cards. It is about the size of a suitcase. This was also brought from the lorry with the aid of one of the slightly drunken helpers, before he finally left me alone in my home with the machine and the enormity of the task ahead.

Each card is 7" by 5". One at a time a card must be fed into the machine. The machine must then be set by means of the 'keyboard', for want of a better word, then the card is punched with its unique set of holes before being removed to make way for the next. This process takes approximately one minute per card. I have an identical but completely empty box in which to place each card after it has been punched, in the correct order of course. The black leather-bound book containing the codes for the cards has the size, weight, and presence of a formidable bible. However, on the front leather cover it has instead the words: Moon Data.

I must say I have maintained my excitement for this project with some enthusiasm, especially when conversing with Mr Comrie. However, now the scale of the project and my involvement in it has become more tangible, some of this enthusiasm has waned. Nevertheless, it is an important project, and I can apply myself to it wholeheartedly. I can't help feeling though that already the dubious merits of the cold moon are being replaced by a keener fascination for the sun and her warmth.

By bringing the machine to me, Mr Comrie hopes I shall be able to complete the task faster than if I were to visit the location where it was kept. With my own studies and work to be attended to, I agreed this was a logical plan.

Spending two hours a day with the machine, I estimate I can be finished by April. I cannot see that I'll be able to spend much more time than this without it affecting my PhD or my teaching duties. I must also give some lectures every week, which need to be prepared and then supervisions for my twelve students are taking up more time than I had envisaged when I agreed to accept this job of work. I will be paid, and this will be a great help, but it is not a lot of money. This work is of great value, I have no doubt about it. To be a part of this enterprise is a great honour for me, it will be beneficial for science in the future and my own career can only benefit in the long term.

Being at the forefront of the new Hollerith card technology is in fact quite an exciting prospect. I began yesterday morning, Thursday. There were a few abortive attempts to begin with, but there are more than enough extra blank cards to accommodate this. I soon got into my stride but it is quite hard work I must say, and noisy too! The buttons on the keyboard are very stiff. This may be due to it being a new machine, the latest model in fact, but I am hoping it will 'wear in' and become more 'operator friendly'. Currently I must push each key with some downward pressure with a finger and in fact my thumb seems better suited.

The handle which one uses to operate the punch to make the holes is sprung with a very substantial steel spring. The mechanical action requires some strength of arm to operate but I am now at fifty seconds per card on average and I hope to improve my technique even more over time. With a quick re-calculation I believe I may be able to finish as soon as May.

It is a means to an end after all, but what an incredible end it is. Comrie will use these cards by feeding them into another dedicated machine and in so doing create an accurate set of tables to predict the positions of the moon for the next hundred years. The mind boggles! When the cards are complete and have been run through his computer, the table is going to be published and will be available for all.

The technology is certainly impressive, but I cannot say that it is beautiful, at least to my tastes. In fact, I have already developed an embryonic fear that the prolonged use of such a device could be sufficient to cause the human operator to metamorphose in a machine themselves!

This is not a danger for me, as I have my music. Without music, where would I be? Is it not music, floating through, around and between all other arts which is the essence of humanity? I love it so and feel I owe so much to those who devote their souls to its creation.

Mr Louis Armstrong not the least! I am playing his record now and listening to the growl of his voice as it rasps its way through the notes and chords, the melodies, and the harmonies. What a man he is! I must pinch myself to wake from my dream of him, to believe that I have heard him and seen him only last night! Alive and dancing in his tuxedo, his spats sliding along the wooden floor and his trumpet always in his hand. He was only twenty feet away from me. His smile larger than life, his band lifting him up, it was so real, and he lifted me up with him. Just incredible!

One Night Only! Louis at The Nottingham Palais! And the man who sat down in the empty seat next to me just before it all began … What a dream … What a gentleman. He drove me home in his fabulous motor car today so that I wouldn't have to get the train. He lives so close by it hardly seems real … I'm only just back and my feet haven't touched the ground …

But I must collect my bicycle from the train station, it's a fair walk and it will be dark soon. I cycled there yesterday afternoon to get the train from Manchester to Nottingham and it has been chained up there, all alone, all night. I must eat something too. The landlady at the bed and breakfast where I stayed last night gave me a light tea before I walked to The Palais and Callum bought me a wonderful, cooked breakfast this morning before we drove home but I still feel so hungry. That's his name: Callum Rondel.

Ana had finished reading this first entry. She paused. The fingertip of her fore-finger had been tracing each word along the page and now it had come to a stop.

I had been listening closely to Ana's voice. I'd heard her read aloud before in the office, when she was reading back to me notes she had taken from meetings or summaries of my dictations. Then the timbre of her inflections had been business-like and even though the content usually related to very dry and sometimes technical and tedious matters, she would always sound bright and positive and would introduce humour whenever possible.

This was naturally different because she was involved on a powerfully emotional level. Nevertheless, her tones were calm and controlled, soft and rounded and fully aware that she would read this for the first time only once. She had been taking great care to read slowly and with perfect clarity.

Sophie was talking and Ana was listening to her mother as she spoke to her across a great distance and time. As I listened to this intimate moment, I was entranced more by the sounds of Ana's soft voice than by the content of the words which it created.

She looked up at me and a kind of short laugh eventually broke the bewilderment which had been on her face,

"Wow, I think you were right. I think she really wants something quite badly, I think she wants her man … Look it says, 'I still feel so hungry …!' Watch out Mr Rondel, looks like Mum has you lined up for lunch …"

I laughed. "That is incredible, what a way to meet. Did you know any of that?"

"Only that they met at a Louis Armstrong concert, that was it."

"Maybe you should read the rest of that on your own some time, you know quietly. It might get fairly personal."

"You're right. This is just weird, don't you think? That this bag must have been up in Aunt Marie's loft all this time with this in it. It's just been waiting, sitting there, unchanged since the day it was written."

She flicked through pages from the back of the book and stopped when they became blank.

"You know, it's actually almost full."

Then she shut it so suddenly with a bang that it made me jump out of the daze I was in.

"You're right, I'll read it later. I'm not sure I'm ready right at this moment to find out what the last entry in it might be. I don't want to get all sad and melancholic. It's my birthday! I keep forgetting!"

I had forgotten about this too, having been busy all morning and dealing with the heating and everything. Also, I had no idea how Ana felt about her birthday and didn't want to mention it until she did, but now that she had, I was able to give her my gift.

"Look, I have this thing for you, I was going to give it to you yesterday and then what with the snowstorm and everything else and me staying here, I thought I'd keep it for today. I hope you like it."

I retrieved the box from its hiding place behind the curtains and handed it to Ana.

"Ooh, now I am intrigued. You squirrelled that away rather surreptitiously."

"It's not a particularly er … feminine thing, I mean it's not exactly pretty or anything like that."

"Now I really I am curious …"

"I mean I don't think it will have a bad smell as such, it's just not soap or perfume or anything like that."

Ana pulled on the string to undo the oversized bow I had made. She did this carefully and painfully slowly as she smiled and then ripped open the brown paper wrapping.

"I know what these are … Just what I've always wanted. Ear defenders! I've seen the builders using these when they've got their pneumatic drills going."

"They're headphones, for music. Custom-made too. Try them on."

"Really, oh my word! Really, for music …"

"Yep, for music, you'll be able to hear music in a whole new way."

She put them on, the large yellow ear defenders from which they had been made standing out like large breakfast bowls from either side of her head.

"How do I look?" she shouted.

I laughed. "Fairly ridiculous actually, but that's not the point, it's the quality of the sound that's important and with these you have some top-end miniature speakers from a company called Bowers and Wilkins … they're the very best. Roger is a friend of mine from Aldermaston, he was the one who made them up from some radio equipment he had."

She pulled one ear defender to one side,

"Sorry, what was that? Can't hear a thing you're saying, old boy!" She let it snap back over her ears.

"I love them! They're amazing! Thank you, Art. Best present, I ever had!" she was shouting again and I laughed.

"I won't have to listen to that damn dog barking anymore!"

She got up and walked over to the mirror in the hall.

"I look amazing!" she was shouting a little louder now, I imagine because she was as many as twelve feet away from me.

She walked around for a while and then took them off.

"Thank you, Art, thank you. I've honestly never had a present like this before. I've got nothing for you though."

"Don't be daft, it's not my birthday, it's yours!"

"I know, but thank you."

She kissed me on the cheek and then distracted herself by looking through the rest of her mother's suitcase.

"It's probably just mainly clothes I imagine, look at these, my god!"

She held up a rather large pair of silk knickerbockers.

I couldn't control myself and burst out laughing. "It was the 40s, I'm sure they were very fashionable back then."

"You could get more than a couple of parachutes out of these, I bet!"

She kept looking and then …

"Hey, wait a moment, what's this?"

From the bottom of the suitcase, she removed a record. It had no cover but was in a square sleeve made of thin plain brown card with a circle cut out of the middle so that you could see the record label. When Ana read the name on the label, she let out a huge sigh.

"I remember this … I can't believe it though. I have to play it right now."

She removed the black disc from its sleeve immediately and placed it on her turntable.

"What is it?"

"You'll see, or rather you'll hear. It's a 78." She flipped the speed selector. "It's shellac, they're really thick and heavy and you only get about four minutes on each side. It's in quite a bad state too, prepare yourself for a few scratches and crackles ..."

Switching it on and setting the turntable revolving, Ana placed the needle onto the spinning grooves with an ease and care made perfect by the practice of doing this many thousands of times over. It made contact with a quiet pop and crackle and then Ana increased the volume. The crackle became louder and was now accompanied by a low-pitched hiss and hum which seemed to go on forever.

"You just listen to this," she said. "It was recorded in 1930. Mr Louis Armstrong, 'Blue Turning Grey Over You'."

It began. I was taken to a place, somewhere in 1930s America, where I imagined the Great Satchmo must have stood in a studio to record this as a permanent gift to culture for all time. The sounds of the piano and his trumpet easily traversed that time and space and when he began to sing, he really was here, in this room with the two of us.

He is still alive and I knew this because we had seen him just recently on the television. Somewhere, I thought, he is singing right now and moving people with his songs. People are dancing and smiling because of him.

Ana and I were looking at each other across the width of the lounge as the words of this song filled the air between us.

Gee, how I miss
Your tender kiss,
And the wonderful things we would do.
Now I run my hands
Through silvery strands
You left me blue turning grey over you.
You used to be
So good to me
That's when I was a novelty.

Now, you've new friends in view,
You've found someone new,
And left me blue turning grey over you.

As he sang to us, I realised Ana was not just here with me and him, she was also in Kodaikanal and she was remembering hearing this music as a child.

When the song finished, she took the needle from the record and smiled that funny smile again.

"You remember it?"

"Yes, I can remember it very clearly, very clearly indeed, I can remember all the words, I can remember the melody and the tune and the feeling. Hang on. I want to try this. I have to do this. The headphones …!"

I handed them to her and she plugged the chord into the amplifier.

"You might have to be a bit careful with the volume, I'd turn it down to start with if I were you."

She put them on and played the record once again. I sat in silence now as using the headphones cut out the sound to the loudspeakers, but in this quietness I felt perfectly invited to watch her listen. Now she was lost in her very own private world, and I could only imagine what it was she saw playing in front of her mind's eye as memories came back to her. Not, that is, until she began talking to me, as she was listening … She was not shouting, I think she may have believed she was whispering to herself but I could hear her voice clearly at its normal talking volume.

"It's my birthday, I am six and I am dancing with mother on the lawn just in front of the telescope in the morning sunshine. I am dancing to this song, playing from this very record on the gramophone on the porch. She is spinning me around and around and around in my white and orange birthday dress. It's not real, it isn't. But it is, she gave me the glass prism which she took from the solar telescope and I'm playing with it, its light

is on the whitewash on the side of the building, a stretched-out rainbow which I paint on the wall. We are walking along the path now, by the house and we are walking along the edge of the forest, to my piano lesson with Mrs Singh. We arrive, my mother leaves, I put the prism on top of the piano and I start to play."

'Blue Turning Grey Over You' has ended and Ana returns to her sense of the room we are both in, removes the headphones, takes the needle from the record, and turns the Hi-Fi off. I'm not sure what I will say to her but fortunately she says something at last and it's a really good idea.

"Art, this is just way too much! Let's get out of here for a bit for heaven's sake! I don't care if it's blowing an Arctic storm out there, I need something else, something that's not happening in my head from seventeen years ago!"

"I'm with you Ana, whatever you want, it's your birthday. Let's just go!"

So, we put on every piece of warm clothing we had and we went out to be explorers in the Arctic wasteland world of Old Basing in the deep December winter of Boxing Day 1962.

37

Left-Handed Mirror Writing

We arrived back at No. 29 around 4pm, the sun was setting now but it was not something one could really see. When I looked to the west it was marginally lighter than to the east but the white-out which still surrounded us would soon be blackness. The falling snow was so thick with its enormous snowflakes that we could hardly see beyond ourselves.

Ana had been thoughtful to leave both the outside light and the kitchen lights on so we could actually find the house, and our way to the front door.

There was no wind at all, none. Following the initial snowstorm, which was full of blustery gales, the wind had now vanished. It was so incredibly quiet too and eerie in this light as Ana tried to find her front door key. She had to take off a glove to get her keys out of her pocket. Fumbling with them she said, "My fingers are frozen solid!"

The car was buried, looking like a small hummock with a shape revealing few clues to an unknowing observer as to what might lay underneath. Thinking of this brought to my mind the computer printout which was still in the boot, I had not thought of it once since I had put it there.

"I'm going to see if I can get the car open, there's something I brought with me I've completely forgotten about."

"Do you remember which way round you parked it?"

"I've got a fifty-fifty chance, I think I'll try that end first. Wish me luck!"

She had managed to get the key in the door and went in.

"OK. I'm going to make a cup of tea."

"All right, I may be some time …"

"Are you sure you've got the right pile? It's not that one over there? I'll shut the

door, to keep the heat in!"

"OK, if I'm not back in an hour or so, send out a search party."

Ana shut the door behind her with a soft thud. Suddenly the quietness seemed to be amplified with only my own sounds for company as I waded through the drift towards what I hoped was my car.

Clouds of condensation caught the light from the kitchen in the stillness of the windless air around me full as the slowly falling snowflakes made the last part of their determined journey from the heavens to Earth. They were so fat and floating down in lines so improbably straight and parallel that I had to stop for a moment to think about it. Perhaps because of their great size they were unusually heavy, heavy for snowflakes that is. If they were people, they would have been dainty sumo wrestlers descending as happy buddhas from a peaceful nirvana.

We really should not have taken the bottle of champagne with us. It had made me top-heavy, and wobbly with it. This contributed to my already difficult quest, and I fell on at least three occasions as I sought to clear the Armstrong of its covering. With the aid of a small sheet of plywood I found by a wall on one of these unplanned deviations to the ground, I managed to locate the boot.

The catch was a little stuck but when I yanked it the boot came open and I was able to retrieve the box. By the light of the kitchen window, I caught sight of the carved wooden baton which went with the singing bowl. It was still wrapped in its cloth but had somehow slipped down into a gap next to the spare tyre. With an instant smile I picked it out and put it in my coat pocket. Shutting the boot, I made my way back to the front door, careful with my footing so as not to fall again and send the paper roll into the elements.

Using a risky manoeuvre, my forefinger extending from one hand while still gripping onto the box, I was just able to ring the doorbell which had been mounted at a ridiculous height. Ana appeared and opened it but for a moment looked at me as if she had no idea who I was.

"Come on, let me in, I can't hold this much longer, my fingers are about to fall off!"

"Not today, thank you Santa. I'm sorry but you've missed Christmas completely. It was yesterday, you're late! Try being on time next year! Anyway, we don't need any more boxes in here, we're all stocked up!"

And she shut the door in my face. I was left standing without the ability to make any thoughts. She opened the door again quickly and was laughing.

"What are you doing out there? Come in you idiot, you'll freeze to death out there."

The last of the champagne had obviously gone to her head too. I went in and put the box down on the kitchen table. Ana had made the tea and was very excited, "Come and have a look at this, I've found something incredible."

Ana had the tea all set up on the coffee table in the lounge. She was insistent that I sit down.

"Just look at this will you … I was going to turn the record over because I had no idea what was on the B-side. So I turned it over and it's called 'The Song Of The Islands'. Now, I don't remember the title at all, and I haven't played it yet, because I want you to hear it too but I picked up the record sleeve and found something crazy on the other side of it. Look, what do you make of it?"

She handed me the brown paper sleeve and then went over to the turntable. As she set the B-side of the record in motion, I was distracted for a moment as I noticed there were some slices of Battenberg cake next to the tea pot.

"May I take one of these?"

"Yes, yes, of course, of course, but look!"

I took a slice with one hand and looked at the sleeve. The music began playing. There were no lyrics to it, only a lovely slow instrumental melody with Louis adding a few of his characteristic vocal improvisations.

Written in dark blue ink, in immaculate neat handwriting on the ten-inch-square sleeve in my hands was a spiral of words. They were written inside the circular impression formed by the record it had contained for the last forty years, the record which was now playing. The words ran in a near perfect spiral whorl towards the centre.

The words themselves were tiny, perfectly formed and in perfectly spaced lines just as the groove of a record. Whoever had written them had done their best to pack them in together just as tightly as they could, and they had done a pretty good job.

With the words so small and the sentences so carefully parallel and close, there must have been forty or more lines, counting from the outer to the centre where the cut-out circle meant they could go no further.

"I can't read it," I said.

"That's my father's writing, I'm sure of it. I have a letter written by him to my solicitor and it's the same handwriting, but here, look … The writing … it's written backwards!"

It was true. The words had been written back to front.

Ana poured the tea. "I can't read it all either."

I looked more closely. "We need a mirror."

Wait there," Ana hurriedly fetched her mother's Aranmula mirror. "Try this, will it work?"

"Of course it will, I'm sure it will. Can you just polish it a bit, it's a bit blurry."

She gave it a quick buff with a soft cloth which she found close by, and the mirror came up quickly to a brilliant shine.

Holding it up to the script at a particular point where the words began on the very outer edge, they began to reveal themselves in a readable way, but I was immediately confused. I had a mouthful of Battenberg as I tried to think.

The first word I read in the mirror was 'prism' with a full stop.

My head was itchy and I realised I was still wearing my woolly hat. I took it off and had a good scratch with my left hand from which I then ate the final mouthful of Battenberg I was holding in it.

I looked at my own left hand, and holding the record sleeve at arm's length with my right, looked at the spiral and turned it around before looking at it up close again.

"Was your father left-handed?"

"He was, my mother too. Is that important?"

"I think it might explain this, maybe ... I'm just trying to work out what it is."

"My Aunt Marie told me that when she had met my father and saw him and my mother together as a couple for the first time, she had said to them that they were a couple of lefties who would probably never be able to do anything right!"

"Ha! I thought so. You know Leonard Da Vinci was left-handed and he sometimes wrote in mirror writing. It's thought he might have done it as a basic way of keeping his ideas secret, but some left-handed people take to it naturally, so that they don't smudge their words as they write. Their problem is that the left hand smudges the wet ink as it moves along behind it. They have to learn how to hold the pen differently, sort of over-the-top I think."

"Art, I'm 'one of them', I'm left-handed as well, it runs in the family I suppose."

"Ah, I see, OK. Then you know about the smudge thing."

"Yep, I know about that, but I didn't know about the mirror thing."

"Ah, OK."

"But, you know, even if he was right-handed, and started on the outside, and wrote clockwise towards the centre, he'd get all cramped up as he got towards the middle. It wouldn't smudge as he went along to start with, but he'd have nowhere to rest his hand as he got towards the middle and thenn he'd smudge everything else that he'd already written. It would become a horrible mess! He must have started on the inside, wrote left-handed and turning the sleeve clockwise worked his way outwards. It's inside out and back-to-front!"

"Obviously, quite obviously. You're quite right, of course it is."

The text was written from the centre, outwards. I held the mirror in my right and tried to rotate the sleeve anticlockwise with my left as I went.

"Do you need a magnifying glass?"

"Yes!"

As Ana went to her desk to fetch a magnifying glass, the music came to an end. Just three and half minutes but the feeling of it, which had a kind of exotic, almost Hawaiian flavour, seemed to stay in the room.

Ana gave me the magnifying glass and I attempted to read the spiral as I turned the sleeve. It didn't work too well.

"I've sort of got my hands full. Can you do the turning?"

"Hang on, I've got an idea."

Ana took the sleeve, walked over to the Hi-Fi, and placed it on the turntable. I followed her over to it.

She rotated the record slowly and I read out loud in my best reading voice, low and quiet, trying to keep steady as the words which her father had written so long ago came to life.

38

Our Spinning Prism Dancer

You have just taken Ananya to bed. A few moments ago, I found her in the hallway, she was spinning around barefoot on the wooden parquet flooring. The steps she made as I watch her dance are small and quick and all a blur. Her tiny feet are making sticky noises. I think Indira spilled some lemonade there earlier during the party on the otherwise highly polished surface which she must have forgotten to clean up. Most unlike her to have forgotten such a thing, I can only imagine she must have been distracted by a more pressing duty. It is a sound that would be incredibly annoying for most adults but to Ananya as she whirls in circles, she might find it to be deliciously new. Held above her head is the glass prism Sophie gave her for her birthday. The setting sun is warm and orange and finds its way here through a gap in the trees opposite the Observatory. Its beam travels through the window above the front door, into Ananya's prism and throws her stars and rainbows everywhere. She is lost in its spirit within her delirious rotations, a rhythmic sticky dance in time with pulsing lights. She is a tiny lighthouse, her rotating beam a beacon of happiness lighting every corner of her world. A sphere of her own energy, within herself but surrounded by a larger space too. I am in this world now, her world, hypnotised. Was she aware I was there? She slows and brings the prism down in front of her eyes, slightly lower still, until she is gazing deep into its heart. She has found something intense there, slowly shifting her look this way and then the other. Bringing it closer and then holding it at arm's length, finally she brings it up very close to one eye. Is she looking straight through it? No, her gaze is fixed on a point inside; an imperfection, an inclusion, a crack, or a bubble has seized her attention. She has stopped moving and is standing completely still. The two of us are standing only ten feet apart. Ananya is a whole world as a person, as a world she is Earth. A vision of the world where we live, its light, its sky, the painterly strokes of it clouds, so thin and delicate running through the life-giving atmosphere, the aura around her soul. The Earth on its axis, she spins again with a joyful, carefree style, the natural beauty of her face only the surface layer of even more beautiful depths. Ananya is in the core of her Earth. A swirling, revolving molten flux, spinning an invisible magnetism field around us all, protecting life from the naked power of the sun. Outside and around her, the mantle contains her energy and protects her unique life. For her, I am this protection. She will always need me. I call to her, softly, hoping not to startle her or wake her from her daydreaming, "Ananya …" She looks up at me with a very serious expression on her face which immediately turns to cheeky laughter. She comes into my study and I give her the little copper cymbals I made for her, to go with her mother's prism. She is delighted and can't decide how to play with both at the same time. I also show her the new passport I have for her. I open it and she holds it but when I tell her she will be able to use it in only a few days' time, when all three of us go to England she drops it on the floor and asks, "Why do we have to go to rainy Old England for a holiday when we already live in Paradise!?" I love you and her so much Sophie, you will always make me spin just as the day our Ananya was conceived, under the copper moon eclipse … in the gardens of The Taj Mahal Hotel … on that balmy summer afternoon. Your love keeps me dancing, and Ananya too! … Cx

39

Islands In A Paper Ocean

Ana was quiet. When I finished reading, she went upstairs for a while. But when she returned there was no trace of tears or sadness, perhaps she had just wanted to be alone for a while to fully absorb her father's words.

When she came down the stairs, she smiled at me and shook her head in slight disbelief.

"It's rather a lot to take in."

Nevertheless, she had already picked up her mother's diary again and opened it at the list written in the front. She read out the entry of the 3rd May 1939.

Callum and I made love in the grounds of The Taj Mahal Palace Gardens this afternoon. The sky was dark and reddish orange in colour, like molten copper.

Ana was shocked. "Honestly! How many people know exactly how and when they were conceived? I'm not sure it's right to have such a fact in your imagination!"

"But if you did find something like that out, The Taj Mahal Palace Gardens in the afternoon under a dark orange sky is not such a bad way to get started in life. I mean I can think of worse ..."

Ana was playing with a smile but had tears in her eyes too. I went over and sat down next to her on the piano stool.

"Are you OK?"

"I'm fine, really I am. So do you think that he loved her then?"

"I think that's a fairly safe bet. He loved Ananya, he loved you. I couldn't write like that, not in a million years."

Ana still looked very sad to me though, still tinkling away on a few keys, single notes sounding out softly.

I sensed she was caught in a place inside herself but that she was so nearly free. I wanted to help her find her way to let go of the trauma and loss of her life. None of the circumstances of her troubled past were her fault but they hung so heavy in her soul and cast a shadow across her heart. I would do anything to bring light to it but was reaching a point where I was clutching at straws with these efforts.

It felt, as we sat there at the piano so close to each other, that there was at least one thing I could do. I put my arm around her, she rested her head on mine and a fine thought came to me.

"I was thinking. I know you were born during the war, but you were actually conceived before it, so technically speaking you're not what one would call a 'War Child'. I mean, you're not like me in that respect. You can quite rightly call yourself a Child of Peace. That's kind of cool, isn't it?"

"It is, yes, it is, that's true. You know I like it when you speak technically Art, I do."

She perked up immediately and gave me another kiss and by her doing so I remembered something I'd forgotten completely. I stood up quickly from the stool.

"I've got something to show you, I haven't even looked at this myself yet. It's hot off the press! I've got the printouts!"

"Printouts? What printouts?"

"From ATLAS! The moon predictions from the punched cards … the ones I took to Aldermaston, remember?"

"Wow!" Ana stopped her absent-minded playing with the piano keys and was immediately alert. "That was sneaky of you. When did you get those?"

"Yesterday, I drove to Aldermaston and picked them up, just before it started to snow."

"Is that what's in the box?"

Ana jumped up with new energy, went to the kitchen and came back with another bottle of champagne.

"I've been saving this. Stupid to save things like this for too long, don't you think? Besides, it is my birthday after all, I mean, come on!"

Within moments she'd popped the cork with a degree of practiced finesse, and we had some beautiful French, cut lead-glasses of Aunt Marie's charged and ready for her toast.

"To the energy of the sun, the copper in the earth and jazz in the moon!"

We drank and soon I had the box open. Sitting on the carpet with the huge roll of printed paper in front of us, I felt the need for some decorum and the need to be serious for a moment.

"Max, told me that the program began calculations from the position of the moon at noon on 1st January 1935 and it goes all the way through to the last day of 1999."

"Is that because no one knows for sure if the world will actually end on that day?"

I looked at her with a very serious face and she just smiled.

"It just means that the last data is from the day of the 31st December 1999."

"That's the day of the apocalypse, Miyu told me."

"Well Miyu is crazy."

"No more so than anyone else. I should think just one of your little atomic weapons going off, evening accidently could prove her right."

"I get it, I do, she's not crazy, I didn't mean that. I always forget about the Japanese thing. I don't think she likes me that much."

"What are you talking about, she thinks you're great!"

"It's just sometimes she really grills me you know, about my 'motives' behind going to Aldermaston."

"She just likes keeping you on your toes. She's very protective of me too."

"Yeah, I know. What's she doing over Christmas?"

"Well tonight she's playing some rather complex Classical music to a rather large audience on a rather large Steinway parked right in the middle of the stage at the Royal Festival Hall."

"Wow… I didn't know that."

"You didn't ask."

"I'm sorry, I know she's your best friend, I should be more interested."

"Heh, don't worry about it. You've got me to think about all the time, right?!"

"Right, that's it!"

"Isn't all this stuff highly classifiable, or classified, or whatever?"

"I shouldn't have any of this at all. If Max were found out about this he'd be in big trouble. If I was found with this, I don't know what they would do to me."

"What would they do, to you that is? I mean specifically, what's the er … process for someone who has, er … effectively committed high treason?"

"As I said, I don't know."

"Would they do anything do me? I mean just because I'm with you, and because the classified data is in my possession, on my property."

"I don't know, really I don't. But it doesn't bear thinking about what they might do."

"Who are 'they' anyway?"

"Be quiet, just listen, please, I'm trying to explain something."

"I don't know, men, they just love explaining stuff to women, there should be a word for it. OK. I'm listening, explain away."

"So, that's the date, and that next number is the moon phase, one to eight for the eight phases. Which are …?"

"Waxing crescent, first quarter, waxing gibbous, full moon, waning gibbous, third quarter and waning crescent."

"Precisely, well done, ten out of ten, eight out of eight I should say, and zero is for a new moon. So, anyway we have to go backwards."

"We seem to be doing a lot of that lately."

"Shh …!"

"Backwards, back-to-front, inside out! Honestly, I don't know what the world is coming to! We'll be spinning the other way round in a minute. You may continue."

"Thank you, I'm trying to."

"So we start with the apocalypse."

"Yes, we start with the apocalypse, which is an … eight!"

"So that would be a … waning crescent."

"That's it, nothing very auspicious about that I don't think, an eight, I mean in terms of the likelihood of the end of the world!"

"True, in fact the number eight signifies balance. The vibrations of the number eight are similar to the vibrations of the planet Earth. The intensity and power of eight's energy can never be underestimated. Eight is also the lucky number of symmetry, which symbolises order. Maybe we'll get lucky and avoid the apocalypse altogether."

"Let's hope so."

"And eight notes in an octave of course."

"Of course."

"Maybe music will save the world. Why don't we try to find out what the moon is today?"

"Good idea."

With some difficulty we started to unroll the roll. However, the paper was so thin and the roll was massive and unwieldy.

I made a quick calculation in my head. One hundred years times 365 days per year, 36,500 lines of data. Plus a few more because of leap years and their leap days.

We finally realised the best thing was just to roll out the whole thing around the room, stopping every now and then to see where and when we were.

When we found ourselves by the drink's cabinet in the corner, we found out that Ana's birthday next year on 26/12/1963 would be a three: waxing gibbous.

Near the kitche door we found my next birthday, which was going to be on 1/7/1963, I was going to be twenty-eight and it would also be waxing gibbous.

Somewhere near the armchair in the other far corner we found today, 26/12/1962. It was another eight, waning crescent and Ana was a little bit disappointed.

"Is that it, a waning crescent!"

"At least it's not a new moon, a zero, you should think yourself lucky, at least you've got something!"

"I was rather hoping for something, a bit more … full perhaps."

"There's just no pleasing some people. What's next? So what was the date of your birth?"

"26th December 1939, twenty-three years ago this very day! But I want to see my sixth birthday first."

"OK, that's 26/12/1945, let's roll!"

We rolled for quite a while and as we got close Ana realised …

"Well, here's the 27th, the day they died, eight: waning crescent and my sixth birthday on the 26th… seven: last quarter. Not that interesting I suppose. Come on, what about the day I was born. Let's keep rolling, I don't particularly want to linger around here for too long."

Eventually we arrived at the day Ana was born in Kodaikanal, and she started getting quite excited before being disappointed once again.

"Roll on 26/12/1939 is a … it's another eight, another blooming waning gibbous! This is getting boring, I'm getting tired of eights."

"I thought eight was lucky."

"Yes, it's lucky, it just seems to be frequently occurring, rather common one might say …"

"How about the day you got started? That day in the gardens of The Taj Mahal Hotel … do you want to have a look at that?"

"All right, let's see what the moon was up to when Mum and Dad were otherwise engaged. The poor moon probably had to watch the whole thing from up there."

"What was it, the date?"

"3rd May 1939."

"A great day, I'm sure. That is 3/5/1939. We're just rolling back the years now …!"

"Very good. Very clever … Very funny."

"It comes easy to me …"

"You're not as funny as you think you are. Come on Armstrong, get on with it."

We were right next to the television set, a lovely thing which Ana's Aunt had bought several years ago, I think it was made by a French manufacturer, it certainly didn't look British. When we arrived at what must have been a most wonderful day for Ana's parents, and not just for the obvious reason. It was a four and Ana was ecstatic.

"Four! Full moon! Jackpot! I knew there was something about me. That's amazing! I can call myself a proper lunatic now. What are the asterisks for?"

Next to the number four there were two asterisks followed by the number two.

"Er … that means there was an eclipse on that day. One asterisk is an eclipse of the sun, two is an eclipse of the moon."

"Really? Are you sure? The moon was in eclipse?!"

"Yep, according to this, that's what two asterisks means."

"That is far out …"

"Yes, it is very far out. Looks like the Earth had to come between the moon and the sun for you to be … to become even possible! Well I never…!"

Ana rocked backwards.

"Yep, but look, there's more, if the number next to it was a one, then it would have only been a partial eclipse, but it's a two so it was actually a full lunar eclipse the day you were, er … dreamt up."

Now Ana lay on her back completely, arms outstretched by her sides. The rolling reams of paper with their perforated edges filled the entire floorspace of the large room. It was a chaos of rolled-out paper sprawling in undulating mountains and creasy folded valleys. I felt like we were in the aftermath of a giant ticker tape parade.

"Art … It's just too much … way too much. What do you think it means?"

"I'm not sure what it means, if it means anything at all. I'm sure an astrologer would have a field day with you. But it would certainly explain the copper colour of the sky that day though. A full moon in eclipse is a kind of an orangey red I've heard, I've never seen one myself though."

"Just imagine it …"

"Maybe that's the reason why they gave you the name they did … Shall we look at the moon for the day your parents actually met, at the Louis Armstrong concert?"

"I can't take anymore, I'm too tired. It was probably a total eclipse of the sun and a lunar eclipse and the planets were all aligned, and Halley's Comet did a fly-by just for good measure."

"You're right, it's probably quite late. What time is it exactly?"

Ana sat up and I realised how tired I was too. Sitting cross-legged a foot or so apart, we were gazing around the lounge. We formed an island in the centre of the room and surveyed the ocean of paper waves we had created which surrounded us on all sides.

When my look came to rest upon hers, she had a sleepy smile on her face.

"I want to show you something. Come with me."

We stood and tried our best not to trip as we attempted to navigate across the treacherous crests and troughs of the paper seas between us and the safe land of the hall. I held onto Ana for balance to stop myself from being dragged under, engulfed, and swept down into the papery depths.

We made it across the lounge accompanied by bouts of uncontrollable laughter and reached the harbour and the beach at the bottom steps of the stairs.

Ana took me by the hand and started upstairs but I stopped in mid-step when I spotted the singing bowl which Ana had placed next to the piano.

"Hey, wait a minute," I said.

"Where are you going? Come back! You can't get away that easily."

"Just wait there, I'm not jumping ship, I just remembered something."

As I went solo back into the abyss, Ana called out after me. "I'm going up to the Observatory, I'll see you up there."

"OK. "

I went to the kitchen and on the table found the fabric bundle containing the singing bowl baton. I picked it up, and on the way back turned the downstairs lights off as I went. I was in the darkness for a while, lost at sea and my rate of progress through the paper was slow but now I had a kind of technique which involved lifting my knees up high. I collected the bowl on my way past the piano and breathed normally with relief once I was on my way up the stairs, the bowl and the baton carefully gripped in my hands.

Ana was in the observation room, which was softly lit by a single lamp, in one corner. She had made a bed for us from several duvets, blankets, and an incredible number of pillows of every size.

"You just did this?"

"No, I came up here and sorted it all out earlier."

"Wow, it's beautiful."

We walked together, held each other close and kissed.

She stopped and looked at me in her funny way again.

"Nice and cosy up here, don't you think?"

"Mmm, whoever installed this heating must have known what they were doing."

"Mmm, I turned the radiators on to full and they've come up hot straight away."

"Ahh, I expect that's something to do with the clever design of the immersion heater and the innovative thermostat of course."

"Probably that."

"Maybe we should shut the skylight though. It's letting all the heat out."

"But I just opened it, I wanted to let some snowflakes in."

"Well, it's your heating bill. I found this."

Handing her the roll of material, she unwrapped the baton and looked up at me with a smile and laugh.

"Ooo … What is it?"

"It's the baton, for playing the bowl. I found it next to the spare tyre in the car."

"How cool is that! Can I see it?"

"It's really cool actually. But let's see if it works, shall we? I wouldn't get your hopes up. When I tried it just the once I couldn't get a note out of it. I think it's probably one of those things that requires a certain amount of skill and a great deal of practice."

We got comfortable wrapped up in the duvets and without any more talking Ana began trying to make music with the bowl. It didn't take her long to create a low sustained note, then a higher one, then yet another.

Ana's touch forms a steady note which finds its way straight to my soul. Her natural skill seems innate and produces a clear and pure tone which grows with subtle intensity as the voices of the bowl's overtones become one.

At first there is only a low fundamental wave, then a mid-tone harmonic appears and then these two harmonise with a further slightly higher tone. I am spellbound by the sound of the vibrations being created and a sensation of humming within my body begins to relax me deeply.

Ana is entranced too, although the meditative state which she effortless acquires seems to be focused. She is concentrating intensely on something within herself, then quietly and softly she begins to speak, in not more than a whisper at first.

40

Languages Of Love

The sounds of the words are calm but there is something in them which gives me the idea they have been hidden in dark shadows. I am looking at her mouth as it makes the shapes needed to form the strange sounds of a language I have never heard before. Her neck muscles are slightly strained to begin with, as if the meaning the words come from a place of a pain.

As she grows more familiar with these words, as they start to flow more freely, she begins to relax. It seems she has discovered a strong light which was previously hidden from her and this is making her become visibly happier and carefree and her words change, or at least the way she speaks them changes, as they become more of the words of a melodic song. Fusing with the song of the bowl, her music begins pouring from her, through the open skylight into the night and upwards towards the moon.

With my head made fuzzy by the champagne, my eyes close naturally to the lyrical song. Ana's voice is soft and undulating now, playful and young, warm and slow.

Was Ana reciting a poem, telling a story, saying a prayer? As the sounds of the bowl harmonise with these most beautiful words, they seem to be coming naturally to her from a faraway place, but nevertheless a place deep within. They are in a foreign tongue which I do not recognise but are clearly of Indian origin, I'm sure. I know nothing of India's dialects or how she speaks with herself but only that this language I have not heard before has a source of great beauty. It is enchanting.

I am almost asleep, but I know the song Ana is singing continues after I have completely fallen, for it endures in my dreams.

41

Ananya's Song

அவர் ச◌ொல்வதகைக் கடே்க முடியுமா என்று எனக்கு ஆச்சரியமாக இருக்கிறது?

Can he hear me I wonder?

நட்சத்திரங்கள் மிகவும் சிறியவை, அவை வெகு த◌ொலைவில் இருக்க வணே்டும், அல்லது உண்மையில் அவை மிகவும் நருெக்கமாக இருக்கலாம் ஆனால் மிகச் சிறியதாக இருக்கலாம். எதுவாக இருந்தாலும் நட்சத்திரங்களால் என் சங்குகளின் ஓசை கடே்கும் என்று நான் நினகைக்கவில்லை.

The stars are so tiny, they must be a long way away, or maybe they are actually very close but just so very small. Whatever the case I do not think the stars will be able to hear my cymbals chime.

சந்திரனால் என் இசயைகைக் கடே்க முடியும், நான் உறுதியாக இருக்கிறனே். வளெிப்படயைாக அவர் பார்க்கிறார் ஆனால் அவர் கடே்க முடியும், அவர் எதுவும் ச◌ொல்லவில்ல, அவ்வளவுதான். ஒருவளேை ஒரு நாள் அவர் பார்த்த மற்றும் கடே்டவற்றில் சிலவற்றை கிசுகிசுப்பார், அவர் மலேே இருந்து பார்த்த விஷயங்களின் கதகைளை என்னிடம் ச◌ொல்லலாம். உட்கார்ந்து பார்க்கவும் கடே்கவும் இது ஒரு நல்ல இடம் என்று நான் கற்பனை சயெ்கிறனே்.

The moon can hear my music, I'm sure of that. Obviously, he watches but he can also listen, he just doesn't say anything, that's all. Maybe one day he will whisper to me the stories of the things he has seen and heard from all the way up there. It's a very good place to sit, and watch, and listen, I imagine.

நான் இப்போது காட்டின் விளிம்பில் இருக்கிறேன், அது மிக விரைவாக இங்கே உள்ளது, தோட்டம் திடீரென்று மரங்களாக மாறுகிறது. நான் இங்கு செல்லும் வழியில் ரோடோடென்ட்ரான் பூக்களின் வண்ணங்களை நான் கவனிக்கவில்லை.

I'm at the edge of the forest now which is here so quickly and the garden changes to trees suddenly. I didn't notice the colours of the rhododendron flowers I passed on my way here.

நிலவொளி அப்படித்தான் வேடிக்கை. நீங்கள் எதைப் பார்க்க வேண்டும் என்று அவர் விரும்புகிறாரோ அதைப் பார்க்க மட்டுமே அவர் உங்களை அனுமதிக்கிறார், சில சமயங்களில் இதுவே உங்களுக்குத் தேவை ஆனால் எதுவாக இருந்தாலும் அவர் உங்களுக்கு எல்லாவற்றையும் காட்ட மாட்டார். நீங்கள் எதைச் செய்கிறீர்கள், எங்கு செல்கிறீர்கள் என்பதில் கவனம் செலுத்த வேண்டும் என்பதற்காக தேவையற்றது என்று அவர் நினைக்கும் அனைத்தையும் மறைத்து விடுகிறார், அதனால் நீங்கள் தொலைந்து போகக்கூடாது.

Moonlight is funny like that. He only lets you see what he wants you to see, sometimes this is all you need but he will not show you everything whatever the case. He hides all that he thinks is unnecessary so that you can concentrate on what you are doing and where you are going so that you don't get lost.

அவர் என்னை இந்த மரங்களுக்கு பத்திரமாக கொண்டு வந்து சேர்த்தார், நான் சேர்க்கும் அனைத்து உண்மைகளிலும் அவருடைய வெளிச்சம் மிகவும் பலவீனமாக இருந்தாலும், அதற்காக மிகவும் கடினமாக உழைத்துள்ளார். நான் அரைத் தூக்கத்தில் இருக்கலாம் என்று நினைக்கிறேன், என் புலன்கள் இன்னும் எங்கோ எனக்கு முன்னால் இருக்க வேண்டும், ஒருவேளை எதிர்காலத்தில்.

He has brought me safely to these trees and has worked very hard to do so, even though his light is quite weak in all truth I might add. I think I might be half asleep and my senses must still be somewhere far ahead of me, in the future perhaps.

சூரியன் விரைவில் உதிக்கும், அவள் சந்திரனை வெடிக்கச் செய்வாள், எல்லா இடங்களிலும் திடீரென்று மற்றும் ஒரே நேரத்தில் வண்ணம் இருக்கும். மெல்ல மெல்ல அவன் மேலே தவழ்ந்து அவனை வென்று அவனை உறங்க வைப்பாள்.

The sun will be up soon, she will blast away the moon and there will be colour everywhere suddenly. Slowly and gradually, she will creep up on him and overpower him and send him to sleep.

அவன் இன்னும் அங்கேயே இருப்பான், அவனுடைய பெரிய பளபளப்பான முகம் அனைத்தும் விஸ்தாரமாகவும் வெண்மையாகவும் இருக்கும், ஆனால் நீல வானம் அவனை மறைக்கும் வகையில் அவனைச் சூழ்ந்திருக்கும், மேலும் அவனைத் தேடாதவரை அவன் அங்கே இருப்பதை எல்லோரும் மறந்துவிடுவார்கள். நிச்சயமாக, ஆனால் அவர்கள் அவ்வாறு செய்தால், பகல் நேரத்தில் அவர் தூங்குவதைக் காண்பார்கள், அனைவரும் சோம்பேறியாகவும் அமைதியாகவும் அமைதியாகவும் இருப்பார்கள்.

He will still be up there of course, with his big shiny face all wispy and white, but the blue sky will be surrounding him, so as to hide him, and everyone will forget he is up there, unless they are actually looking for him of course, but if they do they will find him asleep in broad daylight, all lazy and peaceful and quiet.

இருண்ட இரவில் அவர் அவர்களை எவ்வாறு வழிநடத்துகிறார் என்பதை அனைவரும் மறந்துவிடுவார்கள், ஆனால் அவர் அங்கு இருக்கவில்லை என்றால், அவர்கள் இருட்டில் பயப்படுவார்கள், இரவு நிலவு இல்லாததாக இருந்தால், அவர்கள் சற்று குருடர்களாகவும், விழும் பயத்துடனும் இருப்பார்கள்.

நான் அவரை மறக்க மாட்டேன், ஏனென்றால் அவர் எப்போதும் இருக்கிறார் என்று எனக்குத் தெரியும்.

Everyone forgets how he guides them through the dark night but if he doesn't happen to be there at all, they will be scared in the pitch black and if the night is a moonless one they will be a bit blind and fearful of falling. I won't forget him though because I know he is always there, always.

இன்றிரவு அவர் பிரகாசிக்கிறார், நான் காட்டுக்குள் நுழையும் போது மரத்தின் மேற்கூரை எனக்கு மேலே மூடப்படும்போது அவருடைய ஒளி இன்னும் ஒரு வழியைக் கண்டுபிடித்து, நான் எங்கு நடக்க முடியும் என்பதைக் காட்டுகிறார். நான் நிழலின் திட்டுகளை கடந்து செல்கிறேன், ஆனால் என் வழியைப் பார்க்க ஒளியின் குளங்கள் போதுமானவை.

Tonight he is beaming and as I enter the forest and the treetop roof closes above me, his light still manages to find a way through and he shows me where I can walk. I pass through patches of shadow, but the pools of light are quite enough for me to see my way.

என் கால்கள் தரையில் உள்ள இலைகளை நசுக்குகின்றன, அவற்றின் தண்டுகள் ஒன்றோடொன்று நெருக்கமாக இருப்பதால், மரங்களைச் சுற்றியும் பின்புறமும் இடையிலும் ஒலிகள் எதிரொலிக்கின்றன. என் செவிப்புலன் இப்போது உயிர் பெற்று வருகிறது.

My feet crunch the leaves on the ground and the sounds echo, around and back and in-between the trees as their trunks become closer to one another. My hearing is coming alive now.

நான் என் சங்குகளை ஒன்றாகச் சத்தமிட்டு, அவற்றின் ஒலியைப் பயன்படுத்த முயற்சிக்கிறேன். இது ஒரு லேசான குறிப்பு மட்டுமே ஆனால் அதற்கு சில வலிமை உள்ளது. அது இன்னும் ஒலித்துக்கொண்டிருக்கிறது, மேலும் அது மரத்திலிருந்து குதிக்கும்போது என்னைச் சுற்றியுள்ள இடங்களை என்னால் உணர

முடிகிறது, அது உயரமாக ஆனால் மென்மையான தரையில் பயணிக்கிறது.

I chime my cymbals together and try to make the most of their sound. It is only a light note but it has some strength. It is still sounding, and I can feel the spaces around me as it bounces off the wood, as it travels up high but also down into the soft ground.

இங்கு பயப்பட ஒன்றுமில்லை. இது எனது வீடு, இங்குள்ள அனைத்து தாவரங்களும் விலங்குகளும் என்னை அறிந்திருக்கின்றன. இங்குள்ள அனைவரும் ஒருவருக்கொருவர் நண்பர்களாகஇருப்பதால்நான் சுதந்திரமாகவும் எளிதாகவும் மகிழ்ச்சியாகவும் நடக்கிறேன்.

There is nothing to fear here. This is my home and every plant and animal here knows who I am. I walk freely and easily and happily as everyone here is friends with each other.

சுற்றிலும் காடுகளின் ஓசைகளின் வண்ணங்களைப் பார்க்க முடிகிறது. அடிவானத்திலிருந்து சூரிய ஒளியின் கதிர்கள் தோன்றுகின்றன, மேலும் பல வண்ணங்களைப் பார்க்கத் தொடங்குகிறேன்.

All around I can see the colours of the sounds of the forest. The rays of sunshine from the horizon are appearing and I start to see many more colours.

சூரிய ஒளி எனக்குள் இருக்கிறது, அவளுடைய நிறங்களை என்னால் பார்க்க முடிகிறது. நான் வாழும் உலகத்திலும் ஒலிகளைப் பார்க்கிறேன், வெளியில் உள்ள உலகில் நான் கேட்கும் அளவுக்கு இசையை என் உலகில் தெளிவாகப் பார்க்க முடியும். உண்மையில் உள்ளேயும் வெளியேயும் இருப்பதாக நான் நினைக்கவில்லை, உண்மையில் இல்லை.

The sunshine is inside me and I can see her colours. I see sounds too in the world where I live, and I can see music inside my world as clearly as I can hear it in the world outside.

Actually, I don't think there really is an inside and an outside, not really.

இப்போது லசோக வருகிறது. நான் விழித்திருக்கிறேன், ஆனால் நானும் தூங்குகிறேன். நானும் நடந்து பேசுகிறேன், பாடுகிறேன், ஆனால் மிக உயரமான புல்வெளிக்கு வரும்போது கொஞ்சம் மயக்கம்.

It is getting lighter now. I am awake, but I am also asleep. I am walking and talking and singing too but am a bit dizzy when I come to a small patch of very tall grass.

சூரியன் வலுவடைகிறது, ஒவ்வொரு நொடியும் அவள் அதிக சக்தி வாய்ந்தவள். அவளது அரவணைப்பை என்னால் உணர முடிகிறது, மேலும் காடு வேகமாகவும் வேகமாகவும் எழுகிறது. இது ஒரு முழுமையான ஒளி மற்றும் சத்தம் இப்போது என் மீது மழை பெய்து வருகிறது, நான் உயரமான புல்வெளியில் காலடி எடுத்து வைக்கும் போது நான் நடைபயிற்சி நிறுத்த வேண்டும்.

The sun is getting stronger, every second she is more powerful. I can feel her warmth and the forest is waking up faster and faster. It is a complete shower of light and noises raining on me now and I must stop walking when I step onto the patch of tall grass.

பேட்ச் எனக்கு சரியான அளவு மற்றும் ஒரு வகையான வட்டம் மற்றும் நான் ஓய்வெடுக்க படுத்துக்கொள்ளவும், ஒருவேளை எழுந்திருக்கவும் நினைத்துக்கொண்டிருக்கிறேன். நான் புல் என்று சொல்கிறேன் ஆனால் அது மிகவும் உயரமான புல் வகை. புற்கள் நான் சொல்லும் அளவுக்கு உயரமானவை, நான் நிற்கும்போது அவை என்னைச் சுற்றி இருக்கும் அளவுக்கு உயரமானவை.

The patch is just the right size for me and is a sort of circle and I am thinking of lying down to rest and maybe also to wake up. I say it is grass but it's a very tall kind of grass. The grasses are as tall as me I would say, so tall that they are all around me as I stand in them.

இங்கே யாராவது என்னைக் கண்டுபிடிக்க முயன்றால் நான் மறைந்திருப்பேன், நான் படுத்திருந்தால் இது இன்னும் உண்மையாக இருக்கும், ஏனென்றால் புல் மிகவும் உயரமானது.

If anyone were trying to find me I would be hidden and this would be even more true if I were to lie down, because the grass is so tall.

நான் என் முதுகில் படுத்துக்கொண்டு வானத்தைப் பார்த்து என் சங்குகளால் ஒரு குறிப்பு எழுதுகிறேன். ஒலி நேராக காட்டின் கூரை வரை பயணித்து ஒரு இடைவெளிவழியாக மிகவும் நீல வானத்தில் மறைகிறது.

I lie down on my back and look up at the sky and make a note with my cymbals. The sound travels straight up to the roof of the forest and disappears through a gap into the very blue sky.

புல்லின் தடிமனான கத்திகள் வட்டமாகவும் வலுவாகவும் கோடுகளாகவும் இருக்கும். அவர்கள் மேலே அடையும் போது, உண்மையில் ஒரு விஷயமாக அவை கொஞ்சம் கொஞ்சமாக அசைகின்றன. இன்னும் கூரை போடாத வீட்டுச் சுவர்களைப் போல அவை இருக்கின்றன. நான் என் வீட்டின் தரையில் படுத்துக்கிடக்கிறேன், அங்கு கூட இல்லாத கூரை வழியாக வானத்தைப் பார்க்கிறேன்!

The thick blades of grass are round and strong and stripy. As they reach up they sway a little, quite a lot as a matter of fact. They are like the walls of a house which has not yet had its roof put on. I am lying on the floor of my house looking up at the sky through a roof which isn't even there!

வானம் இப்போது சரியான நீல நிறத்தில் உள்ளது. ஒரு கணம் முன்பு கறுப்பாகவும், நட்சத்திரங்கள்

நிறைந்ததாகவும் இருந்தது, பின்னர் அது கருப்பு மற்றும் அடர் நீலம் மற்றும் நட்சத்திரங்கள் மறைந்து கொண்டிருந்தன, இப்போது அவை திடீரென்று முற்றிலும் மறைந்துவிட்டன என்று நினைக்கிறேன்.

The sky is a perfect blue now. It was black and full of the stars just a moment ago, then it was black and the darkest blue and the stars were vanishing and now I think they have suddenly disappeared altogether.

நீலம் இப்போது ஒரு மென்மையான வெளிர் நீலம் மற்றும் மெல்லிய நீல காகிதம் போன்றது, இது எனது அனைத்து வண்ணங்களையும் உள்ளே இசையையும் வீச முடியும்.

The blue is now soft light blue and is like thin blue paper which I can throw all the colours and music inside me onto.

காடுகளின் மேற்கூரையின் துளைக்குள் நான் ஒரு விமானத்தைப் பார்க்கிறேன். நான் இதற்கு முன்பு பறக்கவில்லை, ஆனால் விமானங்கள் என்னவென்று எனக்குத் தெரியும். அது எனக்கு மேலே உள்ள பெரிய நீல வட்டத்தை ஒரு பக்கத்திலிருந்து மறுபுறம் இரண்டாக வெட்டி அதன் பின்னால் நேரான சுண்ணாம்பு வெள்ளைக் கோட்டை விட்டு மெதுவாக நகர்கிறது. அதன் ஜன்னல்களிலிருந்து பிரகாசமான வெள்ளை விளக்குகள் பிரகாசிக்கின்றன, ஜன்னல்கள் சிறிய கண்ணாடிகள் போல. மேலும் ஒவ்வொரு சாளரமும் ஒவ்வொன்றாக ஜொலிக்கிறது.

Way up in the hole in the forest roof I can see an aeroplane. I have not been flying before, but I know what aeroplanes are. It moves slowly leaving a straight chalky white line behind it which cuts the big blue circle above me in two from one side to the other. Bright white lights are shining from its windows. It is like the windows are tiny mirrors. And one by one each window shines in turn.

நான் ஒரு குறிப்பை அடித்து காத்திருக்கிறேன்.

விமானம் இப்போது சென்றுவிட்டது, ஆனால் அது கரைவதற்கு முன்பு அதன் கோடு சிறிது நேரம் அங்கேயே இருக்கும். அதன் கடைசி சுவடு முற்றிலும் மறைந்தவுடன், நான் மீண்டும் ஒலிக்கிறேன். அந்த விமானம் எங்கே போகிறது என்றோ, அந்த விமானம் ஏன் இவ்வளவு குறுகிய காலம் சென்றது என்றோ எனக்குத் தெரியவில்லை.

I chime a note and wait. The aeroplane has gone now but its line stays there for a while before it dissolves. When the last trace of it has vanished completely, I chime again. I don't know where the aeroplane was going or why the line lived for such a short while.

நான் உருவாக்கிய வண்ணங்கள் அனைத்தும் மறைந்து போகும் வரை இப்போது அமைதியாகவும் மென்மையாகவும் வெளிர் நிறமாகவும் வருகின்றன. நான் மீண்டும் என் சங்குகளால் ஒரு குறிப்பு செய்கிறேன்.

The colours I was making are getting quieter and softer and more pale now until they are all gone too. I make a note with my cymbals again.

நேற்றிரவு விருந்து முடிந்ததும், என் தந்தை எனக்கு அவற்றைக் கொடுத்தபோது நான் தூங்கியது நினைவிருக்கிறது. மலைகளில் நிலத்திலுள்ள பாறைகளில் கிடைத்த தாமிரத்தைப் பயன்படுத்தி தானே அவற்றை உருவாக்கினார். அவர்கள் பிறந்தநாள் பரிசு.

Last night after the party I remember I was sleepy when my father gave them to me. He made them himself using his own copper which he found in the rocks in the ground in the mountains. They are a birthday present.

ஒருவேளை நான் முன்பு விழித்திருக்கவில்லை என்று நினைக்கிறேன், ஆனால் இப்போது நான் இருக்கிறேன். அதை உறுதியாகச் சொல்வது கடினம், ஆனால் நான் என் சங்குகளால் ஒலிக்கிறேன். அவை சிறியவை, வட்டமானவை, செப்பு வட்டங்கள் ரிப்பனுடன் இணைக்கப்பட்டுள்ளன.

நான் ஒன்றை சுவைக்க விரும்புகிறேன், அதனால் ஒன்றை என் நாக்கில் வைத்தேன்.

I think perhaps that I was not quite awake before, but that now I am. It is hard to tell for certain, but I make a chime with my cymbals. They are small, round, copper circles tied together with a ribbon. I want to taste one, so I put one on my tongue.

செப்பு சுவை உணவு உலகில் இருந்து இல்லை. இது நீண்ட நேரம் நகரும் எல்லாமே மற்றும் சுவை ஒரே நேரத்தில் நல்லது மற்றும் கெட்டது. பாப்பா இங்கே இருக்கிறார், அவர் சொல்லும் கதைகள் என் நாக்கில் சலசலக்கும் சுவையில் உள்ளன.

The copper taste is not from the world of food. It stops everything from moving for a long time and the taste is both good and bad at the same time. Papa is here and the stories he tells me are in the taste which is buzzing on my tongue.

புல்லின் ராட்சத கத்திகளின் அடிப்பகுதியில் அது பச்சை மற்றும் உயிருடன் மற்றும் ஈரமான வாசனையுடன் உள்ளது, நான் கூர்ந்து கவனித்தால் நான் நினைக்கிறேன் புல் வளரும். இன்னும் அசைந்து கொண்டிருக்கும் புல்லின் உச்சியை நான் தொட விரும்புகிறேன், அதனால் நான் எழுந்து நிற்கிறேன்.

At the bottom of the giant blades of grass it smells green and alive and damp, and I can hear the grass growing If I listen closely I think. I want to touch the tops of the grass which are still swaying around so I stand up.

டாப்ஸ் மென்மையாகவும் மென்மையாகவும் இருக்கும், நான் என் கைகளை நீட்டி, உள்ளங்கைகளை கீழே வைத்துக்கொண்டு சிறிது நேரம் அவற்றில் சுழலுகிறேன், அதனால் என் கைகளிலும் என் விரல் நுனிகளிலும் அவற்றின் ஒளி தூரிகையை என்னால் உணர முடியும்.

The tops are gentle and soft and I spin around in them for

a while with my arms stretched out and my palms down so I can feel the light brush of them on my hands and my fingertips.

எனக்கு மீண்டும் தலை சுற்றுகிறது, என் காதுகள் அனைத்தும் மங்கலாகி, நான் சிறிது நேரம் அப்படியே நிற்க வேண்டும். நான் அமைதியாக உணரும்போது, நான் என் சங்குகளைப் பார்த்து, அவற்றை ஒன்றாகக் கொண்டு வருகிறேன், அவர்கள் ஒலிக்கும் குறிப்பு நான் வீட்டிற்குச் செல்ல விரும்புகிறது.

I'm dizzy again and my ears are all a blur, so much so that I have to stand still for quite a while. When I feel still, I look at my cymbals and bring them together and the note they chime wants me to go home.

நான் வந்த வழியே திரும்பி நடந்தேன், வீட்டிற்கு வந்ததும் நான் என் படுக்கையறைக்குச் சென்று என் அம்மா எனக்குக் கொடுத்த கண்ணாடி ப்ரிஸத்திற்கு அருகில் உள்ள படுக்கை மேசையில் என் சங்குகளை வைத்தேன். நான் என் காலணிகளை கழற்றி, படுக்கையில் ஏறி தூங்கச் செல்கிறேன்.

I walk back the way I came and when I get home I go up to my bedroom and put my cymbals on the bedside table next to the glass prism which my mother gave to me. I take my shoes off, get into bed and go to sleep.

42

Beauty Sleeping

Art is lying next to me, fast asleep. I'm thinking about him and about us, and about this crazy storm which has blown in.

There is an icy cool chill coming from the open skylight above. I can see my breath rising and going outside. The heating is turned up on full. I think for a moment of shutting the skylight but decide against the idea as soon as I've had it. I'm so very cosy under these duvets lying next to this man.

The shadows of an eclipse move away like clouds drifting and the moonlight returns with a soft, strong music. It flows through my soul as a molten copper stream of memories which merge with the flow of this new life.

Some huge snowflakes are finding their way in. I wonder how it can be true that each one is said to be unique when there are so many of them. The warm air rising meets the cold as it comes in, pushing and pulling the snowflakes this way and that so that they fall in ways other than they might. They are now protected however from the forces of the wind outside and they have become slow and lazy as they scatter and wander and fill every corner of this little room.

I focus on one of the larger ones and follow its path as it floats. Sometimes it seems to wait, deciding which way to go next, then it moves a little one way and changes its mind to move in another. Finally, its journey brings it so very close to my face that I feel I could catch it on my tongue, but then it changes its travel plans once more before coming to rest on Art's ear, melting the moment it touches.

I am sleeping, or at least I think I am sleeping … Sometimes when you are warm and sleepy and content in life it is not so easy to be sure whether you are sleeping … and dreaming … or remembering … and imagining.

The snowstorm subsides for a short while. As the clouds blow away, the skies clear completely to reveal the stars, sharp and brilliant in the pure rich blackness. Each one is an individual of unique light but each one is also a companion to each and every other. Together they create a vision of peaceful harmony and a music of breathtaking peace.

The wind drops to nothing for a moment and the undulating fields of crystalline snow sparkle brilliantly in the midnight moonlight.

TRICORN
BOOKS